'Rakes Resurgent' follows on from
wherein Justin Drake entered the wc
convinced that setting up a practice in his home town of Bristol
will bring riches as well as an opportunity to make the world a
better place. But he found that as he delved deeper into a
world of corporate shenanigans, murky professional
associations, zero hours work and encounters with shysters
and radical activists, that his journey was mired in about-turns
and betrayals. He thought he was the only rake in town, only
to discover that he was surrounded by a nest of them, all
intent on finding a path to free them from the predations of life
in contemporary Britain. Seeking to find a way out of this
tangled web, he succeeded only in dragging his family deeper
into the mess he has created. Through a series of
circumstances, they manage to find a place of peace for
themselves away from major jeopardy, though questions still
hanging as to how they navigate towards an alternative life
together. Rakes Resurgent picks up on their continuing
progress through this bewildering world.

Daniel Doherty: About the author

Daniel Doherty lives in Devon, England, having travelled the
world in search of work and himself. This search continues
through this novel. Always curious and ever restless, Daniel

has written extensively for the sheer enjoyment of it, and also academically. The completion of this first novel is evidence of the fact that eventually – and probably for the first time – Daniel has done what his mother told him to: write a book.

Chapters

Ashes to Ashes

Monday morning finds both Joy and Justin Drake awakening in their suburban Bristol House, feeling pensive after Justin's narrow escape from the clutches of Consignia Finance the week before. As a management consultant, he had overstepped his role by a considerable margin, and was fortunate not to be in deep legal trouble. His one surviving coaching assignment, with Magic Carpet call-centre, is also hanging on a loose peg, as he has pushed his role to the limit in service of the staff, not of management. As they potter over coffee in the silent kitchen, Justin says to Joy, 'how strange it is to awaken without the chaos of the kids under our feet. I do hope they are enjoying their holidays. But I approach another week of Magic Carpet interviews with a heavy, heavy heart. At best it feels as though I am simply treading water, doing a useless piece of work. And at worst I fear I am going to be given the Dolores hairdryer treatment all over again.'

Joy nods in the mutual recognition of what now faces them both, after the escape that the weekend had brought. In some ways she has more to lose, as she works full-time at the Magic Carpet Fulfilment centre, and she too had been pushing management tolerance to the limit. 'Yes, I know what you mean. But at least you have a schedule of interviews to time-mark your personal sense of futility. I will be going back to crisis after crisis. And no doubt a backlog of emails, and of all of last week's crises to punish me for having the ng have the tag "final warning" attached to me. Dead woman walking. That bites deep too. Just one misstep and....'

Justin knows how that sentence ends, without needing to hear it. 'I feel your pain. I do hope the week off has given you some kind of perspective, despite my best attempts to undermine your hard-won tranquillity.'

Joy gathers her bags. 'Yes, you are right. I mean about the fresh perspective brought by a week away from there. And about your best attempts to sabotage it. The week off with the children has been such a treat, a taster of how life might be without the slow burning debilitation of corporate life remorselessly sapping my spirits. But hey, time to go. Separate cars, secret convoy, Brian formation. Watch out for a Magic Carpet delivery van following us with radio transmitters on the roof.'

'Wilco over and out.'

As Justin parks up at Magic Carpet, a sense of weariness begins tugging him ever downwards, deep into his bones. On the drive over to Almondsbury he had felt a surge of redemption, a buoyancy borne of gratitude that Joy had taken the Consignia drama so considerately; in fact relieved and happy that he had offloaded his confession at all. However, this lightening of mood was entirely dispersed by the sight of the Magic Carpet's gates. He drags himself through security, placing his lanyard around his neck, while praying that it will not choke him, physically or spiritually. But he is hardly settled in his now all too familiar room at the far end of the gantry when he is summoned by Dolores, who demands, 'My office, now,' her face like thunder. He follows her dutifully, idly wondering whether she might have spent the weekend rigging up gallows.

'Come in, Justin. I have invited along Diane from Corporate HR to this meeting as we have some really serious matters to talk over with you. Justin – Diane.'

He notices that Diana, in her appearance and demeanour, is almost a carbon replica of Dolores, resplendent in a blue trouser suit, her blond hair scraped back even more savagely than Dolores's. She is scowling at him, as if resentful that this meeting has dragged her from her precious spreadsheets in Birmingham. On the other hand, she might well be looking forward to his inquisition. Perhaps as a child she enjoyed pulling the wings off butterflies. Or drowning puppies.

Dolores breaks off Justin's inspection of her colleague, perhaps hating to see him distracted, even for a second.

'Justin, let us get down to it. Following my concerns raised with you on Friday - regarding the fact that I suspected that you were withholding vital information from me concerning what you have learned from the interviews - I have new information gained from extensive investigations conducted Friday afternoon and over the weekend. These findings are so serious that I have cancelled your entire interview schedule going forward. All supervisors have been notified of these cancellations, which are unlikely to be reinstated unless you know something we don't. You are now stood down. You may not contact any of our staff now or at any time or in the future. Is that clear?'

Justin hangs his head, muttering to the table. 'I see. Yes, it is understood. This sounds pretty final to me and I am really disappointed to hear this. May I ask what is troubling you this time, to cause such a Draconian move? I simply cannot imagine what?'

Dolores gives him her best death stare, suspecting that he knows all too well what is about to be revealed. 'There is more than one thing troubling me. We have unearthed quite a list. Let us tackle them one by one. Diana?'

Diane straightens, as if this were the sort of moment she was born for. 'Good morning Justin. Well, first off, there is the question of you falsifying your character references. Parallelogram were most disturbed when we pointed this out to them.'

'What do you mean falsified?'

'Well, we followed up on them,' continues Diane. 'Richard Finch of Consignia seemed to hardly know you at all. He said that you had done one small piece of work for them, but not enough for him to vouch for you, and they would not be hiring you again. He said that he could not in conscience give you a reference. As for your new so-called supervisor, Bert

Thompson, he was able to vouch for you, in a vague sort of way. But admitted he that he was only recently in post as your supervisor, so his experience of you was time-limited, though he thought you were a 'good egg.'

'I am sure he does,' says Justin, wondering what might be coming next.

Diane presses on, 'at that point we followed up with your previous supervisor Brenda Seagate, whose details we secured from your coaching body. Brenda declared that she was unable to vouch for you at all. In fact, she intimated that she was in dispute with you over your displays of highly unprofessional, intimidating behaviour. Such falsification across so many sources is serious indeed. But hardly surprising as it reflects on the pattern of unethical behaviour that is your trademark.'

'I see,' breathes Justin, alarmed at the completeness of this charge sheet. There is little he can say to rebut this, as it would only dig the hole still deeper. He hardly has time to catch breath before Diane continues, in the same accusative monotone. 'Secondly, it has come to my attention, through searching central HR records, that your wife works up the road in Fulfilment; yet you never once declared this conflict of interest to us. Nor in fact did she. This deception would be at best negligent, at worst evidence of a conspiracy.'

Justin now feels that this is going too far. 'Oh, but, come on. I was given to understand that you have – what are they called?

Oh yes, "Chinese walls." Watertight walls between Fulfilment and the call-centre. In fact, Parallelogram assured me that this was the case, and that I need not disclose my wife's job to you.'

'Yes, we do have such a wall between the two sites, but it is not impermeable,' Diana continues, in a scolding tone. 'You should have known better than to keep secret this family connection across the firm. In fact, given that she works in HR, then she of course was under obligation to disclose your affilation, also. Her failure so to do simply underlines our suspicion that she was in on your deception too. Or should I say your joint deception?'

'But, but, but,' Justin splutters, hardly knowing where to turn. 'There was no such deception. And besides, Parallelogram knew all about our martial relationship – I declared it to them early on, felt I had to. And they duly took note of it, but said it should not change too much because of your secure Chinese walls. They said, "but best not to mention it." They were sensitive to this, yet they pressed for the work, which they were hell-bent on landing, all the same.'

'So you say.'

Diane is scornful. 'But we have contacted them, and they say they have no record of such a declaration of interest. In fact, they are beyond shocked that you did not declare this obvious conflict to them. They are an ethical company, one of our esteemed business partners, and we utterly believe what they tell us. I put it to you that you deliberately withheld your relationship with a member of our HR team to get the work. Or, perhaps to instigate something much more sinister and collusive altogether.'

Justin begins to get a glimmer of where this might be headed, vainly attempting to head it off at the pass. 'I have literally no idea what you may be insinuating here. But clearly you are building a case build on nothing but fantasy. But humour me - what else might you have on your trumped-up charge sheet?'

Diane brooks no interruption. 'If I may continue. The next claim is that you have failed accurately to report back to line management your findings from your interviews, despite your contractual obligation so to do. Dolores has since discovered that much was discussed between you and our staff that you have not reported back on. We take this cover-up very seriously indeed.'

'Really? How might she know that?'

'Quite simply actually,' retorts Diane. 'She has talked directly to the supervisors themselves. She has a good working relationship with them.'

Justin rolls his eyes at this reframing of what a good working relationship might comprise. 'Oh, I see. And they were under duress, no doubt? I suspect that they were put under threat and would say anything to appease management.'

'No, not at all. In fact, the line of inquiry that you have taken has deeply unsettled many of your interviewees. Most of them report that they were glad to get out of the room, for fear of what you might pressure them into saying.'

'I find that hard to imagine,' says Justin, knowing this construction of events is a barefaced lie. But he keeps that truth to himself.

Diane is remorseless. 'Furthermore, and following the same inquiry, we have evidence that you have been inciting unrest among supervisors, through encouraging them to unionise and to stand up against our necessary and humane redundancies programme.'

'Not true!' denies Justin.

Diane continues with the charge sheet, regardless. 'On top of that inducement to unionise, you have been consorting with a troublesome supervisor who was already on disciplinary charges – and who has since been dismissed - when you should have known better, and exercised discretion. The fact that were known to have been talking to at length to such a person on our premises is demonstration that you have you have shown no professional judgment or client centeredness. Did you feel no allegiance, no loyalty to your paymaster?'

'Well of course I do. Do you mean Glynis?' Justin blurts out, then wishes he hadn't.

'Ah, so you know who we are talking about. But of course you do!' jumps in Dolores, who had been contently been watching the show up until now.

Justin searches for some sort of defence, amid all of these distortions of the truth. 'But you never told me that Glynis was blackballed. How was I to know?'

'Because we have reason to believe she told you that that was the case,' says Dolores, crossing her arms for emphasis.

'I see. What else to do wish to fabricate against me?'

'Perhaps most severely of all,' Diana drones on, 'We know that you have been feeding information to the notorious journalist, Dick Bellows - who operates at national press level – feeding him fallacious and malicious rumours regarding Magic Carpet. And that you have been doing this for personal gain, and for political reasons.'

'How on earth might you substantiate that claim?' Asks Justin, his tone querulous.

'You were seen outside the gates by security talking with him, and further we have both of you bang to rights on CCTV footage.'

Justin's refutations continue as the charges mount up, though his resolve is clearly weakening. 'That conversation occurred outside the workplace, beyond the gates. You have no idea what we were discussing. It was a private matter.'

'Well, we have a pretty good idea as to what you were discussing, as he has only one thing on his mind, and that is bringing about the downfall of Magic Carpet.'

'Really? You fantasise,' rebuts Justin once again, but his rejoinder is ignored.

Diane prepares, matador like, for her killer incision. 'Finally, and perhaps most seriously, we have good reason to believe that you are your wife were conspiring to infiltrate and severely damage the reputation of Magic Carpet through the agency of this journalist and other co-conspirators.'

'However might you come to that conclusion?' asks Justin, while knowing that his challenge falls on deaf ears.

'There is no doubt in our minds that you wife was encouraging troublemakers at all levels in Fulfilment to undermine our business. And that she has persisted in doing so, despite the many threat of disciplinary action hanging over her, and that she has continued in this subversive behaviour regardless, even at risk of her own job. She has falsified records, defended the indefensible. But surely you must know this to be true. We feel sure that you two hide little from each other.'

He retorts, 'lunacy,' to this claim, but merely elicits the arching of an eyebrow from Dolores in response, who leaves it to Diane to press on with their litany of charges.

'Our investigation timeline suggests that once she had penetrated our defences, she then inveigled you into the company to conduct a second spearhead within the call centre, to further undermine us and all we hold dear.'

'You have nothing to go on to validate such a fanciful claim.'

'Well, it may look circumstantial to you, Justin Drake,' says Diane, moving around the papers in front of her, 'but out legal team will soon make the connection, believe me. They are good at that sort of thing. Why else would your wife jeopardise her career, with the whole of her family to support? Then there is the connection to the journalist. We believe you two are rallying all disaffected and dismissed employees, with the purpose of mounting some kind of class action against Magic Carpet. And then, from that positioning, to push for unionisation from the inside, when we are clear that our staff are better off without the dead-weight of unions dragging them down.'

'This is simply unbelievable,' he says, while seeing that this paranoid narrative might have legs, in a world where a belief in conspiracy frequently out-trumps any semblance of truth or sober fact.

Diane closes her file, to look him in the eye. 'I could go on. All of these contentions are already with our Legal Department. And Magic Carpet moves quickly on such matters. Once we got wind of this familial conspiracy, we felt the need to isolate not only you but your wife immediately, now she is back from her holiday, to stop you both doing more harm. In fact, my colleague Yim from corporate HR is questioning her in a separate room down the corridor, just as we speak. We intercepted her on the way to work and have now brought her here.'

This news disturbs him more than anything else he heard so far. 'Why isolate her? What has she ever done?'

'Well apart from being married to you …' Diane grins, maliciously, 'she has been consistently undermining management, siding with disaffected employees at every opportunity, when as a representative of HR she should have been protecting executive and corporate interests. She has been running her own little Robin Hood operation; or is she Maid Marion and you Robin Hood? Her charge sheet is pretty long on her delinquent performance alone, before we ever get to her collusions with you. Right now, she is in danger of being instantly dismissed, but far worse will follow once the conspiracy to undermine Magic Carpet is proven. She will be facing massive damages and possibly prison, given that she is a full-time employee - and even worse works in HR – while breaking all ethical rules.'

'May I speak to her right now?' he bleats, for that is all he wants to do right now, all he can focus on, his need to protect her suddenly foremost in his mind.

'No, you may not.' Says Dolores, who has been uncharacteristically quiet up until now, but attentive to Justin's every reaction to their many charges.

'Okay, so you think you have sealed her fate. What might you have in store for me?' asks Justin, knowing as he speaks what the answer will be.

'You? You are of course dismissed forthwith too.

Parallelogram will be informed, as will your professional body, The Coaching Fraternity.'

Despite their tone of certainly, Justin suddenly senses that they may have a chink in their armour. 'No doubt this will be argued endlessly in court. I hear your threats, loud and clear. But where do you want to take it from here? Despite your threats, I hear some sense of prevarication.'

Dolores picks up reins. 'We do not take this lightly. This is one of the worst cases of collusion and corporate espionage to come our way for some time. Possibly worst ever, and all emanating from a premeditated husband and wife operation in their attempt to create a sleeper cell. What we would most like to do would be to summarily dismiss both of you for serious misconduct, then escort you off the premises; then instigate legal proceedings against both of you, jointly and severally. That is what we would most like to do. But over to you, Diane.'

Diane is remorseless. 'We would also like to put stringent gagging orders on both of you, so that if either of you would so much squeal a word of what you know about Magic Carpet to the outside world, you would be professionally dead meat. In addition, we would also like to do our best to ensure that neither of you ever work in HR or coaching again. We are well networked and bad news travels fast. It galls me so much that the likes of you two are free to do damage to the HR profession, undermining the work so many of us true professionals do to maintain standards. It is no wonder that our profession gets a bad name, with charlatans like you hanging around.' Dolores nods in solemn assent.

'So why not do just that then? Run us out of town. What is holding you back?' challenges Justin.

'We would like nothing better than to finish off the both of you - and we probably still will. But there is a problem....' says Dolores.

'Which is?' Justin asks, pleased that his instinct that there may a glimmer of hope in all of this might yet bear fruit.

Diane's tone is level, measuring her words carefully. 'We do not trust either of you to comply with any normal legal restraint. In our view you are both rogue, and too far-gone to be discouraged by common sense or threats to your survival. It is clear you are both desperate people, disguised under the cloak of respectable middle-class modernity. Yes, we have searched your histories, and have unearthed your student left wing activities. The Internet is a very revealing. And for all we know, on the dark web where we cannot penetrate, you might even be running a Marxist sleeper cell from your innocuous house in Westbury. We fear that you are no less than a pair of virtual corporate suicide bombers, intent on leaking classified information and bringing us down, along with as many good companies as you can. And we know you have the ear of radical left-wing journalists and TU agitators.'

Diane sits back, deeply satisfied with the vehemence of her delivery, visibly glowing aliveness.

'This is this the stuff of paranoid delusion,' says Justin, meaning it.

'Hardly. We have the evidence,' says Dolores.

'Yet you hesitate to pull the trigger, even though you are locked and loaded. Because?'

'Because we believe you have a weak spot,' says Diane. 'That is to say, your children and your nice family life in Westbury, and that good middle-class school. That lifestyle is all quite different in kind from your radical aspirations, even if you use your home-life as a cloak. You are well within the conventional bell jar, and we doubt that you truly wish to leave behind the security that delivers. It offends me actually. What hypocrite you both are, wanting the best of both worlds, virtue signalling your radical pretentions while living high on the corporate hog.'

At this Justin, Justin feels under visceral threat. 'What in the name of goodness does my family status and life-style have to do with this so-called charge-sheet?'

Dolores clarifies, 'Let me tell you what … we have run the scenarios. One option is for both parties to go through a whole drag-out legal fight, at risk of you losing everything, while we are seen as somehow guilty by association, damaging our reputation. That option is what we MBA types call the "zero-sum game".'

'Or else? What is the alternative scenario?' Justin asks, eager to hear the answer.

'The alternative is that we lock both of you into a lucrative Non-Disclosure Agreement, an NDA, payable in a monthly basis for 10 years, to ensure we have you gagged and unable to speak against us, for fear of serious reprisals. And believe us, we will watch your future careers, and the careers of your associates, very closely. HR is a very small world. One squeak against Magic Carpet and we will know about it; and we will be down on you with the full might of the law. There is no statute of limitation on this.'

'I see – interesting. Tell me more.'

Dolores continues, 'here is the deal. You walk away with references after you tender your resignation from this assignment, willing given to Parallelogram. And as for your wife? The narrative is that she is clearly suffering from extreme stress. She will be put on indefinite paid leave, and offered employee assistance and full wellness back up to alleviate her condition, as we ease her out of employment. You would both be free to continue to practice professionally without a blemish to your name, unless you transgress this agreement. There would no trace of either of you being in dispute with Magic Carpet.'

'I see…. These choices seem clear. And the condition is that we never offer an opinion on any aspect of Magic Carpet operations – to anyone? Ever?'

'That is correct. Should that happen the previous charges will be run out, and we will throw criminal charges against both of you, especially your wife. Furthermore, you may never even mention that this NDA ever existed - or legal consequences for breach of contract will be brought to bear.'

At that Diane pushes a document across the table. 'Here are the terms we offer for your NDA. Do please read it over. We will pay for your legal fees to expedite this. This offer is not on the table forever. Your wife Joy has been taken through a parallel process down the corridor. Excuse us while we both walk down to see how that is going, while you read the agreement over.'

He is left to consider his fate, once alone more in an empty room. He realises that he is getting used to such pivotal moments, being left alone to dangle. Reading over the agreement, it looks quite legitimate. He concludes that they must be feeling really threatened, to draw up such a generous settlement.

Eventually they return, the identical twins looking poised to seal the deal, with Diane the one chosen to share the breaking news from Joy's holding cell.

'It would seem that your wife fully understands the import of this settlement, and is in broad agreement with it. As soon as possible, we recommend that you both visit the following solicitor's office, which will act on your behalf. If you wish to nominate your own brief, then you may, but we assure you that these solicitors will be impartial. They have done this for us many times before with no complaints. We will pick up the set fees for drawing up the NDA. The solicitor will help you understand this settlement and clarify all your options, including filing a case against us, should you wish to do so.

We are giving you five days to make up your minds. Should you leak any of this then NDA is off the table and legalities will proceed. Any questions?'

'No, not at this point. We will consult with the solicitor then give you our decision from there.' Justin shakes his head in disbelief at this turn of events, but assents all the same.

'No questions?' asks Dolores asks. 'Well, good-bye for now - and let us know as soon as you know. We hate having to make this offer, but we have to realistic. We think it really generous. It protects you and your family from so much unnecessary stress and misery. Let the radical journalists and their trade unionist colleagues fight their own battles. They do not need you. You are simply pawns in their game, sprats to catch a mackerel. If that is it, then you are free to go.'

He staggers out into the summer daylight, so happy to see Joy heading for her car also. She raises one finger to her lips to ensure his silence, mouthing only one word – 'follow.' They drive out in covert convey, again in the fashion of Brian the fixer and his constant shadow, except that now their cover is blown. Joy pulls over in a layby near Henbury Hill, where they step out of their respective cars for a long, heartfelt hug.

'Salutation Inn, perhaps?' Justin inquires, thinking that neutral ground might help them absorb all that has occurred in their separate holding pens.

'No,' she says, with vehemence. 'The only salutation I have for you is "home." Let us close our front door behind us, where I can scream silently.' She hits him with a friendly exasperated smack. 'This is all your fault!!' she says, good humouredly, while starting up the Astra. He follows meekly, duly chastised.

Safely at home, with both cars docked, they collapse onto the sofa in a state of near paralysis. They hug each other closely, their stunned silence broken by Joy, who has a fit of giggles at the preposterousness of it all. She calms herself enough to ask, 'how did it ever come to a head like this? And on all fronts too. Consignia as well as Magic Carpet? I am just so happy that the children are away at camp, far away from the fallout of these catastrophes.'

'At last we might find a use for Neuro-catastrophic therapy,' says Justin, then bites his tongue, immediately sensing that coaching in-jokes are not the best direction in which to take this conversation. 'But then again I think not. Tea?'

'Oh, yes tea.'

Justin asks, 'did you not wonder what was going on in the other room when they separated us? Did you ask yourself if they were asking us each the same questions? Or whether they were following a different tack, to separate and divide us?'

Joy smiles. 'Oh yes, of course I did. I was beaming messages of support through the walls. I really, really wanted to see you, to hear you, to read your mind. But of course they made that impossible for us. That was all part of the tactic to terrify us, to separate us, to make us feel isolated.'

Sipping their restorative tea, they begin, in faltering terms, to figure out what all of this might mean, with Justin suggesting, 'time for a kitchen cabinet. If only we had a flip chart. So what sense do you make of this turn of events so far?'

Joy voices her immediate thoughts. 'Clearly Magic Carpet are paranoid – are you thinking what I am thinking? That maybe there is something else they are afraid of, some threat that we might pose that they're not even telling us about? But what are they are afraid of, that we might know and possibly hold against them? Are they playing some sort of Russian roulette?'

'Hmm... all these unknown unknowns. But in fact we do know a lot about their inner workings already. And that they think we are kamikaze. A joke, I know, but that is what they fear. They are taking chances in the way they organise their workplace, we know that much. They have a lot to lose. And they may have many enemies that we do not know about, though they pretend that they like to play nice all the time.'

Joy feels a surge of vengefulness. 'Maybe we should stoke their worst fears? Go full metal jacket?'

'What a good idea. Not.'

Joy is fully aware that acting out of the need to hit back will get them nowhere. 'I was being sarcastic. But let us not tweak that tail too much more. My hunch is that they think we know something about the leaks. Something serious about the leaks that we are not disclosing.'

'Do you think so? How glamorous. But we cannot speculate too much as to what drives their fevered imaginations. So, what are our options? Realistically?' Justin hands the baton back to Joy, knowing she is better at summarising than he, despite his having participated in the Fraternity's "Make your Summary Shine" module.

'Well, we cannot go back to work for Magic Carpet that is for sure, even if we want to. Which neither of us would ever contemplate doing anyway, given everything.'

'True.'

'And we do not really have the stomach or the resources to get into a stand-up knockdown legal fight, given we are not actuality fifth column insurrectionists.' Joy looks thoughtful.

'Nor are we funded by some shadow Russian organisation. Which is a bit of a shame, given that everybody else seems to be. Besides which, we would lose. We do know that they have vast resources, are feeling backed into a corner, and might even come after our family and our way of life. And we know they are quite disposed to using security, intense surveillance, black ops even, to make life impossible for those that cross them.'

Justin reflects on his own short experience of Magic Carpet to know the full truth of this. 'Oh yes. They love surveillance.

Addicted to it, truth be known. Look at how much they seem to know about us and our family already, even down to our student records. I would think it best not to drive their paranoia to extremes.'

'I agree,' says Joy, 'but on the other hand I feel dirty taking the NDA money. They should not be allowed to hush folk like this. Folk like us. Good people.'

'Yes, a part of me feels that strongly too. I too feel kind of grubby, and somehow silenced, bought, forced low.'

Joy feels the need to be the voice of pragmatism, once again. 'On the other hand, we can live with some of feeling dirty if the deal works for us. Let us look in detail at what they have to offer, work on the facts in front of us; go over our individual copies and see if they match.'

Joy spreads both of the agreements on the kitchen table, where they proceed to play a complicated game of 'spot the difference.' They go over their individual copies, line by line, comparing notes, until they are assured that the documents are in fact identical.

Joy concludes, 'the up-front lump sum is enough to cover our everyday costs while we get set up with something else. Have you noticed how cunningly calculated the monthly stipend is? The payments are enough to cover the mortgage and some of our running costs, but they do not set us up for life, not by any means. The ten years period that the stipend runs for sees the children through - sort of.... though I know that commitment is never fully discharged. But through university and the rest, until they are on their feet. No boomerang children here thank you, never leaving the nest.'

Justin agrees. 'Yes, they have been cunning, and I think I see their motive. We cannot be seen to the outside world to have suddenly come into wealth – questions would be asked that might link this windfall to Magic Carpet, which is the last thing they wish. They do not want to invite any suspicions, rumours, let alone inquiries into their methods of removing troublesome employees. Good, we are piecing together their complex jigsaw quite nicely.'

Joy, too, begins to see the smartness of what they are offering. It has clearly been thought through in fine detail. 'Quite. So we will still need to work, or others might smell a rat if we are living the life of luxury, without visible means of support,' says Joy. 'But beyond being unable to avoid work, I think we both really want to work. We are those types of people, we need to extend ourselves, to do something meaningful, something with a purpose. Neither of us is ready for putting out feet up. And we need to set an example to the kids regarding work and making a contribution. So, we sign up for the deal? It feels like that is the way we are headed?'

'Well, yes we do,' Justin says, 'if the lawyer says it is all waterproof.'

'Yes - and the price is that we give up on bringing down Magic Carpet? Not that we were seriously embarked on that project anyway.'

'True. And that is quite price to pay when every sense of justice say they have it coming.'

Joy puts a finger to her lips. 'But it would be too risky to go after them once we are signed up. We need to let others get on with doing that. They are already vulnerable, exposed on a number of fronts. They will be damaged soon enough, if not fatally ruined.'

A long silence prevails, allowing their decision to sink in. Joy eventually asks the question, 'Are you thinking what I am thinking?'

'Possibly – go on. What are you thinking?'

'Well…' she pauses, 'Maybe Magic Carpet are immune from our predations, but they are not the only capitalistic show in town.'

'Funnily enough, yes, I was thinking just something like that. And.... do go on. Put some words to this thought.'

Joy develops her theme. 'So, Magic Carpet is a no-go area. But there is nothing to stop us going after other neoliberal running dogs, as we used to term them, ironically, in our student days.'

'Quite true. This time around we unknowingly tripped across a subversive role for us. The accidental terrorists. But then there is quite a streak of the freedom fighter in both of us.... so what if?'

Joy surprises herself at her enthusiasm for such fantasy. 'Yes, what if? What if we plan sabotage for real next time around, now we have security from the NDA to see us through? Who knows what Maid Marion and Robin Hood stunts may be out there, ready to be pulled off?'

'The outlaws from suburbia, eh? So, they tried that Sherwood Forest line on you too, did they?'

She nods, saying 'though I think I prefer the Bonnie and Clyde meme. Not least because you really do not suit green.'

'We could even take on the likes of Richard and his CEO and their smug legal team for example.'

Joy feels a need to stick a pin in this fantastic bubble, before Justin is impulsed to do something they will both terminally regret. 'Oh no! Not them. Please! We are excluded there. But there must be other providers of corporate mischief and mayhem for us to hunt down?'

'We would need to find a way to infiltrate whatever target we identify…'suggests Justin.

Joy speaks to a wish that has been growing in her for some time. 'That is all very well. But wouldn't it be best if we were not positioned as agents of management? Besides which I think I have just about have done with defending indefensible management positions and policies that lay the workforce low – and depress and conflict us.'

'Me too. I have enough of the stool pigeon role. We would need to be careful… though it could be fun. But we do not have to overthrow capitalism all on our own, not right now. In fact, I could do with taking a rest from it altogether, for a while.'

Joy grows more confident that Justin is not going to do something crazy. At least not just yet. 'Quite right. But we could plan to take at least a nibble at it some time in the future? If the opportunity crops up? Oh, Justin! I am so happy. Maybe it is the effects of delayed shock or whatever, but I feel released, almost euphoric. And I do not want that feeling to go away. Never mind the whole outlaw life. Sherwood Forest is all well and good, as a fantasy, but just think what this deal means, if it all works out. I have been wanting to leave Magic Carpet for so long. Now I can … I can think of it. In fact not just think about it. I am free right now. They have let me go. The decision made for me. Hurrah. We have the rest of the week to ourselves. We have the rest of our lives to ourselves.'

'I am so happy you are no longer stuck to the sticky carpet too. And now you have all that remedial yoga to enjoy, at their expense.'

'Yes, that is true. Lucky bendy stretchy me.'

'With one mighty bound Joy and Justin are free.'

After a while he breaks this happy silence with a meaningful cough. Joy asks, 'what is it, Justin? What are getting ready to tell me?'

'There is something I have not told you about – full disclosure.'

'I thought there was. Go on, tell me. Stick that fat fly right in the middle of the ointment.'

Justin takes a deep breath. 'It relates to the whole fear of the leaks thing? Well, while talking to renegade Glynis, she slipped me …'

'Slipped you what? For god's sake tell me what?'

'A USB.'

'Stop keeping me in suspense. What was on it?'

'I don't know.' Justin shakes his head. 'I honestly don't know. I have been afraid to look, for fear of compromising myself, so I secreted it away.'

'Where is it now?' She needs to know. Everything.

'The USB is in the toolbox.'

'In a coaching toolbox? I don't get it,' says Joy her irritation rising.

'No, in our real toolbox. The one in our garage. The one full of tools. The metal thing.'

Again, she is aghast at this recklessness. 'God, that is so dangerous. Best we never look at the contents. In fact probably best we get shot of it entirely. It is probably incriminating, and could blow our whole settlement. This is our second dose of kryptonite. But whatever possessed Glynis to give it you in the first place? And whatever possessed you to take it?'

Justin looks humbled. 'You know, I have asked the same questions about her, and about me, over and over. The best I can come up with is that she knew she would be gagged forever, tied up in knots by Magic Carpet, the same as us. She was desperate for this data to get out. She could not incriminate her colleagues. So she decided on the spur of the moment to trust me. It would not have been safe with any one on the inside, and a journalist might be traceable to her. Maybe her gut said that I was on the side of the angels?'

'And maybe her gut said right. But whatever happens, we must protect her at all times. Trust must be reciprocated for it to be trust at all.'

'Yes, we must protect her, whatever the cost,' agrees Justin. 'Though a part of me is hankering to take a look inside the data stick, now that we are out of there. And it could be nothing, probably just a list of holiday rosters or the like that she needed to get rid of. Who knows?'

'NOOOOOO – do not open it, or I will detonate your toolbox.' Joy's stare brooks no argument. 'Then detonate you. Very soon we must make a plan to get rid of that offending item forever, lest it fall into the wrong hands – or even the right ones. In fact ,go and bury it in the garden right now, and bury it deep.'

Though this injunction sounds rather dramatic, he leaves the table to do her bidding. And he could probably do with the exercise. Returning from his mini funeral – it felt as though he were burying one of the children's' pets - Joy was keen to move the conversation on.

'Justin? I take it that it is buried deep? Good, then let us talk about the children. What do we say to them about all of this? I do not want to disrupt this precious, secure bubble that they currently inhabit.'

'Nor do I, especially at holiday time. Perhaps the answer is quite simple, and an approximation of the truth. We tell them that Mummy cannot hack it at Magic Carpet any more, and that she is going to take care of herself, take a rest and do a lot of that self-care and wellness stuff, before deciding what she wants to do next. And Daddy will bumble along as always, keeping the Ponzi factory going. They were never sure what I do anyway, so it will make little difference.'

'Sounds good. Quite a plan. And we stay where we are, the same school? Same house?' Asks Joy, musing on their possible futures.

Justin sees the soundness in all of this, thinking that he is not at all ready for the disruption that a house move would bring.

'Yes, I think so. But we do not need to decide that right now. On the surface everything as normal - except that nothing is as normal.'

The children question dealt with for now – and with the kids currently left safe in the care of the Forest of Dean camp commandant, hopefully with max surveillance – they leave the table to collapse on the sofa. After a moment they reach for each other. Then slowly kiss and embrace like they had not done for a long, long time. She snuggles into him; and with that small, simple gesture he feels a sense of the rising release; feels manly and in charge, not like some haunted, inadequate fugitive dependent on his wife to keep the family afloat.

She murmurs, 'this is delicious. We are free. Savour this moment. And just imagine …'

'Yes, I am imagining'

'Here's an idea. Let us take this moment upstairs. We cannot waste it. In fact we could have a whole week of this, canoodling like teenagers.' She drags him to his feet, for the first time in a while feeling his whole masculine weight. 'Oh, yes I am with you all the way. All the way upstairs. Wild horses and all that. But first we need to phone that solicitor, to see if they can see us tomorrow.'

'You carry on with that then - see you in the martial bed.'

Great Charlotte

In the sanctuary of the Drake household, the previous evening's mood of liberation segues into a bright morning, after Joy and Justin enjoy a wonderful sleep in each other's arms. This new day feels like the beginning of a fresh adventure, the next chapter in their lives. Refreshed after an indolent breakfast, they take the bus down to Clifton Triangle, to meet the solicitor, based in their highly impressive offices in Great Charlotte Street, high on Brandon Hill. Anne Frobisher, their appointed intermediary, is highly professional, taking them through the agreement line by line, to ensure that they fully understand what it is that they are getting into.

Anne says, 'Please understand that at this point I am solely representing your interests, and not Magic Carpet's. All they are doing at this point is picking up the legal costs. You need to know that I am obliged to outline all options open to you before you decide. You are quite aware that you are entitled to take action against Magic Carpet rather than sign this document, should you have a case? Do you feel you have a case that you wish to pursue?'

Joy says, 'for sure we feel we have a case. Each of us has a viable case we could press, jointly and severally. But we have talked over the personal costs and risks of doing that, and have decided that it is best we cut our losses now, and sign this deal, should you think it is the best we can do.'

Anne hears this, but nevertheless persists with outlining alternative courses of action, as is her duty. 'Would you like to tell me about the case you have to press? It may be stronger than you think. And I am obliged to ask.'

Justin responds, 'we could go into the detail, but we have talked this through, and we are prepared to settle. What do you think of the settlement?'

Anne continues doing due diligence. 'This is a really hefty NDA, that is for sure. You do realise that you are seriously gagged, and can never institute action against Magic Carpet ever again?'

'Yes, we understand that,' confirms Joy.

Anne continues, 'but having said that, this settlement is really generous - quite unusually so.'

Joy's ears prick up at this. 'Do you think they have something to hide? Given the generosity of the settlement?'

Anne is glad that her persistence is noticed. 'That could be the case. But do you know of anything specific that might be hidden in the woodwork?'

Joy continues in her self-appointed role of interlocutor. 'Well, we feel sure there is something that we have no cognisance of, but we have no idea what that might be. So best to let it lie.'

'Okay. So, are you both ready to sign?' Anne asks, confident that her role has been discharged with full probity. They both nod to this.

'If so, then I will dispatch the papers straight over to Magic Carpet HR, who will be in touch with you to say that they have countersigned the documents – held by me – and from there they will outline the payment terms and details as agreed in this document.'

Joy smiles, 'Great, so if we are done, let us sign up then breath some fresh air.'

After the handshakes, Justin hesitates at the door for a second to ask another question. 'If you have a moment, I do have another business nasty to deal with, that I may need legal advice on. It is hypothetical at this point, but all the same.'

'Oh, what is that?' asks Anne, thinking she was done with them for the day, but never shy of courting new business. On selling is well rewarded in her firm. Justin tells her of the Consignia saga as briefly as possible, indicating the possible consequences freighted within that saga.

Anne responds, 'I imagine you know that I cannot deal with this matter within the NDA, though I am sympathetic. However, and strictly off the record, it sounds like a fishing trip to me. I imagine it is not you they are after – you are now gagged – but probably their own executive. I would think they have much bigger fish to fry than you. But if they persist with this, then here is the number of someone I feel can really help you, Alison Snell, works in this office. She is a tiger.'

Justin squints at Alison's business card, saying, 'Well, thanks a lot for that. Most reassuring.'

Finally out in the sunshine, Joy says, 'Let us run over to the Boston Tea Party on Park Street. You never know, we could plan to start a revolution of our own. And an aptly named place to plot our future, now the magic trap door is in sight.'

As Justin crunches on an over-stuffed Panini, Joy asks, 'so where do you see your work life going now? I know you cannot bear being idle for very long. Daytime TV and the pub is not for you.'

Justin agrees, saying 'you know, the picture is not as yet clear. But I do have a crazy inkling to do something completely different. Perhaps occupy myself with what the kids might see as my ultimate job combo: and they do have more wisdom than we credit them for, in their own mad way. I could drive my Prius for a living with Uber, and deliver pizzas for Pronto as a sideline. Both are in the gig economy, allowing me maximum flexibility as to my hours of worked. The pay will help the family funding along, and most of all no management responsibility for anything except for myself. It would keep me busy; and I think it will be stress relieving to be doing something real, something hands on, after all of this cerebral, neurotic, corporate bullshit, all so empty and corrosive of the soul.'

Joy had not realised how far he had thought this through. 'Would you do that? Would you really do that? Beyond pleasing the kids, and the exotic adolescent element?'

'Yes, I think I will give it a try. It does not need to be forever, and if it does not prove to be fun, then I can always stop. It could be a honeymoon from serious work, a happy escape while being busy and productive.'

Joy giggles some at the happy escapism of all of this. 'That is true. "When the fun stops, stop," as they say in the gambling adverts. And pizza delivery and Uber could be fine research sites for undermining insidious management practices and establishing employee rights? Kills two birds with one stone. Changing from within. I like that idea.'

'Steady on tiger,' smiles Joy. 'I might just like to enjoy the freedom first, without getting straight into subversive rabble rousing. And you? Is there anything pushing through at this early stage that is catching your eye? There doesn't have to be, but knowing you, but I bet there is a twinkling, somewhere in that fertile brain of yours.'

She places her cup back on the table. 'I am not sure if there is right now. And you are right; I do not have to leap into full-on activity of any description right now. I simply wish to allow this sense of freedom and release to set in, to take care of myself for a bit. Magic Carpet might have wrong about so many things – but not about the fact that I am in need of rehab to allow all that has occurred, all these sudden changes, to sink in for a while. And to assist in doing that that I want to full advantage of all this wellness stuff they have signed me up for – hopefully to be enjoyed at the famous Whole Health Hub.'

Justin is glad that his connection with the Hub is proving of some use; after all he has been subject to there. 'Oh yes of course. It must be your turn for the world of groans and bones. Good luck with that. Seriously, it sounds like that is just what you need. You have been through a lot over the past few years. Let Uber Man take the strain for a while.'

Checking his pinging phone, he finds an email from the Compliance Director of the Coaching Fraternity, saying they wish to see him soonest to a meeting regarding a report of a serious breach of conduct. He reads on hurriedly through all the dross about standards and protocols, to find that Brenda has fingered him. Well, some relief in that, as he was expecting worse. Much worse, He thinks with an exhalation of breath that it is just as well the Fraternity do not know of the other near misses that he has provoked lately.

The Compliance Director continues to write that if Justin does not turn up at such a meeting, then they have no option but to decide his fate in his absence. They indicate that he may bring his supervisor or alternative representative along to the tribunal. Justin thinks this one through. Hmmm – a supervisor. Time to make another rescue call to Bert.

'What is it now, honey?' inquires Joy, noticing him reading the mail over and over again. 'The police onto you at last?'

'No, nothing as bad as that, but the coaching body are. They want to do me for professional misconduct, thanks to chief sneak Brenda.'

'Oh – that "hand from the grave," as we style her, has come back to grab you? I kind of felt that you had not heard the last from her. I can imagine her whipping up a degree of outrage among the coaching guardians of all that they believe is moral and righteous. Gives them some to do, beyond writing rules. What you going to do?'

'I think this is another case for "Better Call Bert."'

'Oh, yes, good idea. He is never short of crafty workarounds. Look, I think we are done here. Other folk are clamouring to take our shaky table. You go off to sort out Bert, while I will mosey on up to the Whole Health Hub, see what they have on offer. I will not mention that I know you at this stage. It might work against me.'

'Very funny. Well enjoy and see you later, back at our empty nest.'

Luckily Bert picks up his call, asking, 'what is it this time? CIA after you?' But he listens closely enough to the blurted version of the Brenda story.

'Hmm. Nothing we can't deal with old bean. I am heading to the Clifton Wine Bar right now. See you there? You said you were in Clifton?'

'Yes I am. Sure thing. I will make my way along and see you there. And thanks again for being my Angel Gabriel.'

He finds Bert snuggly settled in his favourite chair at the back of the bar, proffering the usual mannered handshake. 'Good to see you old chap. Chardonnay, perhaps? Or too early for you? Oh you will, then waiter, please... two Chardonnays, if you will, to wet our whistles.'

The drinks duly served, Bert says, 'Now bring me up to speed on all your various capers. Working with you feels like sitting down to watch a really elaborate box set, full of thrills and spills and unexpected twists. Last I heard Consignia were planning to guillotine you. Did you ever escape from that?'

'Yes, I gained a last-minute pardon. Almost a papal pardon. And on top of that Magic Carpet and Parallelogram have had a go at my decapitation too. But in the end, apart from losing the work, Magic Carpet have settled through an NDA.'

'Oh, good work. Just as well your wife is the sensible one between you,' says Bert, suddenly wishing he not revealed that he had insight into Joy's inner workings.

'You think so? It may interest you to know that she is subject to severe jeopardy by Magic Carpet also.'

'Really? I would never have thought. But she is smart enough to extricate herself smelling of roses, I do not doubt,' says Bert, his mind going back to a memory of his woodland walk with Joy.

'Your confidence in her is well founded,' says Justin. 'She is free, scot-free, with the rest of her life opening up in front of her.'

Bert beams at this news. 'So happy to hear that. She is a singular soul. Never a dull moment when supervising you, is there? I did field a call from Magic Carpet HR, asking how well I knew you, and asking for a character reference. Felt like they were sniffing for more than I was giving them. I hope that my reticence did not rebound. I did my best without perjuring myself?'

'No, you did fine. Your being economical with the truth with them was much appreciated. I could not have asked for more.'

'I am glad to hear it. I did worry some. And this latest palaver from the Coaching Fraternity? You said it involved Brenda? I think we know what kind of huffy chastisement she might be wanting to inflict. A woman scorned and all that.'

Justin shows him the accusative letter on his phone, while Bert reads it through. After a minute or two of inept scrolling, he pronounces, 'Does not look too serious to me, old chap. I feel sure you can ride this one out. My goodness! These jumped-up professional bodies and their pesky codes of ethics, with all of the fancy job titles they bestow upon themselves, making them sound like a mini-corporate. I am not sure that, beyond all the huffing and puffing, they have any power over you at all. It is not a client complaint after all, just a spurned supervisor. Someone with a grudge, an axe to grind. We can run argumentative rings around that lot of amateur do-gooders. You could even counter-sue, on some pretext of another. That is what the accused often do in these situations.'

Justin is reassured. 'Good to know. So what should I do? Engage with this demand and face trial by Brenda – or just let them get on with it? I feel sure it will take them forever, whatever the option. It will surely get mired in the committee stages, while they all happily indulge in sanctimony and file copious expenses.'

Bert goes further than this. 'I am not sure you want to engage with this at all. Purely one of these "he said – she said" things. Write and tell them you are too busy to make a meeting in London. If they want to come to Bristol fine, but I think they are allergic to the provinces. Otherwise say to them that you can sort it out with them by phone and email. You could even elect Tarquin to speak for you. That should scare the living daylights out of them. Besides which, if they do ever throw you out, there are plenty of other coaching bodies you could switch to. And you have your credentials from your various trainings that are separate from Coaching Fraternity's jurisdiction, and portable. No trace of this will ever be left in the sand.'

Justin's eyes open wide. 'Yes, I could. Had not thought of that. And they are all much of a muchness. Thanks for all of your sage advice, once again. You are an invaluable supervisor and a friend in need.'

'I am glad to hear that they are both tied up in one. You are learning to cultivate the right people around you. Like me! But now I must go to deal with troubles of my own. I have run into a spot of bother with the Financial Services Authority, and the Serious Crimes Unit is showing an interest too. Scotland Yard fingering my collar. I need to deflect this as soon as possible, before it builds into something.'

His insouciance over such serious malfeasance helps puts Justin's guilt - and his fears that his respectability might be irrevocably lost - into a wholly different perspective. Bert is always sure there is a way to work around such things, especially if you have the right contacts. Which Justin is aware he does not as yet have, but perhaps need to cultivate.

Bert pauses, portentously. 'Just before you go Justin…'

'Oh, is it about your fee? I can now settle that quite shortly, now I have some dirty money pushing through.' Justin assures Bert, only now beginning to realise just how the Magic Carpet windfall will relieve him of the nagging sense of never quite having enough to pay the bills, of feeling permanently in debt, of deferring payments to the extent that he feels buried beneath them.

Bert is dismissive of this offer. 'That is kind of you and I feel sure you will, I have no doubt about that. You are an honourable man.'

'Justin glows to hear that. 'That is kind of you Bert, but I will settle with you soon. You have been so helpful to both of us in so many ways.'

Bert nods, glad to have it confirmed that Justin is now financially flush. 'But I was just wondering – now you have this

NDA sorted out – whether you wanted to have a chat sometime about some investments I have wind of that could help you make the most of your ill-gotten gains?'

Justin feigns appreciation, while knowing in his gut that the grown-up world of stock market speculation was not for him. In fact he did not understand any of it. 'Oh, that is quite a thought. I had not thought that far ahead. But best to get the money in the bank first. Once the loot is safely secured, then I will for sure give you a call.'

Bert gives a resigned shrug. 'Good man. You do that. And good luck with your latest calamity. Never fear, it will all work out fine in the end. It usually does.'

'I am sure it will. And thanks again.'

 Done with Bert for the time being, but sure he will be needed quite soon for the next as yet unknown calamity, Justin tracks down a bus on Regents Road, eager to hear of the latest developments in Joy's life.

He finds Joy at the kitchen table, pouring over brochures. She bids him a brief hello, waving a hand towards her spread of alternative activities designed to fill her days and her imagination. She enthuses, 'this is all quite exciting, this Whole Health brochure. Though I think I will give the colonic irrigation a body swerve – or whatever it is you do swerve when the irrigators come a-hunting.'

'Quite so. And give the Mongolian throat-singing guy a wide berth also. Mind you, you can always hear him coming, so he is not difficult to avoid.'

Joy grins. 'Thanks for the inside knowledge. Now tell me, how did it go with Bert?'

'Swimmingly, as per usual. He had some fine ideas for to putting the Coaching Fraternity off the scent, so I think it best I just sit one out. It is the least of our worries. Or at least for now it is. Bert is helping me kick the can down the road.'

'Justin, could you now drop these management clichés, now that we are avowed to get away from all of the bullshit?'

'Yes of course we can. Difficult habit to kick though. Thinking of which, I propose as a management antidote something completely different for tonight – a trip to Stokes Croft to hear my new best friend Dave Allenday strut his alternative back stand-up shtick live an on stage.'

'Yes, that does sound like something completely different. Let us do it, take advantage of the children being away. Now.... a cup of tea? But first let me show you the schedules for the yoga and spin classes. I think I can fit both in without clashes.'

'Go for it, girl.' He skim reads the Hub brochure, resentful that his entry is hidden on the second last page. 'They look good, those classes. But don't rope me in just yet. And builder's tea please, I am not ready for the WHH lavender scented variant.'

Joy is relieved to hear that they are not going to become a variant on the happy couple in matching Lycra, yoga mats under arm, exuding conspicuous virtue and glowing health. 'Don't worry; I don't plan to rope you in at all. What I need is some precious "me time," as they say, and not to have that invaded by sweaty males – even you.'

The liberated couple's trip down to Stokes Croft promises them new adventures in a part of town hitherto unexplored. Having time on their hands before Dave's gig, they gaze in surprise at the gaudy graffiti adorning every available wall space.

'Did they have planning permission for these?' asked Justin, somewhat primly.

'For goodness sake, Justin, do stop being so conventional. I really doubt that they even thought of that. Look at the detail though, and the depth of colour. These people have obviously put a great deal of care into the construction of their art works.'

Chastened, Justin agrees, 'yes they are quite extraordinary. I have no doubt that Grayson Perry would delight in deeming these pieces art, by any criterion you might choose.'

As they venture further up the street, every shop-front and café signals a community committed to the pursuit of an alternative lifestyle. Joy says, 'you know it is easy to mock the whole hipster thing, and many of our Westbury neighbours do.

But these murals. They hold such power, for me a sense of the primitive. They have such energy.'

As they amble, they find themselves standing, by chance, in front of the Smoke and Mirrors comedy club, where Dave Allenday is due to perform. The billboard outside the club proclaims it to be "the home of alternative comedy.' Happily paying at the door, they look into to find the small room jammed to the rafters. First up they listen to a black female whose humour is caustic funny as well as insightful. Dave is up next, equally funny, more profane, delivering a whole series of quick-fire riffs on the differences and similarities between "Black Humour" and "black humour."

Joy loves the gig, and the venue, wanting to know more of what makes it so compelling. She takes Justin by the arm, urging him to go chat to Dave, who is standing at the bar with his CDs on offer - but as yet he doesn't have a book to sell, though as they listen to his Dave's patter, they hear much allusion to the magnum opus yet to come. They shuffle along the queue at the merchandise desk; and by the time they get to Dave, the line has subsided. Dave remembers Justin, is even tickled to see him again.

'So glad you came,' Dave says. 'Not too many of my passengers who say they will make the show actually do. Why don't we go to the end of the bar, the three of us, and share a drink? These gigs sure give you a thirst. And this must be?' He says, his gaze turning to Joy.

'This is my wife, Joy. Our first time here, and she is already a big fan.'

Joy winces at this, kicking Justin in the shin, but smiling at Dave nevertheless.

'Well, hello Joy!' cries Dave. 'How did you enjoy the show? Your first time at a black comedy club?'

'Yes, it is. And I loved every second. Thanks for the rib tickle and the provocation.'

Dave beams at this. 'Well, that is my pleasure. Did Justin tell you I am putting together a book on the history of black comedy in the UK? It is all I really think about these days. Every living moment. Even when in the middle of my act, I am in a helicopter up above, separate from myself, asking what on earth is really going on here, that causes folk to come back? This magic must be distilled and written down.'

Joy ponders on how it must be, to be delivering something so immediate while your mind is elsewhere. 'That sounds mind expanding, that splitting of self. And yes, Justin did tell me all about your research. How is it coming on, between Uber rides and gigs?'

Dave scratches his head, 'All the ideas are there, that is for sure, know what I mean? But too many words, just too many goddam words. I have no idea what to do with them all. In fact, I am getting to the point where I need an editor, but cannot really afford one, on Uber wages.'

Rather than commiserate with this, Joy feels the impulse to offer a solution. 'Oh – well, just so you know, I have an English degree, and I am quite good at working with other people's raw material. And I have some time on my hands right now. Any chance you might need my assistance? Not that I know if I would be of any use at all. I do promise I will not give your lived experience a Shakespearian slant.'

Dave's eyes are wide, his grin even wider. 'Joy, I would jump at the chance! A miracle happens. When can you start? Here is my card.'

'Well I can start right away. We both love your work. In fact, Justin is so smitten by you that he wants to sign up with Uber himself, following in your illustrious footsteps.'

'Get out of here! Really?' Dave feigns incredulity. 'Well if he is ready for that life, it would be great to have a buddy in the posse. Justin, is this true?'

'Yes,' Justin says, a little bashfully. 'There comes a time in every man's life when he needs to go down the Uber road. '

'Yep – I do gig economy work all day then gig here at night. Gig, gig, giggity gig all the way for me. Give me a ring and I am happy to help you through the induction process.'

'Thanks for that. I will need all the inside help I can get.'

Feeling a nudge at his elbow, Justin turns to see Tony Crocker from Chrysalis standing beside him.

'Well, hello there Justin! Did not expect to see you here. You got a minute? Oh sorry, you are deep in it with Dave.'

Turning to Dave, he says, 'Oh, hi Dave, great gig as per. Glad we share common friends, venturing here from outside the Stokes Croft massive. Hope I am not interrupting?'

Dave is happy for Justin to be escorted away by Tony, saying, 'no, not at all. In fact, I am needing some quality time with Joy here to chew over bookish things. She is a new miracle that has been sent my way. You can have Justin all to yourself.'

Tony and Justin move to a small nearby table, leaving Joy and Dave to it. 'Good to see you, Tony. So, you know Dave? It is a small world.'

'Yes of course I know Dave. We all know each other down here at the Peoples Republic of Stokes Croft. It is a tight scene. Look, following our last beer at Somerset House, and following the awfulness of the Clifton Club, I have been wanting to catch with you, share some ideas on revolutionising the coaching scene. But first, how is your work going?'

'Oh, it has changed quite a bit. I have been through a series of really scary corporate dramas, but I think I am out of that now, and not wanting to go back. Too badly burned.'

Tony places a hand on Justin's shoulder. 'Don't blame you, mate. I would not want to touch that corporate stuff with the proverbial, from all I hear of it. So, you might have free time to talk over some opportunities in the not-for-profit sector, particularly in the environmental space? That is where I am focussing most of my time at the moment.'

'Sounds good. I would be really interested to hear more of that. Can we get together later in the week?'

'Yes, that would be good. How about Thursday?'

'Perfect. I will come down this way, find out more about what is going on in the alternative scene. I really look forward to it.'

At this point Joy drifts over towards them, released from Dave's charms, as the star-turn of the evening is swallowed up yet again by a pair of fans.

'Hi Joy, meet Tony Crocker. Tony – Joy Drake. Joy –Tony.'

'Oh, hi Joy, yes I heard about you from Justin. If I remember correctly you were struggling somewhat with Magic Carpet, dealing with their control and subjugation battles? '

Joy is surprised, yet not surprised, to find that Justin has been freely sharing details of her work-life with whoever might be listening. 'Well remembered. Yes, it has been dreary. But I am in the process of freeing myself from that. With one mighty leap Joy is free. I hope. With some time and space and funding to decide what next.'

This news of an escape from corporate serfdom is always music to Tony's ears. 'Sounds great. Good for you. Any immediate plans?'

'Well, as of right now I am becoming the proud editor of Dave's tome on black stand-up comedy in the UK.'

Tony stands back, seeing her in a different light. 'Get out of here! Really? Good luck with that. I feel sure he is prolific. And you will need to be strong. Dave is quite a force of nature.'

Tony confirms what Joy has already picked up from her short, chaotic exchange with Dave. 'Yes, I sense that too. He is going to quite a handful, I can tell. And actually, I have little idea of what I am doing, but let me see if it works out with Dave. The patois could be a real challenge. Know what I am saying?' Joy catches herself, looking abashed. 'Whoops. Sorry shouldn't have said that. No mockery intended.'

Tony grins. 'None taken. And Dave enjoys a bit of ribbing. I am sure you will fit right in, once you get used to his little ways. Managing talent eh? Should be quite different from the infernal carpet ride. Look, I need to be going, but I am meeting up with Justin later in the week. If that goes to plan, then we could all be seeing much more of each other.'

Joy offers her hand, which he duly takes. She is not at all sure if this formality hit the right note, in these surrounding. She makes a note to educate herself in the protocol of high-fives and fist bumps. She parts instead with a lame, 'Sounds good. See you next time.'

As the happy couple step out on the streets, the whiff of shared reefers from the cluster of people huddled around the entrance of the club hits the back of their throats. Moving on up the hill, Joy says, 'Oh, it has been a while since we shared a joint together.'

Justin nods, struggling to remember when that last time might have been. 'Yes, it is. And that aroma takes me right back to our student days. We do not get much of that drugs scene in

Westbury, at least not down on our street corners. But not tonight. I am giddy enough already with all that has happened. Let us go and find a bus. It is time for home.'

The next morning, the Magic Carpet Legal Settlement lands on their doormat. Going through it in detail, Joy pronounces it all in order, the paper work confirming what they already know. Joy is glad to read that she will continue to receive her pay-cheque for the next three months while she rehabs – then at that point she will resign with full benefits. The fees for her rehab are all set up, at a health club of her choice, and the settlement lump sum will come immediately, with the monthly payments following thereafter. Lifted to read in black and white what has been verbally agreed Joy is keen to get down to Whole Health straight away, to set up her activity plan, and to choose a personal trainer. Justin offers her a lift, but not until he has contacted Uber.

Uber are more than happy to hear from him, though they say that they would prefer it if he set up the driver registration arrangement up online.

As he reads through all their requirements on the screen, he knows he will pass muster. His state-of-the-art phone is perfect for Uber, and having an up-to-date Prius helps too, as does a clean licence. All it requires is just one simple meeting to collect his Private Hire licence and he is good to go. Shutting the lid on his laptop, he doubts if he will speak directly to a human being in his entire time with Uber once he is set up and starts to work with them, as all his billings will be lodged directly in his bank.

Dropping Joy off at the Hub, he is pleased to find that the licence sign-up at the Private Hire office proves to be a straightforward process. To his surprise he is now good to go, once he gets the hang of the driver's app, which proves less straightforward. But, after stabbing at his phone fruitlessly for a while, a welcoming yellow thumb on his screen tells him he is at last all set up. Justin is delighted to have persisted with this torture to the end, and feeling so satisfied with his technical triumphs.

He points the Prius towards Berkeley Square to meet up with Joy at the Hub. She is happy to see him, wanting to share the news that she as at last finished choosing the hunk of the moment for her personal training, and has also signed up for her series of classes.

'What lovely people they all are' she enthuses, waving her hand towards the rogues' gallery enlivening the lobby walls. Justin turns his eyes to the display, saying, 'Oh yes, no doubt they all are. And do you see my picture on the wall?'

'Yes, I do. Look, right there, just behind the pot plant. Then I guess I have to include you on the list of lovely people too.

Though I am not sure, given the scowl the receptionist was just giving you.'

'Well, she and I have had a few run-ins.'

'I can imagine. My Justin, the one grumpy person amid this galaxy of healing angels. The irritating pea in the holistic princess's bed. And by the way, the kids are right, you do need a white coat. How did it go with Uber then?'

'Piece of cake. I am all signed up.' Justin produces his new Private Hire licence as proof of the same, glad this new line of work will save him the fruitless task of ascending in the hierarchy of the Hub's hall of fame.

'Good to hear. So, I suppose you need a chauffeur's hat to go with your white coat? Once you get the Pronto Pizza blouson jacket you will have the full zero-hours workers collection of Action Man outfits. Unless you want to sign up as a reserve fire fighter too. I would like that look, especially the helmet and boots. With that kit, you could also qualify as a strippergram in your spare time.'

'But you know I can't dance!'

'You would not need to dance, just grind around some, let the girls rip at your Velcro. And I would love to hear your account of such evenings, if you ever return alive. Why not have a full experiential immersion in objectification, learn what we women go through on a daily basis, subject to the male gaze? And I could help you shave your chest and legs before you sally forth. You would need some training in that, unless you want to arrive on site bleeding. Which is something you men never have to deal with. Blood.'

'Just no. Not even in service of my gender awareness education.'

'Justin, you say you want to join the gig economy more fully. You need to look beyond the usual suspects. You could even sign-up to become a Special Constable.'

'Hmm, and spend my time controlling pickets outside of Magic Carpet?

'On second thoughts, best not take that route. Look, let us drop by the Graduate School of Education at the bottom of the Square. See what summer schools might be suiting me.'

'Yes, great idea,' says Justin, wanting to erase from his mind the image of him needing to perform in front of rapacious hen-nights. 'It is about time we both went back to school again.'

The modernistic reception area of the Graduate School is abundant with leaflets and flyers of all kinds indicating how one might fruitfully pass a summer. From this educational cornucopia, Joy picks out three offerings. One is entitled, 'How to Get Published,' the second, 'Creative Writing – getting started.' Her third choice includes details of how to sign up for an intensive post-graduate teaching certificate, which, over the course of one year, would leave the candidate fit to be unleashed on unsuspecting students. The latter requires an interview, but not much more. The first two are easy enough to sign up for, which she immediately does.

Busying herself with the forms, she says to Justin, 'No time like the present. I am on a roll. What is that brochure I spy in your hand?'

'Oh, it is a flyer for a short course on Environmental Activism. Might be worthwhile knowing more, if I am to work with Tony at the People's Republic. And it looks really impressive. I could learn to speak Science. And the other is for 'Alternative Perspectives on Management Development: beyond Neoliberalism,' run by the School of Management.'

She pats him on the arm. 'What finds. Why not sign up for the environmental one? We could walk down to classes together. Dig out our old university scarves. But are you sure about the Management thing? Had we not agreed that we have had enough of managerial indoctrination?'

'Yes, we had, but this one says it offers an alternative view. Or at least it might confirm all our prejudices about the sinful corporate world.'

'It might just do that,' she agrees. 'Lots of confirmation bias. Now, let us ask at reception about the library, as I am going to need library access for these courses. And to help research Dave's book too.' The staff at the Graduate School reception confirm that as alumni, they could have limited library access, and that enrolment on the courses might give them full access. But the receptionist reminds them that, 'While we still use the term "library," in fact most of the research materials are available online.'

Duly informed, they return to the street once more, buzzing with all of the possibilities that are unfolding before them.

'Fancy a coffee in Browns, after all this excitement?' asks Joy.

'Great idea. Isn't that the building that used to be the Student Refectory? Where we used to eat baked potatoes and beans together, when we were young, in love, and fancy-free?'

'The very same. Just next to the Museum. Let us cross over now. Beat you to it.'

'Oh look!' she says, after gingerly negotiating the traffic, and nearly getting run over by their beloved # 1 bus. 'The Vanity of Small Differences is still showing at the museum, that show you were raving about. Could you stand seeing it again? I would love to see it for myself. I might even sign up as a weaver at the Graduate school.'

'Yes of course. My viewing was obscured last time by a busload of tourists from Surrey, so it would be good to have an uninterrupted scrutiny. But only after our coffee.'

Joy is entranced, quite overwhelmed, by her first viewing of Grayson Perry's tapestries, while Justin has time to really focus on some of the smaller detail, taking time to absorb some of the intent behind the juxtaposition of the hangings. Heads together, they whisper as they point at artefacts familiar from their cultural history that immediately tickle them, while other objects cause a squirm of embarrassed recognition, especially the fondue set. 'These tapestries remind me of the anarchic murals down in Stokes Croft,'

Joy says, 'What a shame that the main audience of Grayson's show are largely literate middle-class folk. But then maybe the Stokes Croft murals reach a wider audience. And maybe it is good to know that the murals are an affront to many of respectable bourgeois who have to drive past them going up the Cheltenham Road, on the way to their North Bristol homes.'

Justin looks at her, questioningly. 'I am not sure that you and I are that distant as yet from that social milieu.'

Joy ponders this. 'Have we really become so resolutely aspirant middle class do you think, since our student days, without knowing it?'

'I think that might well be the case. We may well be enacting the vanity of small differences in our Westbury fastness, without knowing it. I think more doses of Dave and Tony might well release us from some of the depredations of the class system.'

'Do you know, I think it might. And what about our children? Do we really want to bring them up class-bound, ever sensitive to the small and larger things that distinguish them from lesser mortals? Do they need to be brought up thinking that needing to be superior is the only thing that really matters?'

'No, I don't think we do,' says Justin. 'And that nearly 'whites only' school they go to probably does not help, even if it will help them get to the right university.'

'Yes, I agree. We should do something about that sometime soon, without completely disrupting their lives. And hey, I think they will be amused – and I hope pleased – that we will be going to school too, and doing homework together around the kitchen table.'

Justin allows himself am image of them all scrambling for space. 'That paints quite a picture. Perhaps the kids could be teaching us a few things in the process. Like how to work my Uber app properly. Or helping you gain entry to the electronic library without crashing the whole university.'

Joy pauses, saying, 'talking of your children, and I know you mean it for the best, but I would prefer it if you resisted the temptation to put pictures of our children up on Facebook. And having them pose, like the pic of them inside Bert's Austin Healey you posted the other day.'

Justin is taken aback by this. 'Joy, you have never mentioned this before. I think the kids love it. And all of our friends are happy to post pics of their kids looking happy, doing wonderful things. I see no harm in this. Our friends always tick 'like' to my posts – sometimes even 'love,' commenting on how cute they both are.'

'I know you mean no harm in this Justin, and yes so many parents do this. But haven't you noticed that these are all images of perfection, of perfectly lived childhoods and immaculate parenting? So, few of these images depict unhappiness or failure. God forbids. I would like us to drop out of the race to curate family life as a state of permanent bliss. Would you mind?'

Justin looks reluctant. 'Okay, if you feel that strongly, then I will stop. I don't suppose you want me to put up photos of them as they come home having failed an exam, or being dropped from the football team?'

'No, I don't think I am saying that, that would not work either. I am simply saying that I would like you to stop, to resist the urge to copy what other parents do. In fact, I would like you to drop out of that race altogether. Even if Amelia wins a Nobel prize. You might learn to live in real time, without needing the fix of your daily quota of "likes."'

A curator sidles up beside them, interrupting this conversation, to say that the exhibit is closing shortly. Wandering through the gift shop, Justin again notices a flyer for 'Human Cargo' show at St Georges Chapel, just down Park Street, opposite their favourite solicitor's office. He says, 'Joy, look, this show caught my eye last time, remember I showed you the flyer? Well it is happening tonight. Shall we?'

'Yes, why not – some slavery action to get my middle- class guilt up a notch should suit nicely, following the assault of these tapestries. And it will help me tune into some of the not so funny themes that drive Bristolian black stand-up humour. From a time when being black was no laughing matter at all. But then maybe it still isn't.'

'Good thought. And supper at Vincenzo's pizza place before? Pretty please?'

'Okay, Justin. But you and your pizzas. Grrrr.'

'I know, I know.' Says Justin nevertheless pressing his culinary case.

'But we so used to love going to Vincenzo's as students, when pizzas were a novelty – and cheap. There was something about the hanging Chianti bottles that captivated us back then. The romance of the Neapolitan vibe, the owner's family chattering away at the table near the servery, the sheer novelty of seeing your food rise in front of your very eyes. Pizzas seem to have become a commodity since. To the extent that the kids have to build their own. More evidence of reducing the workforce.'

They enter the restaurant to discover that the self-same bottles hang from the ceiling still. They find yet more flyers plastered all over the walls, some current, some ancient, below the cobwebbed, straw-bound flasks. 'Look, I think that poster is for a show we saw twenty year ago, in the Anson Rooms,' exclaims Joy.

'I think you are right. Have we aged as much as the band has? Or in fact as much as this restaurant has. Looks like they might be running it into the ground, sell it soon enough for student flats, I wouldn't be at all surprised.'

As they settle for a shared Four Seasons pizza, which is spilling over the plate, Justin's phone pings. It is Uber online.

'Oh, Joy, look.' He shows her his Uber driver's app. 'I have been accepted by Uber and am good to go as a driver. I simply log in when I am ready to drive. Me and the trusty Prius and on the road.'

'That was quick. And well done. Things seem to be moving fast in our lives. Our stars must be in alignment this week. And hopefully for the rest of our lives.'

Finishing their pizzas – and saying they did not remember them being quite so greasy – they walk up the hill to the recently renovated St Georges Chapel, one of the original Georgian concert halls in England, where the renovation has rendered it an impressive fusion of the ancient and modern. They descend to the low-ceilinged cellar bar in the crypt to catch the mood of the assembled throng, picking up yet more flyers for upcoming musical and artistic events as they go. Yet more choice to feast upon. Who knew how much was going on in this city they live in, when they had been so often oblivious to it all?

Justin recognises one of the staff collecting tickets at the door, but cannot put a name to the face, or the place. She sees him too, saying, 'Are you not Justin, from the Chrysalis Coaching network?'

'Yes, I am – and you are?' he guesses wildly, 'Susan?'

'No, Sarah. Don't worry, Chrysalis seems to be jammed with Sally's and Sarah's and Susan's. We can hardly tell the difference between us ourselves. But I don't go to that group anymore. In fact, I feel I have grown out of executive coaching.'

Justin recalls that she was always different from the rest of the coaches, intense, deep, and he is not really surprised that she has dropped out of that iron monkey cage. He says, 'I think I know the feeling. I am having a crisis of faith over coaching myself.'

Sarah looks pleased to hear that another coach has jumped ship. 'Good to hear. It comes to us all in the end, maybe, the process of leaving the elusive promise of highly paid work behind. Now I am doing other things, including volunteering here at St Georges. It is so good for the soul, and you meet amazing people, including the artists. In fact, you might want to try volunteering. And you get to see the shows for free! Meet me at the interval and I will find you a form to fill in and get to meet our creative director and our venue manager.' She is quite insistent, fixing him again with those soulful eyes.

'Sounds good to me. I had never ever thought of doing such a thing. But it seems to be working well for you … I look forward to hearing more, and thanks for the invitation.' She moves on to attend to fellow guests, while he finds Joy absorbed in the Chapel's catalogue of summer events.

'Who was that you were talking to? An old girlfriend? You seemed to be locked in deep private conversation.'

'Not quite, but a fellow coach, Sarah, an apostate who has dropped out and is encouraging me to come volunteering here at St Georges.'

'Amazing. Quell coincidence. And well worth following up on. Meeting reformed coaches will do your soul good, help confirm your decision to leave that behind for a while.'

Settled just to the side of the stage, in seats high in the gallery that surrounds the whole auditorium, they find 'Human Cargo' deeply moving. They are struck once again by the power of live performance, feeling at one with the two artists as they recite and sing accounts of slaves who passed through Bristol over the centuries. These deeply personal stories seem so far away in time' and yet so near. It reminds them of the recent Windrush immigration scandals too, though occurring much closer in time: stories not of slavery but of recent black oppression and neglect.

Left thoughtful but uplifted, they leave with a nod to Sarah, who is busy manning the exits. Justin finds time to thank her for her introductions to the management during the interval, who had intrigued him as to the prospect of volunteering; though with a family he is not sure if he can find the time in the evenings for it. 'Still, lovely to be asked.' Feeling stimulus enough for one day, they find their way to the now customary #1 bus stop on the Triangle, chattering all the way home.

The next morning finds Justin setting out for his first Uber ride, leaving Joy busy pouring over all of the various brochures and flyers they have collected, looking more closely at the courses they like online, and the options and timings they offer. Joy get outs the calculator and begins to work out what all of this might cost, and whether it is affordable. She even thinks of putting the whole schedule and costings on a spreadsheet, but feels that this might be industrialising the process a little too far at this stage. Totally absorbed in this task, she is surprised by her husband coming into the room.

'What a great feeling that was, of being back to work,' says Justin, 'and here I am, my first Uber shift done and dusted.'

'That is marvellous Justin, and I will hear all about it shortly. But meanwhile, give me a moment to sort out the last of these online course bookings while the system is still letting me in.'

Not sure if he can hold back his excitement for too long, Justin instead opens his laptop to capture his inner flow in his online journal.

My first Uber customer. Wow – I cannot believe this is happening so quickly, and all goes well. So far. My first shift begins, though I limit it to three hours, to get familiar with the whole thing. I realise pretty soon that my knowledge of Bristol is going to be massively enhanced, and my knowledge will extend beyond the geography, to getting to know a whole lot more about the variety of citizens who populate this city, too. My first ride is from Henbury through to Temple Meads. The ride is a long one, in time if not in distance, given all the road works jamming up the railway station. I confess to the passenger that this is my first day. She seems sympathetic.

She says she works for the Parliamentary Labour Party, and is on her way to a sub- committee meeting on transport policy at the Houses of Parliament. I learn much of her work on the way. My next ride is from Temple Meads to Southmead Hospital –a junior doctor late for his shift. Finished listening to his tales of the long hours he has to work. Then a ping tells me that my first ride has left a tip. Amazing. I have arrived at the threshold of my new life. I am on my way.

On the way back down Whiteladies I stop at Pronto Pizza, where I discover they are advertising for drivers. I talk to the harassed manager, who seems a little suspicious of my candidature, given my profile is quite different from the usual adolescent suspects. However, he asks me to fill in the requisite form, and says he will try me out soon enough after I have undergone a short training and scooter familiarisation. The delivery boys congregated outside seem to have little to do, but it is early in the day. I ask them how they find their work, as I am thinking of joining them. They look incredulous that I might want to do this, saying that there is a lot of waiting around, followed by insane busyness. 'You will find out soon enough,' says one. 'Apart from anything else, it is not just the customers but the smell of pizza fat that gets to you in the end.'
Whoops,I need to interrupt this reverie, as my phone reminds me I have another ride.

His second shift successfully completed, following a similar pattern to the first, Justin logs off Uber then heads to Stokes Croft for his meeting with Tony. Tony is amused to hear of his Uber career. 'So now you are tasting the gig economy for real, and the wonder of zero hours?'

'Well it is not so different in nature from the pick-up coaching was doing actually, except in shorter time-bites.'

'Well that is true enough, agrees Tony. 'Taxi work is something many from around Stokes Croft are doing – including Dave. Being able to manage your own time while earning fits well with those following alternative callings that do not as yet – and probably never will - deliver secure enough income to sustain them on a stand-alone basis.'

Their conversation moves on from the gig economy to Justin's recent calamities on the executive coaching front, and of his near misses with the corporate behemoths. Justin is taken by the quality of Tony's listening, and by his sympathy and concern, while having to be cautious not to disclose the actual companies he has been ejected from, given the strictures of the gagging orders. Joy's injunctions against him being tempted to spill all to a ready listener ring in his ears, but the temptation is there all the same. It feels mean, not telling Tony the full story.

Surrendering to this impulse, like an alcoholic deciding that only one little drink with a friend will do no harm, Justin weakens to say, 'I am sorry but I cannot give you more detail on the company involved, as I am legally sworn to secrecy, facing dire consequences if I utter as much as one word. But I do need some help, and you could be just the person to help me think through a dilemma. The thing is, a victimised employee from company X has passed me passed a mysterious USB that she wants held secure in safe hands. I really worry that the contents of this data stick that might incriminate me – though I have never opened it - and I need to get it out of my possession fairly quickly. On the other hand, I do not want to betray her trust.' There, he has said it. He feels glad to have put this out there, feeling sure Tony will know what to do next.

Tony ponders long on this. 'I see. Sounds serious. Look, I do not need to know where the USB comes from, or what is on it. But it sounds like you were given it for a reason, and that it would be a shame for it to be destroyed. If you like, you could give it to me for safekeeping. I am really trustworthy in such matters. I will not look at it; just hide it away in my safe, with no attribution. When you feel the time is right to do so, just give me a nudge and I will pass it on, anonymously, to whoever might be able to make the best use of it. And to make use if it for good ends, not to land you or your friend in the mire. You can leave it with me for as a long as you like. I will probably forget that I have even got it.'

Justin grabs Tony's arm for assurance that this promise is not lightly made.

'Would you do that? It would be weight off my mind, and Joy wants rid. If you can guarantee that it is untraceable; and if you can refrain from looking at it; then that would be an ideal solution. Thank you.'

'That is no problem. Sounds as though at some point it will need to see the light of day. Just let me know. Now before you pique my curiosity further, can we move on talking about the work we might do together in the environmental space?'

This conversation proves to be long one, as Tony takes Justin through all of the nuances of his environmental work, in addition to his more regular consulting work with NGOs and charities. Justin discovers that while a number of these interventions are styled as 'coaching,' that in fact, in most cases coaching skills are assumed as a necessary background competence, rather than being placed in the front of the shop window.

Tony is really pleased to hear of Justin signing up for an environmental studies class at the university: but on hearing that the course is part-funded by the World Wildlife Fund, he winces. 'Those Panda people get their paws into all the environmental pies, sucking up all the attention and the money along with their smart logo, and exploiting such a cute, cuddly animal to lure donations in. But the truth is the WWF is a blight on animal conservation. There are far less attractive species than the panda, suffering extinction, while the public's obsession with a zoo animal that takes four years to get pregnant remains undiminished. And do watch out for funding or research work done by the oil majors too. They are well known in environmental circles for their green-washing tactics.'

As this conversation deepens, Justin is slowly growing to realise that environmental activism is politically more complex than he ever imagined.

'This is all very illuminating, Tony. I must say here was I thinking everyone working in the environmental field had the soul of David Attenborough. Now you are telling me that I need to be careful of whom I sup with.'

'Sorry if I am disillusioning you so soon,' says Tony, shaking his head sadly, 'but yes a long spoon is needed to sup with some of the agencies that might sidle up to you offering funding and attendance at murky conferences. But the university course you are signing up for sounds just the right place for you to hone your critical faculties, and to help you choose whom best to partner with. I, for one, am happy to engage you in a couple of upcoming projects where I can coach you in ways to navigate your way through these political minefields.'

'Well thanks for that, Tony, and I really look forward to picking up on this with you next week. Let us make a date now, as it is time for me to be making tracks home, to enjoy the last of my lone time with Joy, before the kids descend once more.'

Black Magic

The Friday morning of their child-free sabbatical finds Joy frustrated by her university library application, but she is intrigued to find that most of the material she is seeking is also available on Google or Google Scholar. She muses, 'I have hardly started but already I am being confronted by warnings from seasoned academics to beware the commoditisation of knowledge, eh? I thought I had got away from robotisation when leaving Magic Carpet. I am reading that artificial Intelligence could soon put not only libraries, but also whole universities out of business. It is a chastening thought.'

'I see. So, are you giving up on the library application already?'

'No, don't be silly. But none of it is as simple as it was in our day, when you would pick up a book off a shelf then read it. Even the process of course application is online, following clunky formats. I am sure it is all really efficient and labour-saving, once you get the hang of it, but I cannot help but feel that my learning will be steered by a series of competing algorithms, fighting each with each other to frustrate me from human contact with teachers or fellow students.'

'I feel sure you will find a way through the automated jungle. I know how resourceful you are. In fact, I am getting to know more of your resilience by the day, since we have been spending more time together.'

Joy nods at the acknowledgment, surprised a little herself at her capacity to move on from chronic stress levels to move quickly on to explore fresh opportunities.

'Yes, I feel sure I will make it through the online library jungle, with my very own digital machete. Oh, and before you log onto your Uber algorithm, Mr Driver Man, could you drop me off at Stokes Croft? I am free from the gym regime today, and have booked in to have my first look at Dave's manuscripts, by way of helping him think how his book might be ordered. He is even willing for me to take his draft of the first four chapters home with me.'

'Well, what a moment, what a turning point in your editorial career. I will indeed drive you down there, before I go on the meter.'

Their conversation continues in the car, with Joy saying, 'I do hope you get paid for all of this driving that you are doing, much as you love it.'

'Oh, I imagine I will be compensated somehow, through some sort of magic transfer that will hit the bank at some point. Or my PayPal account. The great thing is that there is no cash handling. I would hate that.'

Joy tries hard not to think of the mayhem that would ensue should Justin ever be allowed near the folding stuff. 'Hmm... you will be paid, I feel sure, but only after Uber have taken their invisible but pernicious electronic fee from you, to enhance the bank account of some shell company located on a faraway place like the Cayman Islands, but managed from California.'

'Maybe so, but it suits my purposes all the same. Flexibility and all of that.'

'Did you say you had looked into working for Pronto Pizza also?' asks Joy.

'Yes, I have. Less promising than Uber, but a chance to learn my way around Bristol and its people by scooter, rather than car.'

'Or alternatively, you could put one of those big yellow and red Pronto boxes on the back of your pious Prius?' giggles Joy.

'I could do that, but it not quite the Prius-pimping I am looking for.'

'You could always carry the pizzas inside, on the passenger seat, or in the boot.'

'Oh, the smell. Nauseating.' Says Justin, pulling a face

'You never know, your passengers might fancy a nibble along the way. Two birds with one stone, and all of that.'

'Joy, you are a marketer's dream. Product integration. I will park that idea in my desperate synergies bank. Oh, here we are madam – Dave's place.'

'Thank you, driver Justin.'

'How was your ride? Don't forget there is a tip function available on your Uber app.'

'No, I will not forget that – bye bye, my five-star driver.'

As Justin's Uber schedule works out, he is able to pick up Joy on the way home. She climbs in clutching a fistful of manuscripts, filling three box-files that spill over with fragments of paper. 'Just as well you picked me up, thanks. These archives are quite a handful.'

'Looks like you have his entire life story, and those of every black person who has ever landed up on these shores, by the looks of it.'

'It feels like that too,' says Joy looking back at the full backseat. 'And there are audiotapes in abundance too. I am not even sure if we have a cassette deck anymore, though I think there might be one in the attic. The kids will be rapt to see such a mechanical device. Look, two paper bags full of tapes, none of them catalogued.'

'That is quite a task you have taken on.'

'It is more than I reckoned, but Dave's history is fascinating. The stories he has to tell are Homeric. No wonder his observational comedy is so rich. I have entered a whole different world here, and at this stage I am feeling privileged to have been invited. Just to warn you, I am going to need to clear out the entire back bedroom to accommodate this lot. Maybe making it the black bedroom?'

Justin imagines the entire house being consumed by the Dave archive, while Dave luxuriates in all the space liberated in his home. He cautions, 'Some of the more risqué material you may need to keep away from the children.'

'Oh really? How prissy of you. Speaking of which, they are back tomorrow. Our week of blissful freedom nearly at an end.'

'Yes, but we have opened up so many other freedoms yet to be savoured and enjoyed, while they have been gone.'

Back home, they knock up some pasta together, pour a glass of wine, and begin to try to make some sort of sense of the week gone by, before the onslaught of their returning 'here and now' children obliterate it from mind.

'No TV news just now,' pleads Joy. 'Put on some music, some of that Blues your dad liked some much. Besides loving the Blues, I must immerse myself in black culture. I want to immerse myself in black culture. Muddy Waters please!'

'Yep, muddy waters indeed. That may well be what we are getting into.' Justin finds one of his dad's old LPs and places it on their recently acquired retro turntable, the stylus finding some place to settle amid all the scratches.

Joy relaxes in her chair, kicking back. 'Seems quite a while since our time at the solicitor's office on Monday, does it not? Yet it was only five days ago.'

'Yes, and now all that is signed off and agreed - and the money coming in. That is some kind of triumph.'

'Yes, it is,' grins Joy. 'My Whole Health schedule is all set up, taking some real shape, some time structure – and I am feeling better already from my exertions, if not a little stiff. What a prospect ahead, filling my days in enriching and energising ways, juggling all of these wonderful things. Yoga, meditation. Editing, meeting with Dave and some of his chums too. Day classes on writing and publishing starting next week. Children to enjoy while the summer lasts. How did I ever find time for work?'

'That is something retired folk say when they are first released from captivity. That is before the time when their hobbies lose their lustre, and when they begin to miss the sense of purpose that work brought kicks in.' Looking at Joy's reaction to this piece of received wisdom, Justin is keen to dismiss his pessimistic note. 'I only know that because I learned it on one my "coaching for transitions" module. Probably a load of rubbish.'

She grimaces a little at this reference to his canned learning. Justin continues trying to make amends, 'but it is great that your life is so full. I share some of the sense of busy liberation, too. For my part, so much has changed, and so quickly. Getting going with Uber, investigating Pronto, signing up for some classes, having really productive chats with Tony about alternative ways of bringing my coaching and management skills into play, for the sake of the planet. And I am going to book onto that speed awareness class I need to do to clear my licence, after getting booked for speeding the other week.'

'Quite. You now have more than enough on your plate – and don't you forget that you are a father too. You have much to teach our children, just as you dad taught you so much, and not just about music – he encouraged the philosophy of following your bliss, making the most of your gifts. Maybe our kids need to know some of those guiding principles too, rather than pursuing phoney lifetime security at all costs.'

'Yes, I am only now beginning to realise how much wisdom he bestowed on me. And my mum of course, in a different way.'

'Well, now you can brag to your kids of having the two jobs they have always dreamt of for you. They will have a real story to tell their friends in the playground.'

'Talking of Tony? Did you say he had some ideas about the USB?'

Yes, he has. In fact, more than an idea. He was happy to take it off my hands and secure it somewhere safe. I dug it up then dropped it off last week. Put in the safe with my own bare, muddy hands.'

This is just the news Joy wishes to hear, to cap a fine week of resolving impending threats and building fresh opportunities.

'Really? I am so glad that the USB will be gone. I just hope to God that Tony can be trusted with it. But I trust your judgment on him, despite your capacity to misguidedly trust strangers that do not have your best interests at heart. From what I have seen of him, he is not a whistleblowing glory seeker. My honest preference would to have been to bury the wretched memory stick somewhere it could never have been found; but then that would not have honoured Gladys's wish to get the news out.'

Justin is happy to have Joy accept his solution to the unwanted guest decaying in the pet's graveyard. 'Clearly Magic Carpet do not associate us with data leak so we should be in the clear. Besides, they would not think that we would have the balls, post the settlement. Burying it among the remains of the rabbits and guinea pigs was never a great idea, just a desperate measure. But hey, we seem to be rather enjoying being fugitives. Well, at least the initial glamour of it.'

'Fugitives with some financial security behind us. Fugitives with benefits. I am so enjoying the idea that we no longer not need to maintain the mask of middle-class respectability, of having to prove ourselves perpetually in hostile, competitive environments. Most of I am already enjoying that sense of freedom, of being in charge of our lives again, not being run by someone else's invisible rules and schedules. '

She is interrupted by the children bursting through the door, pausing only to wave goodbye to the minibus, then turning to beam at their parents, their over-spilling bags knocking against their muddied knees.

'Oh Mummy, we have so much to tell you. It has been great. And we got so muddy every day. Look at our hands, our nails.' Adam holds out both arms as evidence.

'What is that music? It is groovy,' asks Amelia.

'Funnily enough the artist's name is Muddy Waters, one of your granddad's favourites,' says Joy.

'We love muddy. Can we get muddy again? Can we get muddy to the tune of muddy?' Amelia breaks into a muddy dance, while Adam claps her performance.

'Yes, we can,' agrees her father, 'we can all get muddy together.'

'Did you miss us?' asks Amelia, finished her tribal mud-splattered dance for the time being.

'Of course we did,' assures Joy, 'but you are going to see a whole lot more of us shortly, to make up for that.'

'Oh great. Why is that?' asks Adam.

Joy explains, 'Mummy is taking a break, a well-deserved break from the flying carpet for a while.'

'Yippee. Is it always going to be like last week, on holiday with Mummy, but all of the time? Can we stop going to school? Have Muddy Mummy all the time?' squeals Amelia, inspired to begin her dance once more.

'No, not quite like that, but yes, lots more time with both of you. And even better news. Daddy is taking a break from the Ponzi factory too.'

'Oh, fantastic - to do what? Become an astronaut?' Adam decides to raise his sights on his on his choice of career for his father, while wondering what is coming.

'No, not quite. Not yet. But he is going to become a real taxi driver and maybe a pizza man too.'

'Oh, Daddy, that is just the best. Pizza every night, and a yellow sign on top of your car. Our mates will love that, us being dropped by a real taxi, not by a boring parent. No more Ponzi factory. And more mum at home!' Adam chirps, giving his father's legs an impromptu hug.

Amelia adds, 'Daddy, I am really pleased for you too. And for us. But tomorrow, can we go collect some tadpoles? We have learned all about tadpoles at camp. And chrysalises. We learned about them too. We love sightless creatures that become something else, something grown-up and beautiful. Can we become something else? Please? Can we?'

'Yes, you can. We have plans for you in that direction, but then so does Mother Nature.' Says Justin, reaching out to hold each of their hands, beneficently.

Amelia persists in her wish to share her newfound pond-based knowledge. 'Mummy are you are dad becoming something else too, now that you are changing work? Are you both parental pupa?'

Joy is delighted to discover that learning has occurred, amid all the mud and bullets. 'What a clever phrase. Well, yes, we really do feel that we might be ready to hatch out quite soon.

Watch this space. So, yes to tadpoles and chrysalis, yes to frogs and butterflies. But first go get cleaned up, supper, bed. Then we head off to Leigh Woods in the morning, to squelch through some ponds. Oh, and take off your wellies, leave them outside the door.'

Speed Kills

Justin is tinkering around in the kitchen, trying to avoid his moribund marketing to-do list, when his phone pings. A message from Joanna. He turns his back on Joy, who is busy on her laptop, then casually presses the blinking Messenger icon.

Hi Justin, you free to chat?

Sure, briefly. Just avoiding resurrecting my compelling marketing pipeline for my dying coaching business. Not even sure why I am bothering.

Ha ha. Don't let me keep you.

Don't worry, you are not. I need distraction. And good to hear from you too Joanna. How is your life?

Going okay actually. And I am looking forward to us doing the speeding thing together tomorrow. So happy that we fixed between us to do this on the same day. Sometimes online bookings can work in a person's favour.

Yes it was great how you did that. You being there will brighten up a dreary day.

Well, I am just hoping I can make it out to the wilds of Avonmouth, with my car broken down? Again! Had it back for three whole glorious days then it broke down again.

Well I could pick you up if you like. If that is not too presumptuous. Where do you live?

Henbury? And no, not presumptuous at all. That would be great, it that is not trouble?

No, none at all.

Great. Let me tell you why.

Please do.

Well, to be quite honest, I dare not ask my hubbie Alan for a lift, he is not at all happy about me getting this ticket. I am normally so law abiding. But frankly he is making a meal of this ticket?

That is a shame. But I am still more than happy to pick you up. Hope this doesn't put you off the whole idea... but it would be best for you not to come to the house. Can you think of somewhere? I am not wanting to get us both into something here that might look more than it is

No, me neither. It is okay – just a friend helping a friend – or rather a fellow partner in crime. Look, I could pick you up at the #1 bus stop at Henbury. 8.30. How would that be?

That would work fine thanks. Really appreciate it. Don't want you getting into any more trouble? He he.

I know you don't. You would be welcome trouble anyway, after some of what I have recently been through.

Look, I need to get on with some stuff, but we can chat in here later if you like. Thanks so much for the offer of the ride.

Would you be able to pick me up at the Henbury bus stop,
about 8.30?
Yes of course. My pleasure. Bye for now. And see you there x

The next morning, Joy wishes Justin luck as he gets ready for
his class, though she has little idea what the class might
involve, and she is really not sure that she is that interested.
She just wants it done and over with. 'Oh look, you have put
on your best suit! And a tie. Did the police stipulate that dress
code?'

'No, they did not. But I do feel like I am being called to court,
as the accused. Best to dress for it.'

'Daddy, are you going to prison. Wearing a stripy top? Have
you done something terrible?' asks Adam, suddenly all ears.

'Kids, it is none of your business,' says Joy, in her best school
ma'am voice. 'Just a weird Ponzi thing. Now get ready for
school. And you, my man, go now before you are late. And no
speeding. They take a dim view of speeding at that class.'

Justin fires up the Prius and heads for the Henbury bus stop,
not too far away, aware that his speeding is another secret to
keep from the children. He reflects how white lies, great and
small pile up, perhaps to be excavated later. He is trusting that
his tryst with Joanna will not fall into that category. But then

maybe it already has, captured on some obscure time-lapse device over which he has no control.

He spies Joanna at the bus stop, dressed up casually for her day, wearing jeans and a nondescript fleece jacket. She hurries to the car and jumps in, looking over her shoulder as she goes. 'Hello! And a Prius to boot. I like getting picked up by an Uber! You play the part well. Fake it until you make it?'

'Very funny. But I have already made it. A fully qualified Uber driver, and my passengers love me. I bring them joy.'

Joanna settles in her seat, pulling on her seat belt while admiring the array of flickering dials in this space age, eerily silent car. As they pull out into the slow-moving traffic, she says, 'Talking of Joy? Which we weren't? Did you tell her that you were picking me up?

Justin, taken aback by the directness of this question, pauses. 'No, I have to admit that I didn't. Why? Well, it would only have prolonged the conversation I don't want to have with her concerning my slackness in getting done for speeding in the first place – and the reason for getting the ticket is because I am always late. Justin-not-in- time, as my kids unhelpfully remind me. And also... well I feel that I am entitled to a little privacy in my life.'

Joanna seems satisfied with this explanation. 'I know what you mean – I feel a bit under surveillance at home too.'

Justin can just imagine. 'So what did you get your ticket for?

'Nothing much, really. Thirty-five in a thirty-mile zone, on this very road we are on now. The scene of my downfall. Please keep your eye on your speedo, if you can concentrate on it at all amid all of that disco lighting on your dash.'

'I will, don't worry I will. My offence was not much either. They say it is all a bit of a money-spinner for the police, this caper.'

'That is not what Alan says! Anyway, nice to be person-to-person again, after so much messaging and sharing of writing. Feels a bit odd, to be honest. But in a nice way, odd. Sorry.'

Yes, I agree. But the messaging has been good too. But a bit fragmented, not always sure where it is going. The private writing was at a different order of sharing altogether. Thanks so much for being so open. I treasure it.'

'Oh, it was pleasure. Well some of what came out was an eye-opener. And my writing, so amateur compared to your polished stuff. You have certainly learned how to smear on the varnish.'

'Come on now, don't put yourself down. I spent hours on mine. And the first part was for submission, the second part not so. Your writing was amazing, honestly. I loved it all of it.'

'Really?'

'Yes, really. You have quite a talent for first-time writing, straight onto the page. You held back on nothing, once you got up to speed.'

'Talking of speed, keep your eye on the road, this junction is tricky. Look, who is that rude man honking at you? Should I flip him the finger?' Her giggle rings out above the near silent engine.

Justin looks towards the honking car. "Oh, please not the fat finger!! That is a friend, a casual acquaintance, Jim the engineer, taking his kids to school. I met him on the river ferry, just before you spotted me at the pier.' Justin waves back at his friend, noticing that Jim's kids in the back have their heads down, probably deep in their phones. Or searching for a misplaced harmonica.

Justin takes the right-hand turn, doing his best to drive like a good citizen should, while listening to Joanna's chatter. 'How nice it is to have friend's that know you. This is quite small town though. Who else might have seen us together? I would hate for this to get out. Two criminals on the run, to meet their fate together, all over the Evening Post?' She shivers inside her fleece at the thought. 'Try not to cross the white line. Or any other line, for that matter. Sorry, I was being a back-seat driver.'

He lets this go. 'I know what you mean, but I think this is all quite innocent and explainable. Talking of which, did you tell Alan how you were going to travel?'

She goes silent.... 'No, I thought about it, but chickened out. I am in deep enough water with him already. Just told him I was going to the bus stop, which I do regularly anyway, now that the car is caput. Again.'

'Okay, I get it. No need to explain further. By the way, what you wrote so movingly about your marriage. My lips are sealed.'

'Thanks. It all just spilled out. Best we leave that unspoken for the time being.'

'Fine by me. Look, there is the Police Training Centre. We are nearly late! We had better scamper in.'

'Oh yes. But not together, please,' suggests Joanna. 'You never know who might be there. Best they think us strangers – not a block booking. I will go first, you follow. And thanks a million for the lift. By the way, I have no idea what we are walking into here? I haven't really thought about it. Simply want it over and done with.'

'Nor me. Now off you go. And don't forget your paperwork and your licence.'

Once registered, they are asked to take a place at one of the four round tables that are spaced around the sunlit room. They sit together, enjoying the complicity of being strangers to each other. 'Please don't sit in silence,' says the heavily built tutor in the polyester suit. 'This is not a doctor's waiting room. Fill in your nameplates with the felt tip provided. Get talking to each other. There will be lots of table talk and we want you to make the most of it. We know none of you want to be here – only to clear your licences – but we hope you learn something along the way. There is no pass or fail, just old habits to be left behind, and new behaviours learned.'

Justin and Joanna chat quietly, not finding it easy to play at being strangers to each other. 'Oh hello,' says Joanna, looking at his nameplate. 'Justin is it? I am Joanna. This is quite a step into the unknown for me. Feels a bit like jury service – faced with this random collection of folk, awkward, not knowing what to say – after you say hello.'

'Nice to meet you, Joanna,' Justin replies, offering her his hand, which she squeezes, slowly.

The rest of their table sits in silence, busying themselves with the picture puzzle pre-test in the booklet in front of them. Joanna ignores her booklet for the time being, instead whispering to Justin, 'this set up – it reminds me of all the corporate trainings I have had to endure. You have to go under sufferance, and pretend to get along with each other,'

'I know, tell me about it. I have been on the other side of the pantomime, being in HR, organising seminars for unwilling corporate conscripts,' he says, wincing at the prospect of being on the receiving end this time around. Realising that they are likely to reveal their friendship if they carry on chatting, they turn to pay attention to the tutor, who has recommended his introduction. 'You can go the toilet anytime you like. You do not have to put your hand up, like obedient school kids. We only have two things we want you to observe during your toilet break. They are - wash your hands - and come back.' He pauses for a ripple of laughter, which his captives oblige him with. The tutor, happy with this triggered response, continues his preamble, as if on autopilot. 'No phones are allowed in this room. Anyone spotted doing so will automatically lose six points on their licence and face court on criminal charges,' he warns, knowing this knowledge will hasten much furtive fumbling for potentially incriminating gadgets. Joanna wonders what four hours without a phone might be like, but the threat of prison is enough to cause her to oblige. She knew this might be boring, but this injunction takes that expectation to a higher-level altogether.

'You ask why no phones?' the instructor's rhetorical question is left hanging. 'What happens here is completely anonymous. We do not want you photo'ing or recording each other. Especially if you are a celebrity, but then if you are, then I for one don't recognise you.' More compulsory titters as the silenced phones are buried deep in pockets and bags.

Justin is beginning to think this introduction might last the whole morning. Nonetheless he listens on. 'Most of all we must respect each other. No badmouthing of tractor drivers, cyclists, van drivers and the like. Or police.'

Joanna muses that this requirement was going to kill stone dead the honest, open sharing that they are meant to be engaging in. She is sure that everyone has a category of road user among their pet hates, yet here they are not allowed to speak to such prejudices.

His class duly warned, the instructor continues. 'And no 'isms' may be spoken.' Without explaining this term further, the table members look to each other in puzzlement. Joanna wonders if feminism was off the cards too, given the retro demeanour of their throwback tutor. Finally done with his preamble, each table is asked to share what it was that brought them there, by means of getting to know each other. At their table is assembled a motley crew: a woman tractor driver, a truck driver, and a young woman with a spider tattoo. They all have a hard luck story to tell of how they got done. Mordant British humour is to the fore as they each make light excuses for their law breaking.

Finally done with this trial by group work, the table members are asked to share the biggest stressors that occur for them externally, outside the vehicle.

'Other drivers,' three of them at the table say. The truck driver mimics a one-finger salute, then a vigorous wanking gesture. He is a man of few words but glowering presence, though Justin is not sure if his employer would be happy to see the "Colin's Construction" logo across the back of his hi-viz tabard being advertised to a classroom full of reprobates. The truck driver explains that his job depends on getting this penalty cleared. He glares at the rest of the table, as if they were responsible for this jeopardy.

The tutor explains that intimidatory gestures – the truck driver again simulates wanking, lest anyone had missed it – were in fact illegal, and could be reported. Half the class looks sheepish, deciding that they will stick to flashing lights in future. Only to be told that light flashing is illegal too. As is beckoning on other drivers. As is the honking of horns for no good reason, and certainly not for ventilating anger.

Joanna is left wondering what might be left, beyond silent screaming. She writes in her booklet, 'don't they know that we all turn into monsters behind the wheel?' then pushes her scribbles towards Justin.

Justin writes in his booklet by way of reply, 'apparently not. They should rename this course, "Dealing with your Inner Monster."

She replies, 'or someone else's. Maybe even an inner monster like yours.'

The tutor, noticing this sedulous note taking, nods in their direction, approvingly, as no one else has bothered to pick up a pen. His PowerPoint sequence prompts him to ask his next question. 'What feelings are aroused when other drivers irritate you?'

The tractor-driver says she felt only vile anger towards all other road users. All of them. All of the time. As the stories of road-rage drifts around the table, the tutor encouraged them to think of coping mechanisms that might calm the cortisol racing through their system, though warning that, 'Pilates at the wheel could bring unintended consequences.' Arff arff.

The tractor driver, in a moment of self-awareness, says, 'this is turning into an anger management class. Which is maybe what I need.' The rest of the table nod in agreement, while not wanting to engage in any stereotyping of tractor-drivers. 'Or in tractivism,' Joanna writes. 'I cannot now ever forget what I know what goes on inside a tractor cab when I am trying to overtake it on a country lane.'

The next exercise is to identify stressors that were "internal to the vehicle." The men across the room chime as one: 'driving with my wife! Driving with my partner!' These men are oblivious, clearly, to the women among them. Or else they just don't care. The tattooed younger woman looked miffed. Joanna, thinking about her nagging Justin in the car on the way to the police station, feels a little sheepish.

The tutor confirms this shared finding. 'Yes, driving with the wife beside you is commonly referenced as the most frequent internal stressor. Or indeed driving with someone else's wife.' He guffaws at his worn-out joke, happy to join in with the general misogyny. Joanna turns to Justin, looking uneasy at the truth that lay behind this ribald remark for the both of them, when driving together that morning. Had anyone seen them arrive?

As things proceed in this call and response fashion, the two conspirators continue to write sly notes to each other in their booklets; notes which grow bolder as the morning wears on. They take the coffee break together, outside, to share impressions of the morning so far. They agree that the advice they were hearing was all very sensible, but they did not like being forced to go. Given the freedom to use their phones during the break, Joanna pulls up Facebook. 'Oh, dear,' she says,' more pics of perfect families. Do none of these folks ever write that their kids are driving them up the wall – or that they have locked them in the downstairs cupboard for the weekend?'

Back in class, the tutor kicks off with the question, 'do we humans like being told what to do?' while knowing already that no one in the room does. He then carries on telling them what to do.

'No, we don't like being told what to do!!' scribbles Joanna.

'We don't like being told to do table exercises,' writes Justin, while knowing that he has inflicted just such punishment on management trainees in the past.

For the grand finale of the class, they are subject to a bombardment of statistics concerning the costs of accidents, widths of tyres, deaths, injuries etc. 'I could go on boring you to death with these stats all day,' says the tutor, when it feels like he already has. They are told to turn to page nine of their booklets, to find the goal setting exercise, which is designed to ensure that none of them ever speed again. This is positioned by a short lesson in setting goals – SMART goals.

Recognising this as the ubiquitous acronym beloved of all coaching manuals, neither Justin nor Joanna dare catch the other's eye, for fear of corpsing in a fit of giggles. "Does this man not know that SMART goals look neat but never work?

That human beings do not work along straight lines?' writes Justin.

Log books in hand, and the police data base informed that they were now innocent, they return separately, slowly to the Prius, having left their fellow inmates to speed away. Secure in the car, Justin asks, 'How does it feel to be a free woman then?'

'Feels wonderful. Nothing like absolution! Just like coming out of a Catholic church after confession.'

'I wouldn't know about that. But yes, I do feel a cleansed. Are you... were you a Catholic?'

'"Were" is the correct answer. Though the guilt never leaves you.'

'You feeling guilty now?'

'I feel guilty all the time. Hardwired in.'

'With programme updates from the Catholic Church?' asks Justin.

'Not always. I have installed malware to corrupt priestly intrusions.'

'Funny.'

'Well, free in one way, not in others,' sighs Joanna. 'But relieved to have that speeding ordeal over. And it wasn't too bad after all.'

'Did you learn anything from it?' Justin asks.

'Well yes. Some of the tips for safe driving made lots of sense. I have been lazy, and I really should read the Highway Code again. But I do feel I will be a safer driver – until the learning wears off. Habits are hard to break, as the instructor warned.'

'Yes, he is right. And I really doubt whether bombarding people with "oh ah" stats really changes behaviour. We are not rational beings at heart. Habit change takes a deeper intervention. Which is where I think intensive coaching plays a part.'

'Oh, is this sermon from St Justin? But I think you are right. Such a blizzard of facts – some of them fading in my mind even as we speak. But I do feel – well more accepting that I did something wrong that could have put lives in danger, and screwed up my job, my family life and those of the victims' families too, than I did before the course, when I was just making excuses, like everyone else round the table.'

'I will never forget that round table. And our cheeky secret scribbling to each other, like errant school kids.'

'Yes, we were so bad. Maybe we will always be bad.'

'Could be. Like you, I am out of driving denial. Much more aware of the risks on all sides of a piece of unthinking recklessness.'

'Yep – sometimes small things lead to bigger things. And it was great to have a friend there to share the experience. And to talk it over with afterwards, like this.'

'It was. I feel I know you better. And your inner imp.'

'Look, I have taken the day off,' says Joanna, 'and I'm not ready to go home yet. Do you have time for some lunch, to talk some more about me going into coaching? I would so value your advice. Of course, you may not have the time?'

'No, I would like that. And happy to return the favour. You were so helpful to me during our time in the pub. Somehow you helped purge me of the awfulness of that humiliation.'

'I am glad. I worried I had moved in too close but felt it was what you needed. How about the Henbury Arms?

'That would be great.'

'Now – mirror signal manoeuvre. Look around because I now know, thanks to our tutor, that no one can hear an electric car coming.'

'That is one thing I like about my Prius.'

'I am beginning to learn that no one can hear you coming either. Quite a skill. Justin the stealth bomber.'

'Well, it beats love bombing.'

In the pub, Justin settles for a cola, while Joanna lines up a large white wine, saying, 'let me do the drinking for us this time around. Shall we share one of these monster baked potatoes?'

'Yes, lets. You choose. Monster food for the inner monster.'

Sat at table, she points to the CCTV camera, blinking in the corner. 'Just like the police station. The surveillance society watching us at all times.'

'Yes, I know that on the course they tried to put us at ease, make the atmosphere friendly, but we all knew we were being checked out.'

She nods vigorous agreement, her fork poised over the potato. 'I know it. They even – in a sly way – forced us all to look at each other across the table, to engage in conversations with strangers that might reveal more than we intended, that would cause us to share, to compare – I dunno what?'

'I wanted to coach the tutors in true non-directive techniques. But wishful thinking really.'

'Yep. They were too far-gone with their pre-set, police approved instruction by numbers and awful jokes that we were all obliged to laugh at.'

'Sure, but a cushy number in many ways - no customer feedback...'

'I dream of no customer feedback...' she sighs.

'I can't imagine they have ever had a complaint. Though I am sure they have made a few.'

'This potato really is a monster,' she says, pushing the remains of it in his direction. 'I cannot offend again. Alan, as you know, runs a car parts distribution centre - he says if it goes tits up then I could drive - sorry but that is how he speaks.'

I have heard worse. So, what is piquing your interest in coaching?'

'Well, Consignia are wanting to deal with harassment - we both talked in the office about that, but now they are taking notice. You report might even have helped that along.' Joanna smiles at Justin, appreciatively. 'And I have put my hat in the ring for a job on a special team that will investigate harassment and inequalities. Alongside the job, the firm will fund the successful applicant for some basic training in coaching, leading to a certificate. Your help will be invaluable.'

'Glad to hear it,' encourages Justin, 'though internal change agent jobs can be perilous.'

'Yes, I sense that,' says Joanna, frowning. 'Alan thinks I would be a bit crazy to do all that whistle-blowing, shooting the messenger stuff, as he calls it.'

'Does he now? I think you would be a perfect fit, and should go for it. Apart from anything else you will have new, portable coaching skills under your belt, which will serve you well if and when you move on.'

'Her hands slides towards his, then moves back. 'But look, I have to be selfish here and we are running out of time. Can you recommend a professional body to me?

His response is curt. 'They are all much of a muchness. Coaching Fraternity is okay, they take my money every year, and for that I get the badge.'

'Okay. And are there any good local networks I might join?'

'Yes. We have a local coaching network in Bristol grandly named Chrysalis. You could come along to that if you like, chat to other coaches?'

'Oh, that would fit the bill. How do I join?'

'I will sponsor you. Do not expect too much from it though it will give you a good sense of the many life forms inhabiting the coaching space. It is quite eye opening. I will recommend you this afternoon. I need to write to them about my varnishing session anyway, so it is no problem. I will give them your email.'

'That is amazing. Thank you.' She squeezes his arm. 'Look, I think I need to be going.'

'Me too, probably. But first, moving away from our criminal life, and coaching ...'

'Away towards what?' asks Joanna.

Justin takes his time. 'Well, I know you said not talk about it, but I did want to say thanks for reading my journal entry. It was kind of you to take the time. And your insights into my inner life were quite remarkable. And courageous for you to write them down too. Some of them were confronting, but then some of the best feedback should be just at.'

'Thanks for that, it all just seemed to spring from the keyboard, and I did not want to edit it too much.'

'I am not fishing to talk about what you revealed. I totally respect your wish to keep that private, unless you want to talk about it.'

'Thanks for remembering and respecting my wishes. Though I do see parallels in our accounts of our past and current lives. It was a bit spooky. And I do think we are both reaching for something else. Maybe...'

'Yes, I think so to.'

It is Justin's turn to smile. 'I am glad that we have found each other. I feel I trust you so much. Let us just take this as it comes, shall we?'

'Yes, good idea. So happy we shared the speeding class. That was fun. We have a good capacity to amuse each other, to provide...' she searches for a phrase, her face scrunching little, 'welcome distraction.'

'We do, we do. Early days. Oh, what do I mean by that?'

'I don't know. It doesn't matter. Fire up the Prius and don't forget to check your tyres, just like you should before every journey.'

'I will I will. Are you ready to be dropped off at the Henbury bus stop?'

'I am, I am.'

As he moves to go, she beckons him back to his seat. 'Look, before you go, I have got to ask... will you tell Joy that we shared the class together, now that it is done?'

'Good question, and an awkward question. I am not sure, to be honest. Probably not right away, perhaps not ever. But I would like to. Of course. Nothing to hide here at all.'

'Hmm, me too. I might tell Alan, I might not. He wanted today to serve as a punishment beating, not for me to enjoy myself with an amusing friend. But the fact that we met and are sharing a legitimate agenda around coaching is innocent enough, and true.'

'Quite, same with Joy, too. Though she might go a bit bonkers if she hears about the Consignia association. She might even accuse me of rescuing you?'

'Really? Do I seem like I need rescuing? I am not drowning just yet?'

'I know, I know. I am saying what she might be saying, not what I think our relationship is about.'

With that subject aired, she gives him a peck on the cheek and a short hug, before they return to the car.

Several days after his release from speeding jeopardy, Justin dresses in his best Uber clothes, a dark jacket setting off his white shirt. He looks again at his almost abandoned coaching marketing plan, as much out of habit as anything, but realises that really his heart is not in it. The kids dispatched to school, he thinks that Uber is his destiny after all. Clearing up the breakfast dishes, he makes to log onto the Uber site when his phones pings. It is Joanna again.

Hello Justin – are you free?

Yes, I am, for a little while, and good to hear from a fellow newly released felon. How is your probation going?

Going fine thanks. But then my car is still in dock, so it is going to be hard to amass penalties on the bus. Except if I carry out my inner wish to do violence to fellow passengers, much as I want to. No of course I must respect fellow road users. And never 'ism' them.

Ha ha

So, did you get the email about the Chrysalis meeting tonight?

I did and thanks for the tip off. I am told I get the first session free, for a taster

Good oh. But beware they will come after your money soon enough. The first meeting is the gateway drug to more hard-core coach development. You could end up spending money like you would never believe, unless you are really careful.

I get that, Justin. Look this is cheeky I know, but I would really like it if you could pick me again? Apart from the car problem and my increasing propensity for violence on the bus, it would be really nice to go along with some who knows the ropes, and can introduce me around, I can be quite shy among strangers.

Yes of course I can, same old Henbury bus stop pick up, say seven o'clock?

Dress code - balaclavas?

Yep. And camouflage jackets.

But then they won't see us in the Clifton Club? I want to be a little bit noticed, even if I am shy?

Doesn't matter. It is dark and gloomy in there anyway. And I can't imagine you ever not being noticed, no matter how bad the lighting.'

Seven o'clock would be perfect. Should have the kids sorted out, and Alan playing Nintendo with them
I can just picture the scene,
That would be great. See you then, just text me if there is a problem
I will I will. Lovely to hear from you. I must be getting on the road, earn a crust
I am on my way also. Leave this corrupted spreadsheet behind me. Looking forward to seeing you. And thanks.

At the appointed hour for his pick-up Joanna for the Chrysalis meeting, Justin pulls at the bus stop, finding her dressed to the nines in a smart suit.

'Hello there!' She leans over to give him a cursory kiss on the cheek. 'Thanks again for the ride, Mr Uber Man.'

'That is my pleasure. I have been driving random folk for most of the day, so such a pleasure to pick up someone I can talk to about something other than the traffic or the weather.'

'I have lots to ask you about! Such as …am I going to have time before the meeting to talk to you about my coaching work? I am sure the others will ask me. And I haven't a clue as to what might come out of my unruly mouth.'

'Don't worry, you can rehearse your script with me.'

'That would be good! First question?'

'How is your entry to coaching going?'

She takes a breath. 'It is going well. I have accepted the equalities job, and enrolled for the coaching skills basics course. I cannot believe how seriously the company is taking this. There are two of us on "the team," – have you noticed everything is a team nowadays? - And we are sisters in crime, sharing an office for this special project, which reports to the HR director.' She looks at him expectantly. 'How am I doing?'

'Just fine. That came out well. And you have a good story to tell, especially with the power of the firm behind you.'

He pulls up on West Mall, discreetly – early for a change – and parks around the corner, away from prying eyes, to continue the chat.

'So please carry on with your story,' he encourages her.

'Okay. So, it is good to be away from marketing. The basics course is good. And in many ways the equalities survey is not difficult. The women in the company just want to talk about it all, about being a woman in that environment. Their experiences have been pent up for so long. And it feels my work has purpose at last. Something to look forward to, to get out of bed for.'

'I can imagine. All that feeling welling up. With the women, I mean.'

She is in the groove with her narrative. 'Yes, the womanly feelings do well up, often when you least want them to. The work with the men is trickier. So much defensiveness, but they have been mandated – yes, you heard me right, "man –

dated," to cooperate. And to be fair, some of them – a very small number - are really supportive of the cause. They want to rebalance stuff, even the tougher stuff like addressing inequality of income and career paths. Glass ceilings and all of that stuff.'

'Even better to know. Your brief is wide, not just palliative care, mopping up the mess for a while until the beatings resume?'

`I tell myself so.' She smiles. 'And thanks for allowing me to practice my story. Look we had better get to the meeting. It is time. And I am a little nervous about this. Me a novice among all these seasoned experts. I feel a bout of imposter syndrome coming on.'

'You will not be alone in that. In fact impostor syndrome is often talked about among the newer woman entrants.'

They step out of the car, Joanna checking her appearance in a shop window.

'Don't worry, Joanna, you look great, 'he says, as he steers her towards the door of the Clifton club.

'So, this is where you meet? This place? Just wow, I thought this club was all male?'

'Well it used to be, but not at Chrysalis meetings. You will see that the women coaches in the group far outnumber the men.'

'I believe you. But then numbers mean very little when the power is held by the few.'

Inside the meeting room, Joanna is, however delighted to confirm that the gender balance is just as he had said. Justin introduces her first to Tarquin, who is charm itself towards her, though she would have preferred more eye contact and less scrutiny of her assets from him. Relieved of this necessary introduction, Justin introduces her to a cluster of women coaches who are gathered in a circle at the back of the room, drinking coffee. They offer her a drink, which she gladly accepts; then they ask of her story, which comes out pretty much the same as her rehearsal in the car.

She says how much she wishes to hear of their experiences, too, but all too soon they are called to order by Tarquin. She endures his introductory monologue, speculating that he is primed on a similar autopilot to the police trainer. She turns her attention to the keynote speaker whose subject is Clean Coaching, while clocking who is in the room. From time to time she catches Justin's eye across the room, but not too obviously. He smiles back, looking a little bored, his mind clearly elsewhere, as if he has seen and heard all of his clean patter before.

As the Clean coach describes all the ways in which his clean credential trainings might clean them out of what little disposable income they have left, Tarquin moves to close the session, 'to allow the wild rumpus begin.'

Joanna moves quickly to reform with the group of women circled once more in their usual corner, on her way passing through a gaggle of men muttering of the need for a drink, 'to "clean" the palette.'

As she joins the sisterhood, the women quietly chuckle at the absurdity of the club, and of some of the prehistoric behaviour being paraded within its walls, before welcoming Joanna once again. They include her in a conversation concerning the need for women coaches in town to somehow get from under the suffocating male patronage that drives the coaching conversation. She nods, enthusiastically, all ears to this softly spoken subversion. As the women drift off, she looks around to find Justin. She sees him talking to a scruffy man in the biker's jacket, who has locked him in earnest conversation. Making her way over to him, she is intercepted by an older man in a linen suit and a cravat. He asks, 'And you are, may I ask?' He beams at her, while blocking her path.

'I am Joanna, new here,' she says, not knowing what else to say.

'Well, you are more than welcome. We need all the young female talent we can muster on our crusty old roll call. Brighten the place up. I am Bert Thompson, by the way, gentleman of these parts. So what brings you here, Jo?'

'I am Joanna. Never abbreviated. Justin Drake in fact brought me here. Well I mean he introduced me to Chrysalis. Do you know him? He is sort of my mentor. Informal mentor. Well we hardly meet at all. Early days.'

He chuckles to himself. 'Know him? I know everyone here. But he is a fine fellow. For my sins, I am his supervisor. He will make a fine mentor to you. In fact, If I were mentoring you, I would keep on coming back for more, whether you needed it or not.'

Joanna does not dignify this with a reply, but nonetheless he burbles on. Glancing at her fingers of her left hand, he says, 'I see you are married.'

'Yes I am. But why ask?'

Bert grins. 'Well, marriage is a great institution. But who wants to be locked in an institution? So you are a coach?'

She nods. 'That is why I am here, at this meeting?' in her best sarcastic up-speak.

'Of course. Silly me. So, tell me, what does your husband do, when he is not taking care of you?'

'Well, he plays golf a lot.'

'Oh, good. So do I. Fine game. But what is his job?'

Casting her eyes around for a means of escape, but finding none, she replies,

'He is an entrepreneur – in the motor trade.'

'Excellent. A fine calling. I love cars, got a few myself, and one of them a classic Healey.' Despite her obvious apathy, he presses on, pulling his business card from his tweedy waistcoat pocket. 'Look, would you be so kind as give him my card? I have some motor related investments he might well be interested to talk over. And I could do with his advice car-wise too. Please mention me to him.'

'I will,' she mutters, turning the embossed card over in this hand, rather wondering what the coat of arms signified. The tyrannous Thompson Tribe?

Across the room, Tony continues to buttonhole Justin. 'That woman you brought along? You too seem pretty tight. I saw her catching your gaze across the room?'

'It is not like that.' Justin pushes Tony by the shoulder. 'It is simply that I am supporting her development. She is new in the field.'

'Well, she is lucky woman to have you on her side. And she's really easy on the eye too,' says Tony, winking at his friend.

'Steady on Tony. She is doing some great work within Consignia, on the equalities front.'

'That is work that really needs doing.' Tony's eyes light up. 'Do you think she might be ready to make the jump? With us? To the dark side of coaching?'

'I think in her work she already has made that jump. Joanna shows great promise.'

Hearing her name spoken in vain, Joanna eventually wrests herself away from Bert, who nonetheless leads her by the arm to Justin.

'Justin, old chap, I am handing Jo here back to your safekeeping. She couldn't wait to get away from me. Which I can quite understand.' No one returns his chuckle.

Justin refrains from saying that he quite knows the feeling, but instead says, 'Thanks for her safe return. Joanna, say hello to Tony Crocker. He is a good friend of mine, and on the side of right. Not might.'

'I prefer might every day of the week,' sniffs Bert, 'and anyway I must repair to the bar. See you soon for one of our regular sessions, Justin,' he says, waving a theatrical farewell.

'You surely will,' says Justin, to Bert's retreating form. 'Look Tony, sorry for this, but we... I mean I must be going, must be getting back.'

'Me too,' says Joanna. 'Sorry Tony, that it has been short but sweet, but there will be another time I feel sure.'

'There will be, if I have anything to do with it. And I must be going too.'

Looking around to see that they are the last in the room. Joanna and Justin make their way back to the shadows of the West Mall, then settle in the Prius. 'Free at last.' breathes Justin, sinking into his seat. 'So, how was it for you? Are you always the last to leave a party?'

'Ha Ha,' laughs Joanna. 'Oh, it was good. Far better than expected. But that place – I have seen nothing like it.'

'Hmm. It took me by surprise the first time too.'

She continues. 'Not just the club itself, I mean Tarquin and Bert and all of that, but mustn't get into "isms." They both tried old-fashioned flattery and flirting, quite amusing for a while, I suppose in its own way. Just as well that, with all my time in marketing, that I am well defended against that dinosaur behaviour. Just laugh it off. Sort of.'

'Sorry you had to put up with that though, at a so-called enlightened coaches' gathering. They are both incurable. Unreconstructed. Irredeemable.'

She nods in agreement. 'Quite so. Once Bert found out that I was married he switched from chatting me up to wanting to sell investment to my hubbie. Tarquin did not quite come onto me. But he found it hard to take his eyes off my ... my tits. Sorry but there is no other way to describe it.'

Justin tries and fails to keep his eyes on the steering wheel. 'Dirty old man.'

'He is that. Both of them. But Bert said he was your supervisor?'

'He is sort of, in his own sweet way.' Justin waves his hand, dismissively. 'And he is really useful in other ways too. He is well connected around the city, and good at fixing things. All manner of things.'

She grins. 'I would never have imagined that.'

His turn to chuckle. 'He is a one off. And, besides his extracurricular help, I am happy for him to continue as my supervisor for the time being. But hey, enough of those two. They will never change. What went well in there for you?'

'Quite a few things. I know all about "clean" now. But the highlight of the night was meeting the women for that chat afterwards. They were so welcoming.'

'I noticed,' he says, a rueful smile playing on his lips. 'I thought I would never prise you away.'

'I know. Sorry if I kept you, but they had so much to say, and they really wanted to hear my story. I realise I am so lucky to have the job I have. And don't feel at all an imposter any more – maybe I am the real deal!!'

'Didn't you know that already? You are, you are. And I am proud of you for coming along, putting a toe in the water.'

'No, I am hooked. The gateway drug worked. And I want to hear more and more from those women. One of them even talked about setting up a women's group in town, a support network.'

'Long overdue,' Justin says, encouragingly.

'Oh, this is so good!' Excited, she turns to him, taking his hand, squeezing his fingers as they rest on the gear stick. 'That was great. You are the best.'

Dunno about that,' Justin demurs, as he drives on towards the Henbury bus stop. As he kills the ignition, he notices that her face, caught in the streetlight, collapse a little. 'What is it?'

'No idea really – just want to savour the moment with someone who understands. Don't actually want to go into the house right now. That will flatten all of this.'

'Sorry to hear that.'

'Why?' she inquires.

'Sorry to hear that returning home will dampen things.'

'I know.' She reaches in her bag for a tissue.

'I think I know the feeling. A little the same for me, but not half so bad. And Joy is used to me moaning. But you with you...'

'With me.... what?'

'With you it feels different. It feels so good to support you... sorry, that was not what I mean. Just to be like this. You burst through my cynical crust.'

'Good to hear it. You are too good a person to be buried in gloom.'

'Thanks,' he mumbles, his mind on the hand still resting on his. 'But it is getting late. We were out longer there than I intended.'

'I know. But my new women friends were great. Do you have similar rapport with any of the men there?' She removes her hand, to rest it in her lap.

'Funny question. But no, not really, Tony maybe...'

'Oh yes, I noticed him.' She pauses. 'May I say – he does enjoy proclaiming his alternative status, does he not? By his dress if nothing else? And his challenges in the group?'

Justin nods. 'Yes, well observed. He feeds off it. But hey, he is a mate and has helped me a lot.'

'Wish you had more mates like that in the coaching community.'

'Oh no, not the C word! The community word. Used far too glibly. But no, if I have fellow travellers, then they are among the women not the men.'

She turns to face him. 'I can see that. For a start there are more of us. And you relate to women really well.'

'Do I?'

'Yes, of course you do. I can see that in their eyes. They trust you. And you have read me really well too.'

'Well, I am so glad to know that.' He stares out into the gloom. 'You are... sweet.'

'Oh, not in a saccharine way, I hope. Sickly?'

'No, not at all – it's just that you are growing on me. You are not a project.'

'Good – no Eliza Doolittle me. Please not!' She giggles, turning towards him.

'Don't worry, no Professor Higgins here either. Can't explain. It is just you have grown on me.'

'You me too.'

'What is it?'

'Oh nothing – just thinking how lucky Joy is to be married to someone like you.'

'Really? I am not sure she would agree. But thanks all the same.'

'Justin. Can I give you a hug?' She throws an arm around him, clumsily, and then withdraws, pecking him on the cheek. She brightens, exhaling softly. 'There you are. Your special reward.'

'I felt that. Not like the fake coaching hugs that we often give each other, mechanically. That hug hit home. Thank you.'

'I liked your squeeze back too.'

He shifts in his seat, reaching for the door handle.

She stalls him. 'Look this will never do. Friends ehh – mates?'

'Oh yes of course – for a long time I hope.'

'Sorry that was me going too far again, overstepping, sorry,' says Joanna, holding his gaze.

'It was fine. You were being human. Affection is fine. No harm done and nothing...'

'Agreed. Now I must skulk up the road home, face the music. Well I hope it is not that.'

'What will it be like?'

'More like face the video game's crossfire, while I try to hustle the little ones to bed. And remove the beer can from my husband's grasp.'

'Ha.'

'I will slip him Bert's card, that should keep him amused for a while. Let him know some good has come of the evening, beyond useless coaching cackle.'

She opens the car door, blowing him a light kiss. 'Bye now, and see you in Messenger soon. If not in the flesh.'

He waves a reluctant goodbye, rather hoping that his kids are asleep, and that Joy is already in bed. He needs time to think. But no, more than that, to feel. To allow a rush of emotions that he thought could never be revived, but now course through him.

Hell Hast No Fury

The following day, the Drake's family kitchen is in post-lunch mode, the children playing under the table while Justin taps on his phone, intently. Joy gives vent to a long, resigned sigh. 'Look Justin make yourself useful. We need to research summer camps for the kids. Could you Google that please? I am washing up.'

'Oh okay.' He pulls up his search engine screen, grabbing the first likely-looking tab he finds, 'Oh look here is a good one in Wales. Fits the bill really well?' He pushes his phone towards Joy, who takes the phone, squinting at the screen.

Ping. Ping. 'Oh, you have a fan. Yes, that camp looks good. But there must be others.' Ping. 'How does this message thing work anyway? It says Joanna Cooke? Hmm, I think I have seen that name on your screen before.'

'How come? You are not on Messenger?'

'No, I am not, thank God,' snorts Joy, 'or nothing would ever get done around here. And you do leave your phone lying around. I have seen that name come up more than once.'

He reaches to retrieve his phone from his wife. 'Look, I had better answer that?'

Joy retains her grip on the device. 'Really? Is she more important than planning the kid's holiday?'

'No of course not! Just let me tell her I am busy on family stuff.'

'How urgent is this, Justin?' Her jaw sets. 'Kids, off upstairs for a minute. I need a word with your father.'

The children, sensing the seriousness of this, scuttle out of the way, leaving Justin exposed to whatever was coming his way.

'What is it, Joy?'

'You know what it is. Full well. Who is she, this Joanna?'

He shrugs. 'No one important. A fellow coach I support. Nothing in it.'

'I see. Prove it. I want you to show me the whole conversation.'

'It is private.'

Joy is scornful. 'Oh, for pity's sake. What an excuse. This is like Brenda all over again. Secrets among coaches....'

'It is not like that...'

'So what is it like then? You will not let me read it?'

'I would let you if I could but...'

'But who is she? Where did you meet?'

'It is innocent enough. We met at Consignia, when I was doing my survey. One of my interviewees.'

'Consignia? What were you thinking – Consignia for God's sake!'

'It is no big deal,' he protests, 'and the firm know nothing – she is now a member of Chrysalis Coaching – and she is doing great work for the feminist cause.'

'Hmm. And for the Justin cause too, I bet. I have told you before. Please do not let your head be turned by the attention

121

of woman neophytes. I know how susceptible you are. There is no hope.'

'I won't, I won't. We are both happily married. I mean she and I are both happily marriage. Me to you, she to her husband Alan. She is by no means young...'

'What does she look like?'

'Oh, for god's sake!' blurts Justin, failing to hide his exasperation.

'Come on, what does she look like?'

'You know I am useless at descriptions, not like you,' says Justin, suddenly searching his phone. 'I know! I can show you. She is a friend on Facebook.' He retrieves his phone to find her profile. ' There she is. And her children.

Joy takes back the phone, gazing into Joanna's face. 'She is really pretty.'

'Is she?' asks a surprised looking Justin.

'Yes! Of course she is!'

'Hmm. Well, she looks plainer in real life.'

'Really? So Facebook is not real life. How closely have you inspected? From every angle?'

'Joy! This is beneath you.'

'Sometimes I need to get down in the gutter,' affirms Joy.

'Sometimes you drive me there. So, she has seen all of your perfect pics of our family life too, then?'

'Yep, of course. It is normal.'

'Hang on – look she has just messaged you. Again. She is persistent. It must be love.'

Justin says, 'Just let me switch her off.'

'I bet that is easier said than done. No, leave her hanging while we talk about what is going on between the two of you. So, you are regularly messaging, like a couple of teenagers? I did wonder who you were tapping away to all the time.'

'I have many friends in Facebook, as you know. There really is nothing of that sort going on. This is feeling like your Brenda suspicions all over again. You just said so yourself.'

'Maybe it is a bit,' she concedes, still thoughtful.

'I tell you what,' offers Justin. 'She lives not far away. Henbury. I would be really happy for you to meet her? You can assess for yourself whether anything is going on or not.'

'Are you serious? Why would I want to do that? To scram her eyes out?'

'No, 'says Justin, trying to remain adult, 'but, I would like you to see for yourself, before this much ado about much nothing grows into something.'

'I bet you get our names mixed up? Jo, Joy, Joy, Jo. Must be confusing for you. Do you find yourself calling her Joy? Do you? Or wanting to call me Joanna, inadvertently?'

Justin shakes his head, speechless, allowing Joy full flow. 'Do you think of her all the time? Always anticipating, waiting for her next text? Are you in love with her? Is it infatuation?'

'No. And no.'

'So how often have you met her? How long has this been going on for?'

'I just said. I met her when interviewing at Consignia is all. Kept in touch about her new coaching role.'

'Oh yes... And beyond that?'

'Oh yes, there was another time, just by coincidence, we both attended the same speeding course.'

Joy emits a rasping scoff. 'Oh, some coincidence, I must say. Fellow criminals, co-conspirators. What a place for a secret liaison.'

'Not really, though it was nice to share impressions afterwards...'

'Over a coffee...?

'Yes, sort of...' Justin stutters.

'And where else have you seen her? In the evenings outside of work?'

Well, only at Chrysalis.'

'Chrysalis!' Joy snorts. 'That den of iniquity. Now I know why you are so keen to keep going along to that place, even when your coaching work has died a death. Has Tony met her – does he know?'

'Know what?'

'You know what.'

'Seeing as you ask, Tony has met her there at the Clifton Club, yes,' Justin concedes. 'And he is impressed by her work role, her feminist interventions.'

'Oh, so he is smitten too? Why am I the last to know about this? Has Bert met her too?'

'Yes! At Chrysalis, also, while he was sniffing out potential investors. She has a husband, an entrepreneur in the car parts business, who I understand might well be keen to take a punt on Bert.'

Joy sighs. 'Sounds like Bert's ideal target victim.'

'Could you just stop? Please?' Justin holds up both hands, in a gesture of surrender.

'Okay, okay, I know I am over-reacting.' Joy thinks for a while. 'And I would like to meet her. Feels weird, but I would. Can you set that up? I would be interested to hear of her work. And hear how the coaching world is treating her. God help her, an innocent in the hands of you lot. I could give her a different perspective. And check her out.'

'Of course I can set it up, if Joanna is willing,' says Justin, thinking on her feet. 'There is truly nothing to hide here. Do you want to meet her with or without me?'

'Justin, you are beginning to sound like Bono. But an interesting choice. You know at this stage, I would think I would rather meet her alone. And she may not want to meet me. But then why wouldn't she, if there is nothing to hide? This could be like a witch's trial. She drowns either way. She might even coach me a little. God knows I need it.'

'Sorry,' says Justin, the extent of damage his secrecy has caused begins to sink in.

'You know you should have told me. You should have just fucking told me.'

'Joy, language please – the kids. But yes, I know I should have told you... I was stupid, I am just so, so sorry. There has been so much going on – no, there are no real excuses.'

'No, there are not. It is not so much that there is something going on, but the concealment – that is what hurts. Forgiveness is hard to find.'

'I don't expect...'

'Your coaching world is dangerous. Like advanced seduction techniques disguised as rapport building. Some twisted form of advanced, intellectualised speed dating.'

'Not at all. You fantasise, Joy. It is nothing like that, and you know it.'

'Really? I think the fantasies are all yours.' Joy rolls her eyes. 'Teenage dreams. I kind of wish you had chosen a younger woman, one of Tony's cast-offs, or one of Bert's past their sell-by date wives.'

'Pardon?'

'I mean, what a choice!' says Joy, with another eye roll for emphasis. 'I mean she is married, lives down the road, children – probably a possessive husband. Works at Consignia for heaven sake. Hangs out with you at all of these coaching meetings, where folk can see you canoodling together and gossip about the two lovebirds. What a choice of a girlfriend. Could you not have made it messier, more complicated? How could you do this to me? How could you?'

'I know,' says Justin, his expression suggesting that the penny is at last dropping on his folly, in the face of Joy's ire.

 'You know that I normally trade in sarcasm, probably to disguise my true feelings, but now I am just angry. After all I have done to support you. I feel betrayed. Hurt. Exposed. Shamed. Rejected. How could you?'

'I haven't done anything,' Justin vainly pleads.

'And it is not about her, or about the two of you, as much as about you. And yes. Before you tell me to be calm. I will be calm when I meet her, icy calm. Give me her number and I will set it up, if she is willing.'

He writes down the number of a scrap of the children's homework paper.

Joy looks set on her course of action. 'Now, enough of this for now. Get those children downstairs. I need to go out for a walk, to deal with this alone.'

Later that afternoon, alone in the house, with Joy still gone on her unspecified walk, Justin cannot resist texting Joanna.

Hi Justin – what's up?
Guess what - Joy knows about us and wants to meet you.
Oh, so you have told her then. I think I am glad. It was feeling a bit much, the secrecy. When there is nothing to hide

But she nearly intercepted your message. It was a close-run thing.

Oh, I am sorry I should have thought before texting you at home.

I know. It is okay. I text at all sorts of odd times, to quite a number of people

I know. I know. Me too. But I take risks with our timing.

Have you told Alan? About us?

No not yet – now I think I must do. And he, like Joy, is suspicious of the texts and stuff. Anything I should be worried about when meeting her?

No not really. She does want to check you out though – only human – I have no idea where she might take the conversation.

Alan might want to do more that check you out

Oh My God

This gives me good reason to talk to Alan about us. Oh - there is no us.

No there is not! Well, sort of. I won't tell him about the speeding class though. That is not an event I ever want to bring up with him again. I can't leave the house without him throwing the Highway Code at me. It feels demeaning.

I bet it does. Joy is just glad I did not get the points on my licence. But it was one more thing she could do without. And now this

So okay, if I do meet her – how will you set this up? This is a really weird idea by the way. No idea what possessed you.

Well, I have given her your number - you can set it between you. Or you can forget the whole idea.

Sure – I wait her call, if she ever follows through. This is really weird. Me meeting her. You know that don't you?

Yes, I do. Good luck. I miss you Joanna

You too Justin, you too. Now everything is threatened. Not sure why I wrote that.

Everything is okay. Everything will work out.

Returning from her walk, Joy decides that she will follow through on the offer to meet with Joanna. After a somewhat awkward, but not disagreeable phone call, Joy agrees to meet Joanna in a cafe in Westbury, adjacent to their homes. Hardly knowing what she might be running into, she makes make her way on the appointed Saturday morning, to find the café bustling. Joy immediately recognises Joanna from her Facebook photograph. She rises from her seat to meet her, gesturing towards the vacant chair.

'Hello Joanna,' says Joy, as Joanna nestles her shopping beneath her feet, making a show of her busyness. 'Shopping done at last,' she explains. 'It never stops. And hello, Joy, nice to meet you too. Thank you for arranging this. I like the idea of us getting to know each other better.'

'My pleasure. What can I get you? Coffee? I know how taxing Saturday shopping can be. All those baby buggies. And those pensioner's electric carriages.'

'That would be lovely, thank you.' Joanna surveys the menu blackboard. 'A simple flat white for me.'

'Okay. I am never quite sure what a flat white is, but I am sure this nice chap with a beard can rustle one up.'

Ordering Joanna's drink, they face each other across the condiments and the menu. Joy breaks the ice. 'I know this probably seems strange, but I have been hearing of you through Justin, and I am sure we have a lot in common. Lots to talk about. Always happy to make new friends in the neighbourhood. And I just thought...'

'No, no it is a good idea. And I hear a little about you too.'

'All good, I hope?'

'Of course! Justin thinks the world of you. So, we live close by. Two women faced with the juggling act of work, careers, family and the rest. Livining the dream, as good suburbanites should,' says Joanna, working to keep the conversation upbeat.

'Well summarised, Joanna. And it would be good to share notes on the way we live out our lives. I am always too busy to find time to make new friends.' Joy casts her eyes around the café, as if seeking someone else that she might enlist on her random friend's roster. With her eyes settling back on Joanna, she says, 'Justin tells me that you are now working as a coach, in a gender equality unit at Consignia? Sounds like noble and necessary work. Gruelling at times, too, I would imagine?'

'Yes' it is. But it is so rewarding. I love it.'

'I can just imagine,' Joy sighs. 'I would have craved such a unit when I worked at Magic Carpet. Mind you the inequalities issues there reach well beyond gender. Many of the managers are women, but that does not have much impact on the macho culture. Woman taking on male personas. Sheep in ram's clothing.'

'I see. It is different in Consignia – we have very few women managers. I was one of the few, but now I am out of line management for a while. Mind you, I plan to return and make a difference, hopefully from a position of influence – if not power. I do not kid myself too much on that score.'

'Good luck to you on that. Though I am not sure I ever want to go back into corporate management again.' Joy stirs her coffee. 'Unless it is to a company amenable to progress.'

'Hm. So few of them are. This coffee is good. 'Joanna looks around the packed café. 'Never been here before. Don't know where all these trendy people come from.'

'Nor me. This neighbourhood is changing day by day. Lots of them working from home. Cybernauts.'

'I notice that too,' says Joanna, scanning the clientele. 'I am glad we moved here, to Westbury, before we got priced out.

And so convenient for getting into town, to go to the glass-fronted treadmill where I spend my working days.'

'Is that how it feels?' Joy raises her eyebrows.

'To be honest, a lot of the time, yes.'

'Sometimes we just have to...'

'Yes. we do. It is hard.' Joanna's smile fades.

'Justin says how much he has enjoyed supporting you in your new role. He says you show great potential as a coach. In fact, he sings your praises so highly I thought I had better meet you. I could learn something.'

Joanna smiles again, politely. 'Well that is nice of him. And nice of you to extend the invitation. And he has been really helpful and encouraging, in an informal way, behind the scenes.'

'What scenes?'

'Not those type of scenes.' Joanna blushes. 'I meant behind the scene at work. The formal, up-front scene, forever being assessed.'

'Okay, I get it. We all need that. Justin supports me well that way too, when he is not lamenting the state of the coaching world.' Joy catches Joanna's eye. 'And he has sponsored you into Chrysalis?'

'He has – into that bastion of white male privilege. That Clifton Club is a revelation.'

'So I hear,' says Joy, stiffening in her seat, as she sticks out her chin to emulate male gravitas. 'I must take a look inside someday, when I am feeling strong. What did you make of the coaching fraternity gathered there? I hear of that cast of characters often, but have only met a few, and none of them are in the mainstream.'

'Really?' says Joanna, looking surprised. 'I would have thought you would have met loads of them. I have had the great good fortune to spy the whole coaching ensemble up close and personal the other night.'

'And how was the tableau?'

'From close distance, they come in all shapes and sizes. Hard to generalise. All in the coaching business for lots of reasons, some agendas declared, some not.'

'A diverse ecology?' asks Joy.

'Yep, but not all pond life.'

'Just some of them?' Quizzes Joy. 'So where do you think you fit into the species, if at all? You may be an outlier.'

'Hmm.' Joanna ponders the question for a moment. 'Well, I think I am different. I realise that in many ways I am lucky, to being doing the work within an organisational framework, with job security behind me, and an opportunity to work for long-term change. That is different. Not many of those jobs about.'

'Fortunate indeed. Many of those wishing change are at the bottom of the pond, poking around among the low paid weeds.'

'Indeed. I would not want to be in the shoes of the independent coaches that I meet at Chrysalis, not only having to scramble to get the work, but also knowing that they could be shown the door at any point with no reason given, and without having made any lasting impact on the workplace culture.'

'Too true. Justin would agree how precarious and stressful all of that is. He must have told you. And all of that stress impacts me and the family too of course.' Joy picks up her cup, inspecting the dregs.

'Yes, he has, but not in too much detail.'

'Well it does affect me. Not just the stress of getting work, but him spending lots of time with strangers, when he cannot share with me what is going on. It is unsettling.'

'Some of that comes my way too, at home,' agrees Joanna, without knowing where her disclosure might lead her.

'It comes to us all.'

Joanna's phone buzzes on the table, making a move towards the sugar bowl. She reads a WhatsApp message from her husband on the home screen.

'Anything important?' asks Joy.

'No, nothing. Just my husband wondering where I am. I did tell him.'

'Want to reply?'

'No, it is okay.' Joanna frowns, turning her phone upside down.

Joy asks, 'did I hear you went on the dangerous driving – sorry the speed awareness course - with my husband?'

'Yes, I did. Quite a coincidence,' says Joanna, colouring slightly. 'We couldn't quite believe it. Just like that.'

'Yes, he did tell me. But took his time about telling me, mind. Not quite sure why the delay. But then, sometimes, the longer you leave these things, the harder it becomes to tell the whole story.'

'Could be. Mind you, it was good to have a friendly face at such an ordeal.'

'Ordeal? Not how he painted it. And I am not that sure that he is taking it the lessons seriously, even when his Uber driving depends on him driving sensibly. Typical. His mind wonders to all sorts of places, when he should be concentrating on the task at hand.'

'Really? Well it is quite different for me. And my husband Alan is perpetually reminding me that I must never be caught again. He is most insistent,' says Joanna, seeing her upturned phone making yet another determined little jump towards her, like a scary baboon spider she had once seem on a nature programme.

'Oh, he is on your case then?'

'Oh yes, nearly every time I go out the door with car keys in hand.'

'If I can ask,' solicits Joy, 'is this nagging purely driving related, or is it wider?'

'Look I am loyal to him, and he is a dedicated father and husband, at least when he is not preoccupied with running his business, which is taxing.' Joanna looks away at an adjoining table, where a bearded father makes a fuss of conspicuously chatting to his child. 'But yes, he does get on my case about things, gets a bit fixated, then doesn't let go, even when he should let things that have happened be left in the past, then moved on from.'

'Such as?' asks Joy, channelling Justin's minimalist questioning technique.

'My new role for example. He has so many reservations about that. Worries that as a whistle-blower, my career might suffer. He worries about everything.'

Joy leans towards her. 'There could be some truth in that, beyond habitual anxiety on a spouse's behalf. But isn't the risk worth it, to see the results you might achieve? Maybe he is feeling threatened?'

'Yes. Could well be, but not much I can do to allay his fears once they are up and running. And nothing I can do to stop him lecturing me.'

Joy pulls a sympathetic face. 'If I may say, this all sounds quite controlling. Not unusual, but controlling all the same. Does he know you went to the speeding thing with Justin?'

'No, I never told him,' she shrugs. 'He can be quite possessive.'

'Sounds like it. Though, having met you, I feel sure that there were no reasons for suspicion.'

'None whatsoever. Justin is always the perfect gentleman with me.'

'I understand you are Facebook friends? He showed me your pics.'

'Oh no, how embarrassing.' Joanna squirms in her seat.

'Some of those photos - I should never have posted. Just put them up on impulse. But then everyone does, I suppose.'

'Not me, I am afraid. I stay away, but Justin loves it. Always tapping away. Does Alan know that you and Justin are chat mates?'

'Oh, not really. But he asks me all the time who I am chatting to. He is like you, not on Facebook, he sees no great reason for it, and he may have a point. He thinks that my being in his company should be enough to satisfy me, and he thinks it takes my attention away from my mothering. But I confess it is a nice escape for me, to get away from the everyday, allow myself some inane, inconsequential chatter.'

'I have never tried it.' Joy looks doubtful, distracted by the bearded dad force-feeding liquidized kale into his mewling child. "Some men never give up, do they?'

'No, that is true,' says Joanna, watching the father still attempting to force the bottle down his daughter's throat.

'Even when all the signals say stop.'

'So, Facebook?' Joy sees the phone makes a determined little leap again towards her companion. 'I can see that there might be benefits, allowing conversation to flow in an anonymous way, without consequences?'

'Yes, there are. Without consequences.'

'I see. It does sometimes really annoy me, when Justin is chattering away to strangers, letting it all hang out on line.'

'Well all I can say that he is really supportive of me. Nothing risqué, if that is what you are asking?'

'Well that is good to know, and he is well-intentioned man, offering help all the time in fact, even when it might be harmful to him. No good deed of his ever goes unpunished, as the Danish say. I feel sure you are safe in his hands.'

'From what I hear, he thinks so highly of you. And your lovely children.'

'I know he does really. And in some ways he was born to listen, and to support. That is a really good quality. And he makes me smile a lot of the time, even when I am annoyed with him.'

Joanna smiles at the dad failing to assemble the ocean-going buggy. 'Talking of children, I really must be getting up the hill. Alan is expecting me back from this girlie chat soon; he is off to play golf. Again. But lovely to chat to you, and thanks for the coffee.'

Joy bustles home then back into the kitchen after her time with Joanna, her face a mask of impassivity. Justin, who had been playing anxiously with the kids while awaiting her turn, knows from her demeanour that there is little point in asking her how it went, lest he give away any fears that he might have been found out; while Joy avoids the topic of her meeting completely, simply saying, 'I see the kids are fed. Good. Now come on children, time for that walk in Blaise Castle that I promised you. Wellies on please! Enjoy your afternoon shift, Justin.'

After this blur of activity, Justin is left alone to speculate as to what might have occurred between the two women in his life, over coffee. Unable to live within this information vacuum any longer, and with his imagination running riot, he succumbs to the temptation to text Joanna, despite the reservations running in his mind as to the wisdom of this impulse. Nevertheless, his fingers reach for his phone.

HI Joanna, nice to see you are online.
Yes, you too, Justin. Always good to see you in here too.
Can you chat?
Sure thing. I am alone. Alan is out playing golf. I have the children, and they are playing on the trampoline in the garden with friends. Maybe our children might play together, now that I have met Joy. That was a good thing to do, by the way, thanks for setting it up.

Okay, glad it went well. Joy has taken the kids out to the woods, leaving me to get on with the chores before hitting my next Uber shift.

I see. Busy man.

Joanna, just want you to know that I am not prying into your time with Joy. What passed between the two of you is really none of my business, unless you wish it to be.

That is decent of you. And no details. But I think it went well. I picked up that she is unhappy that you and I chat in this way.

Well that is a general unhappiness, not confined to you... she does not much encourage me to chat away aimlessly with virtual friends when I could be doing other more useful things

Yes she... No never mind.

She what?

Well, I think she feels quite threatened by us chatting – anywhere, but especially in here. And I felt deceitful, when I know much more about you, and even about you and Joy than I was letting on. Managing that boundary was really tense. I was worried what I might leak – and she is a really attentive listener and general all-round body language expert.

Hmm. Many women are. It comes with the territory. But sorry to have put you in that spot.

Well I allowed you to, I guess. We have both shared loads, privately. And I was happy to reveal things to you about my life that I tell very few, and especially Alan. He is naturally

suspicious I think, and inquisitive. Controlling was the word
Joy used, and she might well be right.

Sounds like she was being very direct.

Yes, she was. And I don't really know how much further we
should go with our relationship, beyond the safety of
professional conversations. I do feel quite guilty. There are
things we know about each other that cannot be let out.

But they never will be?

But people will know. They always do.

Maybe, but it is none of their business. And we have been
counselling each other, supporting only, nothing more. What is
said in that context must be private. I make that clear to Joy,
though she doesn't much like it.

I know that is all true.

God, do you know what I am thinking?

No, not a clue.

I am thinking that I should never have put my hand on yours
back in the pub, the first time, when you were so bereft. I
mean it felt the right thing to do. And I know you did not read
anything more into it – or showed no indication of doing that –
just that it worries me when I think of that.

Why would you worry? It was such a kind human thing to do.
In the moment.

I know. It is just that I liked doing it. And I liked you too, in that
moment of your showing your vulnerability. I liked the warmth.

Yes, me too

And then I went on to put my hand on yours in the car in my excitement, after Chrysalis, and then a hug.

I do remember that well. Thanks for it

Sometimes I worry about the power of this coaching thing to reveal secret feelings, to open Pandora's box. It felt so close in that moment, out of my normal experience.

Yes, it is powerful. And it has its dangers, quite easy to run into trouble. To give you an example, I soon have my hearing with the head honchos of the Coaching Fraternity, who will do me for bad behaviour.

Oh yes, you mentioned that before. Good luck with it.

Thanks – but you didn't mean that coaching was dangerous in that legalist sort of way, I suspect?

No, you are right. I was thinking of how it takes relationships outside the norm. Please don't think I have some sort of schoolgirl crush on you, quite the opposite. But I do feel a strong bond, like we broke through some kind of barrier?

'Yes, we did. And you broke through to me big time. Cathartic. It was powerfully healing for me, if outside of the recommended coaching catechism. Please do not let that eat you with guilt, Joanna.

But it does, I am afraid. I am actually thinking that maybe we should stop chatting in here. Keep the contact to email maybe, for professional reasons.

Hmm. I did not realise how strongly this was running for you.

There you go again. You see there is no "this" – or if in fact there is a 'this," but I don't want to live with this 'this' any longer. I want it to go.

That bad?

Justin, I feel dirty about it, even though there is nothing dirty about it. Just a strong feeling. I just want this to stop… before it builds up to something that we find impossible to stop.

I get it. Of course I do. But I feel sad when you write that. A bit at a loss. Feeling a sense of loss about it.

You must let go of this, Justin. And help me to let go of this too. I hope we have not gone too far already.

Okay, okay I will. Keep "us" to Chrysalis and such like.

Yes, that would be good. I guess the other thing is Consignia.

Oh yes

I do not know the whole story there, but sense that you are no longer discussable in the organisation. You are like the Flying Dutchman that once passed through the corridors, but is now a consulting ghost ship. People see it glide by, see its traces, but no one dare mention the name of the ship that has you as figurehead on the prow.

Vivid. I have never been a ghost ship before.

So being in touch with you is a bit dangerous on that score too. And I think I may be protecting you in this Consignia thing as much as me. I really do. And I do care about you enough to be protective.

I know that. And yes, it would probably be dangerous to have my ghost ship materialise for real. I get it. So that really restricts our conversations doesn't it? No Messenger, no meeting alone outside of events, no revealing all to each other?

That is right. I mean it, help me with this.

Okay

And while it was nice to meet with Joy, sort of, it was really tense. I do think it was mainly her checking me out, and I have no idea how I did on that score. No idea. But she is a lovely lady, a fine wife and mother. I have no wish to disrupt that at all.

Of course you don't.

Nor I think do you, in your heart of hearts. Having initiated the meeting on the pretext of a feminist solidarity meeting, it was that but some much else was going on under the surface. She didn't suggest she and I meet again, and nor did I. So that is that. No more please, I do not want to face her questions again. She is too good at those.

She certainly is.

Oh my god. Sorry Justin. One of my children's friends has fallen of the trampoline and hurt her leg. Her mother is lethal, sued one of my friends once before. I must go. Bye. And love. And thanks for everything you have been wonderful. I will never forget your support.

Yes bye. And I need to go drive customers around the town. Help take my mind off this parting. Love to you too. Enjoy your first aiding.

Revealing the Digital

Tony sits in his threadbare Stokes Croft office, taking stock of his current state of affairs. He sees nothing strewn across his littered desk to lift his spirits. Energy bills. Obscure scientific papers on the collapse of the planet. Invitations to protest marches that look right up his street, but that he cannot afford the fare for. Not much on his screen either. The pamphlet on climate change that he is working on, the one that he knows will go viral once published, stays stuck on the same page where he left it the week before. He looks at his introduction to his masterpiece and groans. Who is he kidding? It reads just like everyone else's climate change pamphlets. And there are thousands of them out there. Nothing to see here.

Tony faces the grim realisation that much of his heroic, one-man efforts to save the planet and defeat capitalism along the way are going down the pan.

He worries that one or two of the young women who previously were devoted followers of his funky radicalism have gotten wary of him and his leadership style, instead drawing upon their own resources to create a style of activism that has their own stamp upon it. His source of once plentiful girl-friends has dried up; and those that might still team up with him are penniless, which does not fit his current profile for a partner at all. Could be time for a rethink on the girl friend front too. Maybe someone older, with some resources behind her. He makes a note to trawl dating sites for older women looking for love and rejuvenation; and preferably with a house and car. Turning to an almost empty folder titled "coaching leads," he is forced to admit that his coaching efforts are in dire straits too. Clients are few, and those that do survive cannot pay. One or two have left him for supposed breaches of confidentiality. And Stokes Croft is a small world, where word travels fast, and reputations get tarnished quickly. His dream of leading a reimagining the coaching space, based on radical lines is fading too. In the early days he was so taken by his banner of "alt.coaching." There are plenty of disillusioned coaches around who are sympathetic to this project, but he has found that growing a groundswell of interest is really hard. He realises also that in the process of declaring war on conventional managerialist coaching, he has gotten up the noses of those leading professional bodies and networks, who are now deeply wary of him too. In fact, these bodies now simply ignore his prods and snark, making it very clear that he is no longer welcome in the conversation.

Tony realises that his desk, full of stillborn projects, is going nowhere. He feels blocked at every turn. With one decisive sweep of his arm, he pushes all of this detritus into a black plastic bin bag, leaving him looking at his now clear desk, empty save for his whirring desktop computer. He decides to ceremonially cremate his past ambitions in the brazier down by the homeless shelter, where those with little hope in the world would make a fitting witness to the death of his dreams. Turning away from this soon to be funeral pyre, he scans the rest of his office, looking for more candidates for this symbolic ending. His eyes fall upon his safe, unopened for many months, not least because he has had no money to put in there.

Swinging open the rusty old iron door of the safe, he decides to empty the contents of that into the bin bag, too. Documents, proposed legal actions, plans for sit-ins, once thought precious, he now admits have no life left in them. Blindly scratching around on the safe's top shelf, unable to see what might be contained within its darkest recesses, his fingers fall upon something small and sharp. He pulls this out. It is Justin's USB, the data stick that may well cause the downfall of Magic Carpet. And maybe even cause a disruptive tear in the fabric of capitalism. The USB that he had quite forgotten about. He had promised to Justin that he would safeguard this treasure as though his life depended upon it. But now, amid the ruins of his future, this find could open up a fresh pathway to fame and fortune.

Disregarding his vow never to scan the contents without first alerting Justin, he pushes the USB into a slot on his computer. It opens immediately, displaying a number of sub-folders, none of them encrypted. His eyes open wide at the titles of these clustered folders.

- Executive emails
- Customer records and bank details - encrypted hyperlink
- Legal files – NDAs, Dismissals
- HR Records and manpower plans
- Tax planning

Scanning each folder in turn, Tony discovers that this is a treasure trove indeed. The executive emails reveal so much. Cover-ups and concealment of actions against each other and staff. Plans for the shut-down of distribution centres and for centralisation. Customer records containing all customer's personal details, and contacts, bank records and credit checks. The Legal and HR folders document details of all actions being taken against employees and managers, together with a listing of current actions being taken against Magic Carpet. Tax planning enumerates records of tax strategies, including off-shoring and tax evasion. The immensity of this find, its comprehensive sweep, hits Tony right between the eyes. He begins to understand why Magic Carpet would be so afraid of this leaking; and can also well understand the fears of the whistle-blower who had fenced it to Justin.

His every instinct tells him that this is too good not to share. For a moment he contemplates ringing Justin, then decides against it. He simply does not have the time for his inevitable agonising and prevarication. He does not need Justin as some middleclass conscience, parked on his shoulder. But if not Justin – then – of course! Dick Bellows, a friend and the journalistic scourge of Magic Carpet. A quick call finds Dick in, at his office just around the corner. Tony summons him immediately with the bait that he has a goldmine of data that Dick and only Dick will know what to do with. Dick says that he will be around right away.

Dick sidles through the door silently, his brusque manner indicating that he has no time for social niceties. 'Great to see you Tony, and thanks for the heads up. Now what is this burning news that I need to see?'

'I will reveal all in a minute,' Tony teases. 'You are still on the case with Magic Carpet?'

'Yes, of course, but the trail has gone cold of late,' says Dick, shrugging off his frustration. 'After early breakthroughs and much tweaking of them around the edges, I have been losing impetus of late. I simply cannot put the whole picture together, from victims' first-person accounts, which is all I really have at this point. All too subjective, too many fragments. Are you daring to say that you may have something beyond that?'

'Yes, I do. Something big. Something really big. The same big picture that you are seeking, all documented on official files.'

'That is great, but stop tantalising me, Tony. Time to open your kimono.'

'Hmmm. Before we proceed – given that this is my find – how would you manage the publication of such data?'

'Well, that is a hypothetical at this point.' Dick puffs, clearly impatient with this dance, but playing along for the while. 'The normal process would be for me to take it to a paper that would handle such incendiary material. Probably the Guardian. They would then have legal crawl all over it check for jeopardy. Then they would involve the Editor in Chief to devise a publication strategy, plan to network with other publications, such as the Washington Post, who specialise in whistleblowing stuff.'

'I see, that is helpful. How about negotiating a fee for this release?'

'That depends on the scale of the scoop,' considers Dick. 'Often journalists do this for pure public interest disclosure, and then get the story, the by-line, and the glory. And, of course journalistic immunity would need to be granted, to ensure security for sources. Why do you ask?'

'Well, I want to bring down Magic Carpet as much as you do. And would appreciate your help in doing this. But while not wishing to seem mercenary, would I, as owner of the data at this point, not get a cut of some kind?'

'Possibly. Depends what this is.'

'Okay, another question,' Tony persists, 'and in no way disrespecting your professionalism, or our friendship, comrades in arms and all of that. But how might it be if I were to go it alone on this?'

'Well, nothing to stop you. And in some ways, I would be happy for this to get out. Whatever it takes. You could post all you have got online and sit back and watch the chaos, Wikileaks style. But you would be traced, even if you did not put your name on it. And your sources could be in much danger too. Not sure how you would make any money out of that, and your career could be wrecked. The press would go after all the dirty secrets they could find in your personal life, girl-friend disclosures and all of that. You would probably end up in the Ecuadorian Embassy for the rest of your life. Apart from that – fill your boots.'

'Best avoided then,' says Tony, not wishing to even contemplate the embassy scenario.

'Look Tony, you are a mate and I am grateful for you bringing me in on this. But I am getting a little impatient with all of this preliminary sparring. I am happy to be fully open with you on payments, and to cut you in, be assured. But at this point, if you want to go with me, then you need to trust me, and follow my advice to the letter. There are other independent journalist you might go to. Or you could go to the papers directly, but that takes much skill to negotiate. Your choice.'

'Oh no, it would have to be you. Okay, so a trust basis it is, with you. Exclusivity, I guess?'

'Yes exclusivity. Now show me what you got.'

Tony moves aside and invites Dick to the screen. Dick scrolls through in silence for a full fifteen minutes, clearly rapt with this discovery. He eventually turns to Tony, who sits on the edge of his seat, looking at him expectantly. 'Tony, old mate, this is gold dust. This is everything I might have dreamed of finding. No wonder the Carpet have been so cagey. Maybe they just knew it was floating around, somewhere. And now you have it. Wonderful. How long have you been in possession of this?

'Oh for a few weeks now, maybe longer.'

'Why did you hold back on it, if I may ask?'

'Because my source needed safety while negotiating an NDA with Magic Carpet. But I believe that is all through now,' says Tony, hoping to convince.

'Have you let your source know that you are planning to go public?'

'No not yet, I wanted to talk to you first, to plot strategy. I don't think he would care anyway. We need never mention his name.'

'Perhaps it is best that we never do, even between us. But I would be more that interested to know the trail.'

'I will let you know sometime. Not now. But it is amazing content, is it not?'

'It truly is, and well done you for sourcing this. Have you taken copies?'

'No, not yet.'

'That is good. And if you do not want to be implicated, then probably best you never do. Once you hand over the USB to be me, then I suggest you erase this record from your hard drive. In fact, you might want to destroy that ancient Amstrad computer altogether. You cannot claim the journalistic immunity open to me.'

'I see – so I let go of this data forever?

'Yes, you do. Does your source have a record?' asks Dick.

'No. In fact I know that he has not even looked into it all for fear or prosecution.'

'Wise man. I assume he was fencing this on someone else's behalf, someone who might have much to lose? A Magic Carpet employee perhaps, who would have been close to the hacker?'

'Correct.' Says Tony. 'And the whistle-blower's protection must be absolute.'

'Believe you me, Magic Carpet will launch all efforts to find out who leaked this material. Interesting to speculate as to where it might have come. Could even be that the CEO has been having an affair with a staff member, perhaps his executive assistant. He dumps her; she downloads all she can find then squirrels it away. Looking at these files, I would say that they have passed through a number of hands before the final collection was assembled. With each iteration, the original source or sources had gotten more deeply buried.'

'Fascinating. So what next?

'Leave it to me to sort this one out. This one needs some cold-blooded thinking through.'

Tony pleas, 'don't you need my help?'

'With all due respect, no, not really. And that is said for you protection. It is between the newspaper's legal eagles and me now to sort out the authenticity of all this, then decide on an angle of attack. Slow release, or dump the whole package? Alerting the Criminal Prosecution Services etc. All a bit beyond your experience. Sorry, no offence.'

'So that is it then? I simply hand over the USB, and that is me done?'

'Well nearly, but not quite. You need to clear this with the fence, face to face for preference, no electronic or phone trail. Once he or she has cleared this – and I do not need to know who this is – then let me know and we can proceed.'

'I will do that immediately. In fact, I am seeing him today. I am sure there will be no problem.'

'Good to know. Thanks for bringing this to me by the way. This feels such a payoff for all these years of conducting guerrilla warfare around the edges. This is going to do irreparable damage to Magic Carpet at so many levels. It will tie them up for years.'

'It won't do you any harm, either,' smirks Tony. 'When will I know of your reward? I still want to have that conversation about my split?'

'Please be patient here. You will get your share. But that must be an untraceable payment, camouflaged as something else.'

'Okay that is fine' says Tony. 'You off now?' asks Tony, watching Dick place the USB deep in his jacket pocket.

'Yes, I need to go. I can see me pulling a couple of all-nighters on this one. And thanks for the scoop. You know that this in good hands. But be aware I cannot predict how long this will take to go through due process. Please do not mention this to a living soul while I clear the ground for publication.'

Tony is left alone with an empty desk and a blank screen. He puts fingers to keyboard, strenuously tapping on delete to ensure that there is no trace of the folders anywhere to be found. He is driven by a desire never to be directly implicated in this release, consoling himself with the knowledge that - though the data is now gone from him forever - he will be reminded soon enough of the content, once the leak hits the wider world. He registers some disappointment that this discovery will not, after all, cover him in glory, or reap immediate financial reward. But he needs to trust Dick to see him straight.

And as for informing Justin, he sighs. After all, Justin will not necessarily know that the source of the scoop was the USB. It could have come from anywhere. No, there are lots of reasons for keeping Justin in a state of innocence, his natural state. He will just let Dick know that this side of things, his tipping off the informant, is sorted. A short, coded text. A little white lie. Which he decides is probably best for all of their protection, moving things along nicely. Done for the day, Tony picks up the bin bag and heads for the homeless shelter, deciding that along the way that he will reward himself with his favourite guilty pleasure, a giant-sized greasy sausage roll.

White Face, Black Heart

Justin is out for a walk by Harbourside, taking a break from Uber rides to watch the canal water lap in small waves against the pier side. He feels content that he and Joy are, at long last, out of choppy waters, and ready to move house to pursue a more modest way of life. A "minor adjustment to prosperity," as Joy had so sensibly framed it. He feels relieved, too that the tension and drama of Joanna in his life gone too, and that the meeting between her and Joy seems to have allayed Joy's suspicions. He reflects on the last time he was here at the docks, distraught, haunted by failure and fears of destitution, before Joanna had offered him solace, when he could easily have sunk without trace. The scene unfolding before him is blissful, all shimmering buildings and small bobbing boats. He is alone but not lonely, with his thoughts for company. His eyes rest on the quay, wondering whether to take the ferry once more, just as he did before for his trip with Jim and his family, but this time in far better mood, reconciled and in control of what is before him.

He wonders, idly, how Jim the engineer and his family are doing now. It would be fun to see him again, to exchange some friendly manly banter. He thinks that maybe what he needs right now is a dose of undemanding, unconstrained blokishness. Joanna was right about one thing; he does need some male company. Bert, as a friend, is too much looking after his own less than hidden agenda, which is to get his paws on other's funds, and along the way have a go at seducing their wives. In contrast Tony is more like a true friend, and on the surface so supportive. But it is never relaxing in Tony's company, with his running of radical agendas, at times just too intent on toppling the establishment to offer easy companionship. And though he enjoyed male company for serious conversation, Tony was all too easily distracted by the rebellious young millennials he seemed to attract around him, as if he were the redeemer. Once one of those girls floated by Tony's gaze, Justin noticed that he was all too soon ignored, as Tony encouraged the girls in their accounts of the awfulness of their parents, their siblings and their schooling.

As he is about to alight the ferry, the phone rings, announcing a call from Joanna, quite out of the blue. He panics. Since she had met with Joy, they have both been true enough to their word not to contact each other again, never even exchanging as much as a single yellow-handed wave on Messenger. What could she want? This cannot be a casual call. He thinks of shutting off the call, but then he is curious. He has to know. 'Hello Joanna.' He says, trying to keep his tone light. 'Surprised to hear from you. It has been a while.' He thinks of mentioning that he is strolling by the quay, scene of their first fateful meeting, by way of easing into the conversation, but decides this reference might strike the wrong note altogether.

'How can help you? What is up?'

Her voice is quavering, a small choke. 'Hi Justin, I know I shouldn't be ringing, we did agree. You would be well within your rights to shut this call down. But please, listen to me for a minute, I have news. And some of that might affect you too. Sad to say.'

'Oh okay,' he says, bracing himself. 'I am alone right now. What is it then?'

'Well it is more than one thing. It is a number of things. In fact, I don't know where to start.'

'At the beginning?'

'Okay, first of all, I am in deep water with Consignia, and my job is under threat.'

'Oh, that's not good. And there I was, thinking that you were doing so well, in your new role. How has this turn of events come about?'

'Well, my work on Equalities, the way I have been doing it, has become very confronting of the status quo. Richard Finch, the ex-Finance Director, who is now interim CEO despite all his sins, has caught wind of what I have been up to, and is very much on my case. He is accusing me of trying to destabilise the whole firm with feminist propaganda, and has put me on gardening leave.'

'That is dreadful,' he says, hearing the tremble in her voice. 'But you said that was not the only thing?

'No, it is not, not by any means. I have only just got started. But it is good to spill my guts to someone.'

'I am here.' He watches as a small boy picks up a loose pebble and throws it into the canal, the boy fascinated by the ripples spreading. And spreading.

'You know how Alan had always warned me of the folly of taking this risky job, when my career was so stable, so secure?' she asks.

'Yes, I remember you saying. And...?'

'Well, he is now full of "I Told You So's."' She barks this phrase down the phone, with venom. 'He says I have become radicalised somehow, and he blames the whole coaching thing I have gotten mixed up with for that.'

'But it isn't.'

'I know that!' she says, impatient to continue. 'But when I argue back, he says that I have become hysterical, permanently hormonal, always the angry woman. He says I was asking for it. And he is not surprised that the firm finds me too hot to handle. Because he has begun to believe the same thing too. It is too, too bad. I feel assaulted.'

That is so unfair. And I feel sure it is such a distortion. Poor you.'

'Yes, poor me.' Scorn in her voice. 'He is full of anger, and he is hitting out in all directions, especially mine. The other thing he blames coaching for is...'

'What?'

'Bert! He blames coaching for Bert ever coming into our lives.'

'He would not be the first to do that. But how has that come about? You hardly know Bert.'

'Well, I introduced Alan to Bert, who in his own sly way sold Alan down the river to the tune of ten grand, on a really dodgy investment that has gone south. We will never see those funds again. Or see Bert, who seems to have gone to ground. Of course, I am forever to blame for introducing Bert to him in the first place. And the rest of you coaching types are to blame for me meeting Bert. So it goes on. Blame blame blame.'

'What a mess.' The little boy turns around, looking for his mother.

'Not the half of it. It gets worse, I am afraid. When he did get his chance to interrogate Bert, Alan asked him about you and me.'

'What on earth?' Says Justin, a quiver of fear rising in his voice. 'What did Bert tell him?'

'He said that from all he had seen and heard, that you and I were more…well more than friends.'

'Hmm. Bastard. Did he imply we were lovers?' he asks, watching the boy run to his mother, another pebble clutched in his hand. "But I can't believe this of Bert. Alan must have made up the whole story.'

'More than implied, I think. And I know how good Alan is at the Olympic event of jumping to conclusions, and of manufacturing self-serving gossip.'

'Partners can do that. I know.'

'Then Alan really started to give me the third degree.' She develops her theme. 'Forced the confession out of me that I had met you through Consignia in the first place, and taken things from there, where you had... had seduced me into the Chrysalis coaching web and so much more.'

'Does he know about us and the speeding course?'

'Well, thank goodness for small mercies. No, he does not. But he has complained to Consignia that you overstepped your mark. Neglected your duty of care in your rush to seduce me.'

'This is so bad. I hope it doesn't go anywhere, Joanna. Sounds like hearsay.'

'Well that is as maybe, but Alan is still on your case. He says you have enticed me into some sort of radical cult, masquerading under the guise of coaching, brainwashed me. This is not good for you or for me.'

Justin says, 'please don't worry on my account,' as the mother tells the boy to put back the pebble where he found it.

'I know, but I do care about you being in harm's way. And right now it is me Consignia are after. Even worse. Just when I need support, my sister in crime on the equalities team has bailed out completely. Fearful for her job, she is saying that I have led her astray from the original purpose of our team. How bad is she?'

'My God, you are in it deep.'

'I am. Worst still, remember our last Messenger chat, when I asked you, implored you to break contact?'

'I remember it well. It was sad. I was hurt. But you were right to stop it then. And thank god we did, or we could be in hotter water than ever.'

'Justin, this is not about our break-up, but about what happened later that afternoon.'

'Oh okay. I have no idea...'

'Do you remember as we chatted, a neighbour's child fell off our trampoline?'

'Well, vaguely. I thought maybe that was just an excuse for you to terminate a difficult ending.'

'Unfair,' rebukes Joanna.' No, it was more, much more than that. The same accursed child broke her arm. And her vindictive mother is now taking me to court for neglect.'

'I have read about this type of thing...'

'Well you could be reading about it again, but this time with me in the frame. The unfit mother. Her kids are saying that I was not supervising them, that I was on Messenger instead, neglecting them.'

'Too bad. And?'

'When Alan heard of this – of course he wanted to know who I was chatting to. Don't worry, I did not drop you in it. But it confirmed all of Alan's suspicions that I was having – am having – an affair.'

'Not with me you're not.'

She takes a moment. 'Well the upshot of this horrific sequence of events is that Alan - in a fury – has stomped out of the house, taken the children to his mothers. This was in full view of the neighbours, he was shouting at me, and the kids were terrified. Now they are gone.'

'Not forever, surely. What is Alan's mother like?'

'Like? My worst nightmare. She is all too willing to believe that all of his accusations are true. She hates me. So that is it. For now. Well no, it is not quite all.'

'He is on the warpath?'

'Justin, of course he is. He says that he wants a divorce, says I should not be allowed near the children, or their friends. He wants me out of the house. He will sell the house and have me out on the streets, no job, no kids, no nothing.' She breaks into deep sobs.

The small boy comes to a halt by Justin, offering him a stone to skim, which he declines, while rather thinking that the boy's game is a better prospect than more absorbing of the agony coming his way. 'I don't know what to say that will make it better. So sad.'

'Really?' Joanna bites back. 'I am not sure if you sound sad enough. Sorry that came out wrong. But I kind of wanted you to say that you would fly to my side. Be my hero. A ridiculous idea I know. But I have no one to turn to. Nowhere to turn.'

'I know. It sounds like one thing on top of another for you, all piling in. But I am not sure how I can help.'

'You sure?' says Joanna, a note of pleading replacing her questioning of his sincerity.

'I am. You need to understand my position,' says Justin, flatly, feeling desperate for a decent way out of this demand.

'Which is?'

'Look Joanna, I am just climbing out of my own mess. Still climbing. It is a long way up. I cannot be dragged down by... by anything.'

'Please Justin. I know I am pleading. But I want you to be there for me just this once, just an hour of your time. Not a lifetime commitment, for God's sake.'

'I know that.'

'Justin, listen. I don't want to say it, but I was there for you, when you were in distress.'

'Oh, that in so unfair! That was different. Totally different. Just a small work problem, a brief moment in time.'

'I know, sorry, below the belt. My bad. But I need someone that really knows me. I at home alone right now. And lonely. I hate doing this over the phone when I could be seeing you, be comforted by you. Is that too much to ask? I have told no one but you of this full awfulness. No one.'

Justin is aware of his inner rescuer twitching in every part of his being. But he must resist. He just must. He cannot take this risk. And he knows that if he saw her, he would melt. Not out of pity, or the need to rescue, but out of something more primitive entirely. He must be strong. White face, black heart.

'Joanna, you know that in ordinary circumstances I would.'

'Hmm do not finish that sentence. Do not embarrass yourself. I know you won't see me. Probably want to get off the phone right now if you could.'

The ferry sits patiently in the dock, as the passengers queue to board. 'It is just impossible, Joanna. I do feel for you, but, but.'

'I know that but. You cannot afford the risk. Too much to lose. I know. I can hear it.'

'Joanna, listen to yourself. You finished things with us. Now you want to flick a switch and have me over to comfort you. And we both know it be more than a short consolation hug?'

'Well, I have no idea it would be more than that. That's in your mind alone.'

'Perhaps it is. But I doubt it.'

'Look Justin, just go your own measly way. I have things to deal with. Alone. I am going to put the phone down before I make more of a fool of myself. Sorry to intrude on your good nature. I will be strong. But this is the end. Sorry I ever called. Goodbye. Enjoy your day.'

The boy throws the stone anyway, as his mother lifts him, tenderly, onto the boat. Justin throws his ferry ticket in a bin, as the phone pings. Uber. He has a pick-up to make.

The Powers That Be

Over dinner at the Grand Marriott, Evelyn McQueen, President of the Coaching Fraternity, and Andrew Rice, VP Standards, review their two-day trip to Bristol. 'This is quite a spread they lay on at this hotel,' says Evelyn, a broad smile of satisfaction playing across her face. 'Maybe the colonies are not quite so provincial after all.'

'A bit pricey, maybe?' asks Andrew, always a little conscious of how Fraternity members might view their extravagance,' but there again we are volunteers. We give up our time for nothing when we could be out there earning. So I would say we can console ourselves with the thought that this luxury is payment in kind.'

'You are quite right, Andrew,' agrees Evelyn, 'And if you, as Standards VP, consider this permissible, then I can put any feelings of guilt to one side. There is no one on the executive who would ever question your judgement. And we really work hard on these trips. I had quite an afternoon up at the University of Bristol, vetting that new management course that they are putting on in alliance with the Better Bank.'

'Oh yes of course, that looked promising. You showed me the brochure on the train. How did it go? Did they sign up?'

'Fine, actually,' answers Evelyn, 'they want full accreditation from us, for which they will pay handsomely. The university were behaving themselves, none of that academic criticality stuff. And Better Bank was suitably respectful too. A senior marketing guy, Dominic Cross, who was riding shotgun for the Director of People, was most convincing on the subject of the digital learning platform. We sealed the deal over lunch at Browns.'

'Great news. So, another victory for us to chalk up in this month's online newsletter? Our rivals, the Coaching Alliance will be green with envy. World domination is within our grasp,' says Andrew, brandishing his fish knife in a gesture of victory.

'He he. Don't say that too loudly though. Please remember that our mission is to make the workplace a more human place, not to fight to the death with competing professional bodies.'

'Thank you, Madam President, for the sobering reminder,' says Andrew, making a mock doffing of the hat. 'And while you were out there being wooed by the bank, I was left shuttered in my suite here, pulling together all the evidence that we gathered this morning from the witnesses in the Drake case. If only our members knew of some of the dreary tasks we executives have to face. And I got lonely while you were away, being wined and dined at Browns.'

'Aww, that is so nice of you to say so, Andrew. But I feel sure I was not missed that much,' she says, raising her eyes to his. 'But yes, that was quite a listening marathon we both endured this morning. What are you concluding? I admire you for sticking with it. Such dedication to the Fraternity cause.'

'Conclusions?' mulls Andrew. 'Well I must say, they are quite a rum bunch, the coaching fraternity here in Bristol. There was that chief witness Brenda Seagate? I never thought she would stop bleeding all over us. Such sanctimony. And all that trauma she claims to have suffered, forever blowing into her box-full of ethically-sourced tissues.'

'Yes, I found that all that a bit melodramatic,' sniggers Evelyn. 'But there again I would say she has a case, a strong case for ethics violation. We cannot have members trampling over our accredited supervisors. They are our first line of defence in ensuring conformance to standards.'

'Yes!' says Evelyn, 'we need to show we have teeth. Pour encourage les autres. And what did you make of her claiming that Drake had sent his wife in to spy on her, post his temper tantrum?'

'That was bizarre,' says Andrew, 'but plausible from all we hear of him. His wife put the frighteners on Madam Seagate, that is for sure.'

Evelyn nods vigorously. 'Then there was that guy from Consignia legal, Damien, trying to unravel that whole saga about the husband of the staff member who accused Drake of consorting with his wife, while she was an active client of his.'

'Damien didn't look as if his heart was quite in it,' suggests Andrew. 'It felt like a malicious prosecution to me, that one. But none the less, no smoke and all of that?'

'Quite so,' says Evelyn, reaching for her wine glass. 'I am taking it seriously though. We cannot appear to be soft when a major corporate brings such a complaint to us. That accusation carries more weight than the complaining supervisor in some ways. Shame Consignia did not come forward earlier with this though. We did not have the time to get the papers to Drake.'

'Not to worry,' assures Andrew, 'there was not much of a paper trail anyway. Just third-party accounts of what may or may not have happened. I am sure we can test Drake on this one, see how reacts. What did you make of the witnesses for the defence?'

'Hmm.' Says Evelyn pushing her scallops around on her elegant porcelain plate. 'I did not make much of them at all, to be honest. I was not convinced by that Tarquin Crouch. He was dripping condescension. He seemed to know Drake. But his suggestion that we would be best to leave this case to him, to deal with at a local level, when he is not even a member of the Fraternity, seemed clutching at straws.'

'I agree. He was quite bumptious. And as for that Bert Thompson character, Drake's new supervisor. He seemed more intent on bad mouthing Brenda than defending his supervisee. God knows where Drake dug him up from.'

'Didn't we rock him back on his heels, though?' Evelyn smiles at the memory. 'And his face when I put it to him that inferential claim from Consignia that Drake had introduced him to the aggrieved husband of Joanna Cooke? And that Bert had gone onto diddle the poor bloke out of his life savings. Therefore Drake was to blame for that too.'

'That was quite a stretch, I must say. But it had the desired effect on Bertie boy. He became belligerent, defensive at that point, especially when we asked after his non-existent FSA licence. Ha ha.'

Evelyn fills her glass again from the beckoning ice bucket. 'That was fun! A direct hit. Even if it had very little to do with the case under investigation. But Andrew, you did at least put the finger on Bertie Wooster's dodgy coaching practices. You were magisterial at that point,' she says, lightly stroking her cheek. 'Then he didn't help himself by saying the Drake should be counter-suing the prosecuting partners - and us, for goodness sakes - for reputational damage. Suing us! The very thought. That boot will never be on the other foot, not while I am President. And then there was that Tony in the biker jacket?'

'Oh yes Tony. He really was from left field. His challenging of – what was it again?'

Evelyn sniggers. 'I think it was the hegemony of the Fraternity...'

'Yes, saying that to the President did not seem like the best move. And then there was his – I did make a note - his "renunciation of supervision as a malign neo-feudalistic construct." That will play well at our next executive board meeting. Though it might help them know some of the forces of darkness that might threaten us all here, in the Wild West of coaching.'

'He was comical really. Some sort of Marxist cartoon character. I was glad to see the back of him. And he did Drake no good whatsoever, saying that Drake was totally aligned with his radical cause.'

'More asparagus?' Andrew offers her the fine china bowl, lightly coated with butter.

'Oh yes please. What a treat. And splash me some more of that splendid Riesling.'

Allowing her to savour the wine on her palette for a moment, Andrew then asks, 'so, tomorrow we have the man himself in the dock. It will be interesting to hear what he has to say. Where do you think this is heading, Evelyn?'

She considers this carefully. 'Well, we have had very few complaints that have gone this far. And our procedures are quite – shall we say immature? So we need tread carefully. But from all that I have heard, I think Drake is guilty as charged, unless he comes up with some really powerful, unanticipated defence.'

'Couldn't agree more, Evelyn. An excellent summary. You are not the President for nothing. Let us see what he has to say. But I would say that he is heading for a long suspension, at least.'

'You know, it would be good for us to have been seen to show some muscle,' says Evelyn. 'The membership needs to know that the executive is not just here for the ride, waiving any old misdemeanour through. We need to be seen as much more than symbolic leaders, to be enforcers as well as nice guys, from time to time. Tempt you to pudding, perhaps, Andrew? The profiteroles look to die for.'

'No thanks all the same.' He looks across at her. 'I am ready for bed. How about you? Can't wait to try out those Egyptian cotton sheets.'

The next morning, Evelyn McQueen is sat at the round table in Andrew's suite, her papers stacked neatly in front of her. A glance in the long mirror across the room confirms that her choice of an austere black suit, set off by a pristine white blouse, should set the tone for this, her first disciplinary inquiry. Hearing a tentative knock on the door, her tone is imperious. 'Please show Mr Drake in, Andrew.'

Evelyn rises to shake Justin's hand, pointing to the chair opposite them. 'Please be seated, Mr Drake, and welcome to this meeting. As you might know, I am Evelyn McQueen, President of the Coaching Fraternity, and this is Andrew Rice, VP Standards. We want you to know that you will have a full and fair hearing here today. We know you are a fully paid up member of the Fraternity, and we respect that. But these charges against you are of a serious nature, and must be considered with utmost gravity. Andrew, would you be so good as to run Mr Drake through the allegations?'

'Yes of course. And good morning, Mr Drake. Cutting to the chase, these allegations are two-fold, both concerning deeply unprofessional behaviour. The first is from Brenda Seagate, your ex supervisor - the second from Consignia Finance.'

'Consignia?' Justin cannot conceal his alarm. 'What have they to do with anything?'

'Oh yes, sorry, we did not have time to prime you on that one. The complaint only came in late yesterday. But we can go through it all today, since we are here in person. I feel sure that you will recognise the accusations in question. And a paper trail will follow in due course. Which you can of course challenge. Be assured that you will be allowed a full and fair hearing.'

Andrew Rice then proceeds to run through the Brenda Seagate case, in full and lurid detail. He pointedly reminds Justin of the disturbing scene that he caused, in the sanctuary of her study, and of the devastating damage done to her life as a result. Having laid this before their appellant, Andrew asks, 'did you, or did you not lose her temper with her on that occasion?'

Justin has little choice but to tell the truth. 'Yes, I did, but I was so provoked...'

'And did you or did you not, in the course of your verbally violent outburst, not malign the Fraternity and all that we stand for?'

'Did I? Not sure. But in my anger, I might have done. We all say things in the heat of the moment?'

Andrew looks at Justin steadily. 'And were you aware, in the course of this outburst, the effect your attack was having on Ms Seagate?'

'I suppose I was, yes.' An image of the brown tapestry floats in front of Justin's eyes.

'I see.' Andrew closes the first bundle of papers in front of him. 'So you agree these charges?'

Justin shuffles his feet under the table. 'I suppose I do. But really, she was being of no help to me. Quite the opposite. No consideration at all.'

'And then there is the not inconsiderable matter of you sending in your wife to see Ms Seagate on an undercover espionage mission, post her complaint? With the intention to further upset and destabilise your supervisor?'

'This is scandalous,' blurts an astonished Justin. I ordered no such thing. This is a complete fantasy borne from Brenda's paranoid imagination.'

Andrew fixes him with an unblinking stare. 'So, you deny this episode ever occurred? When Ms Seagate is very clear that your wife fixed to see her under a pseudonym, on the pretext of an initial chemistry meeting, then bombarded her with hostile questions. Brenda only discovered her true identity by searching your Facebook page, seeing images of the two of you happy together.'

'This is totally fanciful,' says an ashen Justin. 'Can't you see that?'

Andrew is unmoved by this plea. 'Moving along to the Consignia accusations,' he says opening the second bundle, 'this relates to you meeting a certain Ms Cooke, a Consignia staff member, out of hours, on a number of locations, while you she was a client?'

Justin blanches at this, unsure where it is heading, while glad that Joanna had forewarned him that Alan had made his accusations public to her company. 'Where are you getting this from? I am not sure if she was a client or not, at the times when we met.'

'So you agree that these meetings occurred during the course of your assignment there? And afterwards, once you had been dismissed by Consignia?'

'That is true, but for goodness sake…'

Andrew turns over to the next page in the bundle. 'And had you not, in the course of an NDA, agree never to meet with anyone from that company ever again, as a key consideration in that NDA?'

'I did. But no one is meant to know of this NDA! That is why it is termed non-disclosure! And it does not affect my professional integrity as a coach.' Justin tries to catch Andrew's eye, but he is busy with his folder.

Satisfied he has his facts straight, Andrew continues in the same monotone, 'that may well be you view, but we are afraid it does reflect very badly indeed. Consignia is, after all a major corporate player, and you have violated their express wishes. Which then reflects really badly on the Fraternity, under whose auspices you were flying at the time.'

Justin shrugs. 'This all seems like a fabrication to me. A tissue. Did you not talk to my witnesses, to attest to my professionalism?'

'Yes of course, we interviewed then in turn yesterday. And while they gave you good character references, nothing that they said mitigated the accusations as they stand. What do you have to say for yourself?'

'Not a lot. I am dumbfounded. Do carry on. This is a lot to take in.'

Evelyn takes up the reins. 'Can you say where you are practicing now? Which clients? I notice you had not asked any of your clients to come forward as witnesses? It would have been helpful if you had produced a client or two who would aver to the ethicality of your practice.'

'There is probably a good reason for that, for as of right now, I am mainly taxi driving, actually. I am doing some coaching with NGOs, nothing mainstream.'

'Thank you,' says Evelyn, catching her reflection in the mirror once more, before rising from the table. 'This all seems quite clear cut. Could you allow us a moment while we recess?' Justin is left alone in the room, looking out the window, forlornly, at the youngsters falling off their skateboards on College Green. He chews on a complimentary peppermint, seething inwardly at the array of charges set against him. And thinking it foolish that he ever agreed to come along to this meeting in the first place. Soon enough, his two nemeses return to the suite.

Andrew begins. 'Well, Mr Drake, we have now heard your witness, and we can only conclude that you accept the charges set against you. We have made our decision, which is to suspend you from the Fraternity, allowing you time for an appeal. Should you not appeal, then we are minded to move towards a judgement of full exclusion.'

Justin swallows hard at this. He feels some welling of tears, but rising behind that impulse to cry is a groundswell of considerable anger. 'You two! You ought to be ashamed of yourselves. Who the hell do you think you are? Poking about in my private affairs without my permission. Sitting in judgement on me as if you were representing some higher power, when in fact you are self-appointed nobodies, free-wheeling at your members' expense. It is you that should be on trial, not me. You make me sick.'

'Mr Drake, kindly control yourself,' admonishes Andrew. 'You are doing yourself no good at all with this childish tantrum.'

'Really? I think it is you lot who are not looking good here, not me. I should never have agreed to come here to this kangaroo court, to have my good name trampled on by both of you. President!' he spits. "VP indeed. Such grand but empty titles. Stop showing such crazy entitlement.'

Evelyn rises in her seat. 'Mr Drake. We are giving you one last chance. Can't you see that you are demonstrating the extremely aggressive behaviours that caused Ms Seagate to complain about you in the first place? I am finding this distressing. You are frightening me in fact. Andrew, could you protect me from further attack please?'

'Yes of course, Evelyn,' says Andrew, offering her a handkerchief. 'Can't you see the damage you are doing here, Drake? Of course, you are aware that this outburst will be added to the evidence against you. I need to ask you to leave right now.'

Justin remains firmly in his chair, stubbornly clutching the solid mahogany arms. 'Sorry, but I am going nowhere. Why don't you two leave instead? You are the ones causing all the damage to a member's good name and livelihood. Let you feel how it is to be shown the door. I am going to stay put, as you have no right to do any of this.'

'Mr Drake,' says Andrew, doing his best to sound controlled. 'You are making yourself look ridiculous. Can't you see how

you are upsetting our President?' Evelyn sniffs beside him.
'You leave me no option at this point but to call the hotel
security.' He moves across to the desk, to pick up the phone.
Justin sounds disdainful. 'Well why don't you then? And I will
take a photo of my being manhandled out of the door. Strong
armed by the Fraternity executive. I feel sure the "community"
will have a field day with that.'

Justin clenches his fists at the table, surprised at the strength
of his resolve. He stares at his accusers, who do their best to
avoid his gaze. Evelyn retreats to the ensuite bathroom,
leaving Andrew to open the door to security. After a whispered
conversation with his uniformed accomplices, one of the
security men turns to Justin, saying 'we are going to have to
ask you to leave sir. We understand you have been causing a
disturbance in this guest's suite?'

'Really? His suite! It is the likes of me that are paying for all
this indulgence! You are going to have to drag you out. I am
not coming quietly.' With this, Justin pulls out his phone, to
take photos of Andrew picking up his bundles, then of Evelyn
coming out the bathroom. The two security men advancing
towards him provide yet another photo opportunity.

Evelyn looks across at her colleague, barking, 'Andrew, I
really cannot take any more of this nonsense. Please take me
downstairs to the safety of the lounge. Leave Drake to
security. And you, Mr Drake.' She eyes him coldly. 'You have
not heard the last of this.'

'And as for you, Madam President,' says Justin, his voice laced with intent, 'nor have you heard the last of this either. Nor have you.'

Justin stands on College Green, listening to the clatter of the teenagers' skateboards as they crash into the cathedral walls. He feels shaken by his encounter with the powers that be, but proud of his defiance. Why should he always be the one to be shown the door? The adrenalin still pumping through his system, he is pleased that he had the forethought to arrange a post-mortem on the hearing with Bert and Tony at the Quinton House pub, his wing men, just at the top of Park Street, though he was now deeply doubting Bert's loyalty to him, from all he had heard at his inquisition, just hoping that none of it were true. He finds his way up the hill, his heart still pumping from his display of sustained anger back in that room. At last at the pub, he finds his two witnesses sat at table, sharing what looks like an uneasy silence.

Tony looks relieved to see any face other than Bert's. 'Hi Justin. How did it go? You look like you have been put through the wringer.'

'I feel that way too, believe me,' says Justin, collapsing in a seat with a heavy outbreath, unable to look Bert in the eye. 'How did it go? I am afraid to say that both of your witnessing counted for nothing, while the forces of darkness think they won the day. But I found the strength to counter-punch at the final knockings.'

'Good for you, my son!' says Tony. 'How did your pushing back work out?'

'In the short term, not well. It merely convinced them that I was a bad un. They are going to exclude me.'

'That is too bad, Justin,' says Bert, cradling a large glass of red. 'I didn't trust those two slime-balls from the moment I saw them. They have given themselves ridiculous powers – and just make up the rules as they go along. I said to them that you should counter-sue them. You need to do that, if you can be arsed.'

'Oh, don't worry,' says Justin, looking across at Bert. 'I think I might just do that. I stood my ground. Even to the extent of them getting security to evict me. But I made it clear that they were out of order. I even have photos.' With that, Justin pulls out his phone, to show his friends the evidence.

'Oh Justin, that is so cool,' exclaims Tony. 'Look at her face, coming out of the bathroom like she had just wet herself. A picture. And those security men? You stood up to them?'

'I did,' says Justin, puffing himself up proudly. 'I didn't think I had it in me. But that whole thing riled me so much. I was a man possessed! Well not quite, but you know what I mean.'

'A picture tells a thousand stories,' says Tony. 'Looking at those two faces again, I hate them. They did not even try to understand a single word I was telling them. This treatment of you confirms my worst suspicions concerning that lot. I will never join such a neoliberal set up. They have enjoyed humiliating you.'

'You reckon? That sadistic eh?' ponders Justin.

'Oh, for sure. They will be back at HQ to bragging about how they shafted a provincial bumpkin – just to show that they have teeth. You did well to get mad at them. And there is no need for their approval for you to work in the environmental or radical world.'

Bert looks sideways at Tony. 'Well, funnily enough, there is no need for such folk or their policies in my commercially inclined bloke-centric practice either.'

'Perhaps we have something in common after all, then,' says Tony, squaring up to Bert. 'Although I do not attempt to sell bogus investments on the back of my coaching.'

'What? What do you know about that anyway? Fake news.'

'Not so fake, Bert,' replies Tony. 'While giving witness yesterday, I was asked about you putting pressure on Joanna's husband to part with all of his hard-earned.'

'They got that all wrong!' protests an indignant Bert. 'That quite legitimate selling was not on the back of my coaching. Quite separate. True, I met Alan through Joanna - whom I met through Justin. It is quite an obscure trail. How else do we all get to meet each other?'

Justin, disappointed that he is not the centre of attention after his epic drama, decides to intervene. 'Yes, Bert, I heard about that too! Last thing I was expecting to come up. What did you tell them, Bert, about me and Joanna?'

Bert is quick to reply. 'I played a straight bat, stuck the facts. And besides, they have no jurisdiction over me, as I am not a member of their Fraternity. Nor is Tarquin. We would not touch that bunch of power-crazed bastards with a barge pole.'

'Come on! They have no power,' says Tony, 'but the FSA do. And the Fraternity could report you to them! They did ask me about the legality of your sideline. I said I didn't know.'

'Yes, they could! But then I am fighting a rear-guard action against the FSA anyway,' says Bert, now all bristling defensiveness. 'So, more fuel to the fire from a poxy institution will not make that much difference.'

'So how much trouble are you in this time around, Bert?' asks Tony. 'Deep?' 'Lots this time. Pretty deep.' Bert shakes his head. 'CPS are involved and this time I may go down, if my brief does not get his act in gear. I just need to find a way to get the judge's ear. We shall see.'

Tony considers Bert's predicament. 'I wish I could say I feel sorry for you. But every ethical hair in my body stands on end at the thought of what you are getting up to, on the back of a bogus coaching practice.'

Bert snorts. 'You are entitled to your opinion I suppose. But you sanctimonious bastard, Crocker! You have nothing on me beyond your worthless opinion. I have had quite enough of you Trotskyites from Stokes Croft undermining the whole mercantile basis of this city, stinking the place out. Why not fuck off to London? I am off.'

Justin decides to pile into this. 'Not so quick Bert. Before you go, I need you to know that what you did with Alan Cooke has backfired badly on me. In so many ways. Not just through the Fraternity but also through destroying my relationship with Joanna. Whatever possessed you to tell Alan that I was having an affair with his wife? Is this taken from your playbook of investment selling?'

Bert is scornful. 'Oh, I knew it! I just knew there was something going on with you and that married woman. And to think that Joy told me on our intimate little drive in the country that she had complete trust that you would never have an affair?'

'How they hell did you get around to that? She said no such thing!'

'She did!' says Bert, winking slyly at Justin.' You wouldn't believe what we talked about. And I knew something was going on with you and Joanna. Sniffed that one out from a mile away. I think Joy did too. These women always know.'

'How dare you! You know nothing. As my supervisor, you have a duty of care for me. Not to be selling me down the river, and interfering with my private life. Can't you see that you are fucking everything up?'

Bert stands up. "For God's sake Justin, grow a pair. Stop being such a victim – you brought it on yourself, hiring me because you wanted a quick result without the red tape. Saw me as a lifeline. You are a nothing. And I have more pressing matters to attend to.' With that Bert stomps out slamming the frosted glass door behind him, saying, "I have had enough of having to wipe your arse, Justin.'

Tony and Justin are left in the pub alone, recovering from Bert's bombardment. After a silence between them, listening to the bartender clinking glasses back on their shelves, Tony says, 'Well mate, if it is any consolation, you are better off without that snake in your life.'

'Tony mate, I could not agree more. Wish I had never invited him in, but there you are. Live and learn and all of that. Cantankerous old bastard. He deserves what is coming to him.'

'This has been quite a day for you, Justin. Standing up for yourself for once. Telling them all where to get off. It is not before time that you did that. Good on yer.'

'That is true enough. And it goes against all the voices in me that I should be a good boy, not to make a fuss. Tell you the truth, I have really enjoyed it, letting that noisy side of me out to play. But it has been quite an effort. Taken it out of me. Taken its toll. Not sure how some people manage to stay angry all the time. I need this beer.' He raises his glass to

Tony, who clinks his in return, saying, 'anyway, for better or for worse. The Fraternity is gone out of your life. And Bert is gone too. And if there is any justice in the world, he will end up behind bars.'

'If only. I wish. But here's the thing.' Justin looks rueful. 'Bert is so well connected, spent his whole life wriggling, snake-like, out of things that would have the rest of landed in prison, or stony broke. And I would include in that charge-sheet four really expensive divorces, leaving a trail of abandoned wives behind him.'

'Hmm. The path of the charming charismatic bully then.'

'I am afraid so. And I should have spotted it. Please don't get me angry again,' says Justin, grinning.

'Well, it is what it is. He is out of your life.' Tony feels a need to move the conversation on, before Justin starts to rant again. 'How are things otherwise, beyond this blot on the landscape that is the Fraternity? Which you are better off out of too.'

'Bad. Things are bad, Tony. Joanna is humiliated that the whole world has decided we are having an affair, when we are not. Alan has kicked her out, contacted Joy, contacted Consignia, contacted the Fraternity and God knows whom else besides. The Lord Mayor probably. He will not let go until he has brought down the two of us so-called illicit lovers.'

'That is really bad scene mate.' Tony puts an arm on his shoulder. 'If it is any consolation, Justin, I stuck up for you with the Fraternity. Probably did more harm than good. They do not like the likes of me encroaching on their space at all.'

'I am sure you did. This will not affect our working together, will it?'

'No not at all. You getting mad with them makes you rise even further in my estimation. And will give you chops with the radical scene too. My mates will love those photos of yours, exposing their brutality. You could get hold of Dick Barrow and tell him the story. He would love to get behind such injustice.'

Justin's face brightens. 'Yes, he would! You are quite right!'

Tony is pleased to see some signs of life. 'Better to attack their likes from the outside, rather than you trying to fight them from the inside, where they make the rules up as they go along.'

'But I cannot fight them alone. I just know that there are other members in the system that would love to bring them down...'

'Yeh, but they prefer moaning to activism. They will sympathise, but those good-boy coaching badges means a lot to them. They have invested a lot in getting the credentials.'

Justin raises his eyebrows. 'Well so have I, mate, so have I. I have made the same investment.'

'I know I know. But sunk cost mate – move on. Put it behind you.'

Justin allows the sense of smouldering injustice to subside.

'You may be right – and contacting Dick is a good idea.'

'Just by the bye, have you heard from Joanna?' asks Tony, changing the subject. 'She seems such a decent person, keen to break away from the ties that bind?'

'I didn't know you had taken such an interest in her,' replies Justin, looking sceptical. 'But yes, she is a really good person, but now she is in danger of losing everything. Husband, house, kids, a job, a new career in coaching. In fact, I have heard from her. She says she is desperate and has nowhere to turn, except to me. Or so she says. She really wants to meet up.'

'Oh and – that sounds so risky,' says Tony, clearly keen to hear more.

'Yes, it does. What I said her was that while I was compassionate to her plight, that it would be impossible for me to see her, that it would only make things worse, for her.'

'Yes, it would. And worse for you too.' Tony adopts his best judicial posture. 'Unless the bond between you both is so strong that you would just sling in everything, give up on what you have built and set up with Joy....'

'No Tony, stop just stop.' Justin holds the palm of his hand towards his friend. 'It cannot come to that. The bond is not that strong. I hardly know the woman. I cannot risk supporting her, even on the phone. It pains me to leave her alone like this, when every empathic bone in my body says go to her, but really I cannot. We are both too vulnerable, too needy. I have no idea where it might end?'

'Bed?'

'Behave yourself Tony! But it sounds like she is utterly alone. I just hope that her suburban friends rally around because her parents won't, not from what she tells me.'

'Could be,' says Tony, 'but I can't imagine she will want to share too much with that competitive suburbanite lot. They would commiserate of course, but I bet they would be inwardly gloating. Schadenfreude. '

'Tony, you are right – it is tragic, but there is not much I can do to make it better for her.'

'No there is not. I have an idea.' Tony's speech slows. 'This might sound off I know. But would it help if I met her, offered an ear and a tissue? To help out a mate?

'Uh ho. That could be an idea, and nice of you to suggest it.' There is doubt in Justin's eyes. 'But I think not, not at this stage.'

'I get it. Message received. Talking of a much more important woman in your life, how is Joy doing with all of this?

'Well, we were recovering well after so many knocks backs, but today's disaster with the Fraternity will not help things at all. What should I tell her about today?' asks Justin. 'I am lost at this point.'

'I think best to tell her the truth, mate.' says Tony, peering dolefully into his empty pint pot, and clearly in need of a refill.

'Yes, the truth, that is good advice Tony. Telling less than the truth has got me in trouble before. But talking of Joy, I need to be getting back. Apart from anything else we have exchanged contracts on the house far more quickly than we thought with a couple who are keen to move in as soon as. They have been around this afternoon, talking about buying curtains and such. Joy has had to do that all alone while I have been out facing the Spanish Inquisition.'

'Best get on with it, mate. Call whenever, I am here for you. And we will see each other anyway next week.' Tony makes his way to the bar, alone, to make small talk with the bar tender, while Justin shuffles off to find the bus.

'Hello Joy,' says an exhausted Justin, making his way into the kitchen.

Joy gives him a perfunctory hug. 'Oh good, you are back! Your turn for the kids!'

Justin asks 'How did the selling of the odds and ends to the incoming couple go? Sorry to leave you to all of the messy end of moving house.'

'It would have been good to have you here for that. That went great. They want to buy most of what is in here, and much of the bigger furniture too. As you know the happy couple are just returning from Dubai, with money to burn.'

'Well, they did offer a great price, at such short notice. We had not planned to sell so quickly, before we have a new place lined up,' reasons Justin, 'so happy we are all set up on that.'

'Yes, it is good news, but a shame you were not here. Now I can't imagine for one minute that you return with good news from the Fraternity?'

'Afraid not. In fact, it was worse than I thought. And it seems like my principal witnesses just made matters worse, in their own polar opposite ways.'

'Really? Not surprising though, given those two. What was the upshot, Justin?'

'I was given a chance to defend a suspension and exclusion,' Justin hesitates '…. but then I blew my top. I was just so angry at the whole set up. And now there is no way back.'

'Oh no, not again, 'sighs Joy, 'same scene as with Brenda? You lost it?'

'Hmm yes. You have no idea of the provocation though. And thinking about it, I am better off without them.'

Joy chuckles, exasperatedly. 'What a post-hoc rationalisation that is. You would have been better off staying at home and helping me. And – let me guess – you went for a pint with Tony?'

'Guilty as charged, me lud. And there is worse to come I am afraid. No wonder I needed a beer. The Fraternity are the least of our worries.'

'So, what else?' she asks, while looking like she really does not want to absorb any more miserable surprises at this point. 'Could be something or nothing. But today I learned, through the Fraternity of all places, that Alan Cooke has squealed to Consignia. And they know I have seen Joanna since the signing of the NDA. Which means they could rescind NDA and come after us too. Opening up once more that can of legal worms that I thought I had left well behind in Knowle. Sorry, but that is what I know for now. Sorry again. Hope it doesn't go anywhere, though. I don't think it has legs. I have hardly been trying to bring Consignia to its knees.'

'This is really getting us deeper into the pit that I thought we were climbing out of.' Joy looks crestfallen. 'I was feeling sad earlier at the prospect of leaving this home, and all it has meant to us. But now I think I am now glad we have sold the house, gotten the monkey of the mortgage off our backs. So now we can hide the proceeds from the house sale somewhere. Whatever else might be coming back to bite us? Why are Consignia so sure they have a case? Have you seen that benighted woman since?'

'No, I have not.' Justin's tone is adamant.

'Wanted to?'

'No not at all.'

'Been in touch?' persists Joy.

'No not at all. Nothing at all? Not even a weensy text?'

Justin shakes his head as Joy presses on. 'You tell me there was nothing going on between the two of you – and I believe you, especially having met her and put her through a minor grilling. Unless you both have carried on since, behind my back?'

'No never, I would not have done that.'

'I think I believe you. But my god, the trouble you have landed yourself in with this supposedly benign coaching lark. It is shark-infested waters.'

'Joy, talking of doing things behind people's back. Brenda concocted this ridiculous story about you visiting her under a pseudonym, and proceeding to scare the life out of her. That should bring a smile to your face. What an idea! What is it, Joy? You don't seem to be seeing the funny side of this paranoid delusion.'

'Hmm, Justin. Maybe it is not as fanciful as it sounds...'

'Wait a minute. You did, didn't you! Why Joy why? I can't believe you didn't tell me.'

'I know, I know,' says Joy staring at the floor. 'It was a moment of madness. A crazy dare from Sharon that I followed through on and shouldn't have done. So sorry. I just had to know what Brenda was really like. My curiosity got the better of me. But I covered my tracks so well. How did she track me down?'

'Easily enough, Joy. Through a swift reccie of my Facebook page.'

'Justin, I should have told you.'

'Oh, well, that was a crazy thing to do, but hey ho, my goose was well and truly cooked with the Fraternity anyway. So, you are not that squeaky clean after all?'

'No, I am not, never claimed to be. It was a terrible thing to do, but a part of me really liked doing something so bad, so out of character.'

'Hmm... the shadow side of Joy Drake. So, could we now call it quits on accusations of secret doings?'

'Yes Justin, I think we can. An amnesty. The Drake family truth and reconciliation commission is now in session.'

Justin laughs at this. 'Our souls are laid brave, cleansed through confession... Oh, and I forgot to tell you. There is some good news amid the carnage. I finished with Bert in the pub. For good. He has roared off into the sunset, out of our open-topped lives for ever.'

'That is good news. He has landed us in deep enough water as it is. So, lots of coaching bridges burn this day, eh? Bert gone is music to my ears.'

Read All About It

Dick sits in his office, well pleased with all his efforts to make sense of the Magic Carpet data leak. It has taken a while to fillet this find, but the deeper he has dug, the richer the seam. The legal and tax disclosures are potentially explosive. All that he has read confirms his deepest suspicions regarding the

Carpet and its nefarious strategies. He has no idea how all of this has been hacked. A disillusioned IT person, perhaps, who might have used someone else on the inside or outside to get it out. Not that that matters.

What matters is that the sources have been protected, with Tony assuring him that his source has agreed the release. Having crawled all over it, and matching it with his own efforts at discovery to date, Dick is convinced it all looks authentic enough to him. Having sorted the data in priority order regarding which of revelations would do most damage to Magic Carpet, he decides that he has spent enough time doing due diligence on the findings. Now is the moment to go to press. He lifts the phone to set in motion what he senses might prove to be a turning point in investigative journalism. On his tip-off, the Guardian immediately summon him to London, where he is more or less confined to a hotel room while he huddles with legal and the Editor in Chief. Legal are insistent that they involve the Criminal Prosecution Service who are more than interested, saying go ahead and publish, because the exposure might even help them build a water-tight case.

Dick negotiates his immunity and fee, but what he cares about most of all is getting the by-line. Settling on a generous fee, his mind turns to payment for Tony. He decides on gifting him ten percent of this initial fee, appropriately money laundered. He is not at all sure of Tony, who can be a wild cannon. But he is grateful that Tony came to him – and also impressed that he protected his source until the coast was clear. However, he was quite aware that Tony always has an eye for the main chance and was wary of involving him any more than was necessary. Besides, with the legal all clear, he needed to get down to work with the sub-editors, cleaning up his prose, laying out the data in tables, and deciding on headlines.

On the chosen Monday, the scoop hits the front page, as well as pages five, six and seven of the Guardian, supported by a major detailed spread online. Simultaneous with this release, they were also able to report that the police were moving on Magic Carpet headquarters, seizing documents and computers, as well as interviewing suspects at every level. All Magic Carpet customers, both current and historical, were advised to change their log-in details immediately, and also asked to ensure that their banking and personal security elsewhere had not been breached.

In their living room, Justin and Joy are fixated on the unfolding Magic Carpet narrative, whooping along with a mix of incredulity and deep delight. Each hour brings new revelations, as they learn that the CEO has resigned along with many of his executives, while customers leave in their thousands. Consumer groups are up in arms, while illegally terminated employees are finding plenty of space in the news cycle to ventilate their grievances.

Tearing her eyes from the screen, Joy asks Justin, 'Do you think the garden USB might have been behind this?'

Justin ponders. 'I doubt it…Tony would have asked me for permission before release of the USB. That was the deal.'

'Maybe you might ask him? Asks Joy, then pulls back abruptly. 'No, let me walk that question back from whence it came! That would be such a bad idea!! It is best that there is not trace at all back to us.'

'I agree. Let us just assume that a benign force is at work in the universe.'

'Oh, but this this is wonderful, after all the damage I have seen that Magic Carpet do from close range…but …'

'But what, Joy?'

'I do worry about the fact that innocent folk will be laid off a result of this.'

'Yes,' muses Justin, 'but probably management mostly, not the shop floor. Besides the company is too big to fail is it not? Customers say they leave but they will come back. They always do.'

'True enough. I wonder what will happen to the awful Dolores?'

'Hmmm, yes, there is news of her,' replies Joy. 'The last I heard from Sharon she is now head of the euphemistically termed "Performance Enhancement" division at Birmingham HQ.'

'Oh Dolores, The lady of the Dolour's, the Lady of the Pain – or perhaps more appositely the Lady of Dollars. Dolores of the perpetual dollar. That cockroach could survive anything, crawling about underneath the carpet after all other life forms become extinct.'

Joy shakes her head, 'Poor people – at least those that might remain – will still suffer under her machinations. Forced into pitiless matrices, tied in knots by seemingly innocuous algorithms. And Parallelogram are still her ministering angels of darkness.'

'Really?' says Justin. 'I heard they are going through a major rebrand – though I suspect only because no one could spell their name. They are now branded simply as "Para".'

Joy mimics hanging onto to the lines of a parachute. 'Sounds like a marine commando unit – but then that is largely how they operate - swooping in on a major SWAT mission, then getting out quick before anyone came name the faces under the process improvement balaclavas.'

'Well, I have never heard from them again, I am pleased to say. I never did get my picture on the sidebar of associates on their website.'

Joy says, 'no, you never did, thank God. What an odious company. They deserve their comeuppance. Oh look, be quiet for a moment. There is the slimy Carpet CEO now, resigning...... listen to him droning on.

"We have fallen far below the standards we have set ourselves. All customer leaks are now patched. You can continue to trade. We will clear this up – and all who have lost out on the employment front will be compensated, we will make sure of that. I am stepping down now, but my interim replacement will put things in order. He will clean this up from bottom up, and address root and branch culture change at the same time."

The Earth is Not Enough

Tony sits in his dingy Stokes Croft office, ploughing his way through a turgid report on air pollution in South West England. Sure, he feels passionately about this – as he does about so many examples of environmental degradation – but once again the hard science defeats him. Standing up to brew some coffee, he gives up on even trying to understand how particle volumes are measured. Instead he muses on how well Dick Bellows has done out of MagiLeaks, as he now grandly calls it, his face everywhere in print, online, and on TV, while his part in the data release continues to go unnoticed.

Sure, he has tried hard enough to tout his role in the undercover operation to the press, to steal some of the glory or at least get some payment for the same, but no editor he went to would touch it, and he knew that his recent attempts to go behind Dick's back and sell his side of the story to the media would land him in the deepest of waters. He had been warned off several times by serious media players and he deeply feared any reprisals from Dick. He had already spent the monies Dick had forwarded to him, and he was slowly realising that there was no more mileage in MagiLeaks for him. He had run out of road.

Doing his best to put this missed opportunity behind him, he lets his mind wonder instead to his recent conversation with Justin regarding Joanna Cooke, and the problems she is facing. And of Justin having to knock her back. He is not quite sure why she has been preying on his mind. But she just has. He does not know her well at all, but some part of him is curious about her, wanting to get to know her better. This is an instinct that often occurs for him around attractive women, but in Joanna's case, this urge to know more feels different. He feels for her, lost in pain as she is, and with no one to turn to, now that Justin has decided that she is too hot to handle, and must be cast adrift.

She is new to this world of coaching, wanting to take an alternative direction with her life, but now has to pay the price for sticking her neck out, and in the process of that courageous act, has lost her job. He knows that he can help her, wants to help her. How could she resist such an offer? After all, this approach, of offering support to women has worked well enough for him in the past in similar situations to be confident it will work this time around too.

He thinks on further as to why she was occupying so much headspace. Yes, she is attractive, which is not bad thing. For a brief moment he admits to himself that his motives are somewhat mixed.

But then, so what? Few people are pure of motive, he tells himself, and if the task is professional support alone, then what is the harm? And if there were the opportunity for something more intimate to evolve – consensual of course – then that would be welcome too. But how does he make an approach, without seeming too forward, too keen? The more he dwells on this, the more he knows that the Joanna challenge is an itch that must be scratched. An itch that takes priority over learning more about carbon monoxide emissions on the Bristol bypass any old day. And me needs to stop feeling sorry for himself that MagiLeaks had not found him the glory that he felt he so thoroughly deserved.

His first challenge, then, is to track her down, and set up a meeting.

But he has as yet no contact details for her. He can hardly ask Justin, who was lukewarm, to say the least, about him wanting to offer her support. Scratching his head over this, a plausible way in occurs to him. Chrysalis! He swills his coffee, congratulating himself on his ingenuity. Chrysalis might know, and Tarquin has all the details of each and every member, past and present.

Keen to pursue this angle of attack, a quick call to Tarquin's office confirms this hunch. After the application of some well-oiled charm with Tarquin's secretary, Tony explains that he is conducting a survey of all new members, in part for research, but also to make them feel more at home. The only problem is that he is short of a number of contact details. He tells the secretary that he has mentioned this initiative to Tarquin at the last meeting, and that the chairman is fully supportive of his move to integrate new members. After some tooing and froing, he at last receives an email from the obliging secretary containing a listing of the details of the last five new members, including today's star prize, the email and phone number for Joanna Cooke.

The first hurdle successfully navigated, his next decision is whether to email or to phone. Thinking this over, he decides that email would be too impersonal, too easily misinterpreted, or most likely be allowed to sink to the bottom of Joanna's inbox. Phone it must be. But if it is to be voice-to-voice, then what does he say after he says hello? What would induce her to meet? It was not as if he were asking her on a date. Well not really. It would have to be offering her the opportunity to assist him with the newbies survey; the survey bearing the formal sponsorship of Chrysalis.

Without planning the conversation further, he wastes no time in picking up the phone and dialling her number. To his to delight, she picks up immediately.

'Hello? Who is this please?'

'Oh, hi there Joanna, this is Tony Crocker here, not sure if you remember me? We met at the Chrysalis meeting the other evening?' As he speaks, Tony is banking on the fact that she might remember him without him having to reference his friendship with Justin, which might set off all sorts of alarm bells in her mind.

'Oh yes! Tony. I do remember you. The man in the biker jacket. What a surprise!! How may I help you, this fine day?'

'Wow, I am glad you remember me. You must meet so many people. Must have been the jacket, my old faithful. Sorry to spring a surprise, out of the blue like this – but can we talk? Are you free? I want to talk to you about a survey I am conducting.'

'Oh, I see. Well I am somewhat free – but first of all, how on earth did you get my number?'

'Oh, that was simple enough, all legit and above board. Chrysalis are sponsoring a new members survey,' he says, 'and, given that I am a trusted long-term Chrysalis member, they were happy to give me a listing of recently joined members to interview.'

'I see.' She pauses. 'Goodness, do they just give out numbers willy-nilly? What about data protection and all of that? Could anyone get my number from Chrysalis? Then start marketing all kinds of coaching support services and training at me that I don't want?'

He had not anticipated this challenge. 'Oh, I would hope not. But you do have a point, and sorry for the breach. I will let Chrysalis know to be more careful in future with personal data. They can be careless I know, a bunch of amateurs to be honest. But I was quite specific in asking for the details of a selection of new members for my survey – and you would be the bull's-eye in my target population.'

'Well, I am not quite sure about the idea of being a target, but you are forgiven for now,' she says, with a chuckle in her voice, 'but go on, tell me more about your inquiry.'

Tony, realising that charm alone will not win the day, pursues a more measured approach. 'Well, there are two purposes behind this inquiry. The first is that we know - from chatting around at Chrysalis meetings - that many coaches are wondering what happens after basic training, in terms of support and development. They feel that they fall off a cliff. And that those follow-up offerings of the same old courses from commercial providers find that those tired formulae do not fit the bill.'

'In my case that is true enough.'

'And also true for others like you,' Tony continues. 'They wish for something deeper, but nowhere is that offered. The premise for this survey is that if those who are on a development path beyond conventional courses, are supported in clarifying their true needs, then we could design next steps together for this niche.' He realises this is a mouthful, even as he says it.

'I see. Having been through basic training, I would agree that there is a gap. But you mentioned a second purpose?'

'Yes, I did,' he says. 'There is a secondary purpose, which is one I do not want to major on too early. I am interested to discover what coaches might want as an alternative coaching association, beyond the existing Fraternities of this world, of which there are many – and to ask how that could be set up.'

'Well good luck with that. Coaches seem really good at moaning about the state of the profession, but not...'

Tony interrupts, 'Yes, exactly. You have hit the nail on the head, Joanna. Coaches need to look beyond current dissatisfactions with the way the profession is set up – those grumps are well rehearsed – towards visualising an alternative frame, a radical frame, for the positioning of coaching in the world. For the betterment of the world, not simply to line the pockets of those making commercial pitches.'

She considers this. 'Take my case. Chrysalis does provide some of the exchange I am looking for, but I would enjoy something alternative, or additional, away from tired network rituals.'

'You are on the money,' replies Tony, instantly regretting the financial allusion.

'Hmm. Well, I am already involved in talking to a group of women coaches in the region. We are looking to set up our own support hub, away from the male gaze.'

'Great! That is exactly the kind of thing I am talking about! Alternative forums and formats. I would just love to hear more of this women's set up.'

'I feel sure you would, though it is in an emergent state at present. Happy to talk about it. But we do not want this group to be hijacked by men,' Joanna warns.

'Oh, that would not happen, at least not by me. I would support you completely, without interference.'

'Well that is noble of you to say so,' says Joanna, cautiously, 'but we are not looking for male permission to do this either. It is ours alone. We women are tired of being reflected in the male looking glass.'

'I get it,' says Tony, not getting the looking glass reference at all.

'I hope you do. I am happy to listen to your alternative ideas, but I do not want this conversation to turn into another form of disguised hard sell.'

'Oh, no do not worry. This is simply an inquiry at this stage – and survey responses would shape the outcome of whatever emerges. It would certainly not be for profit.'

'Well not so far. Though I would like to be sure that your intentions are good.'

'They are, they are,' breathes Tony, winningly, though not sure if his confident air is getting him anywhere at all.

'But surely you know, Joanna, that these emergent entities in any field do have a habit of becoming a monetised thing. As a wise man once said, "It all starts with a vision but ends up in geometry."'

'Are you sure it was a man who said that?'

Again, Tony is wrong footed by the power of this push back. He seeks to reassure, saying, 'I am well aware of the institutional nature of professional bodies. But my vision is that this survey could materialise different organisational forms – such as your admirable women's group – that would be based on very different principles.'

'I see. All very fine aspirations. So you would seek to displace existing bodies?'

'No. Good question, but that would be unrealistic at this stage. We would not be a direct rival in that sense. I do not think whatever we might create would drive the big guns into the ground. But it would be safe space for others who are lonely in their work, without feeling that they are being driven down a marketing funnel.'

'Oh yes I recognise that term. I have spent long enough in marketing to know how the funnel is designed, to capture its unknowing victims by stealth.'

'Exactly! As I say this is at an early stage, but already there is quite a ground swell of interest in these ideas.'

'Okay. On that basis,' says Joanna, anxious to get back to her work, 'cooperative rather than hierarchical, no Ponzi, count me in. So, what is next?'

'Well, what I would like would be for us to meet for an interview – informal of course. And I could help you assess your needs, and help us shape the bigger picture. Together.'

'I think I could be up for that, though I am busy – but it would be interesting to hear more of your work, and of your thinking, before I sign up.'

'So, we shall we meet then! Good! Could you manage this week or next? I am keen to get this moving.'

'Sure. In fact, how about tomorrow? Late morning – I am in town and free.'

'Great! Park Street? The Boston Tea Party?'

'Elevenish?'

'Yes, that would be fine, see you there. And thanks for agreeing to do this.'

Putting the phone down, Tony reclines back in his creaking chair, hands behind his head, smiling in the satisfaction that his plans to get to know Joanna better are moving along with such rapidity. He just knows that face-to-face, he will find out more about what really makes her tick, beyond the fine feminist words. His mind turns to the next day? What should he wear?

Something cool, a little downbeat. But not his biker jacket again. She had seen that before, and he saw her looking at it askance. Perhaps his Extinction Rebellion hoodie? That should fit the bill. And thinking of rebellion, he feels renewed enough to tackle the pollution report afresh, though secretly hoping that somewhere on the Internet, he would find a summary for eco-dummies. More that satisfied with outcome, he decides to reward himself with a nice fat sausage roll.

Tony enters the Boston Tea Party, happy to find that the quaint upstairs area is still quite empty. He takes a rickety table near the window, the sun streaming through onto the distressed oak tabletop, illuminating every dark crack. This is the perfect setting for this encounter, he decides, just as Joanna appears at the top of the staircase.

He stands to greet her, offering her a coffee.

'Well thanks Tony, and nice to see you,' smiles Joanna. 'Is this café a regular haunt of yours?'

'Oh yes, it is. I really like it. Truly organic, not just playing at it. An ethical green entrepreneurship thing – eco-preneurs really. The first café in the country to ban single use coffee cups.'

'Really? That is radical,' says Joanna, casting her eyes around the artfully disorganised layout.

'True. It has hurt their business but they have carried on regardless,' nods Tony, 'and now the big chains are following its example. Talk about influencing, nudging...'

'Yes, I quite see. But talking of chains - did I not see you emerging from Greggs, the sausage roll emporium just up the road there? I was just behind you on the Triangle?'

'Oh yes.' Tony gulps. 'Guilty as charged. Nothing really to read into that. I was early for our meet, felt peckish?'

'Is Greggs your guilty pleasure then?' She grins at him, awaiting his answer.

'No, not at all. Probably my first time in there. Needing food for fuel. And I cannot really afford the sandwiches in here, lovely as they are.'

Joanna ponders this dilemma. 'Yes, I guess being ethical and making money comes at a price?'

Tony looks sheepish. 'Okay. Ah good, here comes your coffee. Nice of them to bring it upstairs. Such service as well as totally green. So, could we get straight down to it, talk about alt.coaching?'

'Alt.coaching?' asks Joanna, arching a sceptical eyebrow. 'Is that what you are calling this thing you hope will come from your survey?'

'Well, I am not really set on that name. Alt.coaching is simply a working title, a container, to keep the thing distinct in my own mind.'

'I see. You gave me the bare bones on the phone, I get the drift,' replies Joanna, looking not entirely certain. 'What was it you want to ask me, by way of the survey?'

'Sure, let us get into that. Let the interview begin,' Tony grins. 'So, what has been your coach training so far?'

'Basic. Own brand "Essentials" type of thing. No frills, stripped down. The Greggs the Baker of coaching education.'

'How was it?'

'Good in many ways. And I got the tee shirt. Licence to operate and all of that. And the company paid for it!'

'Do you mind if I make a few notes?'

'Be my guest,' she waves at him, while blowing the froth off her coffee.

'And your professional support post training? CPD?'

'Not much. Chrysalis. A few podcasts that turned out to be sales pitches – none of them feeding a deeper need. In fact, that click-bait annoyed me a lot. Not going there again.'

He scribbles in his notebook. 'You mention your deeper need? Which is?'

Joanna pushes back her chair, the legs scraping on the uneven floorboards. 'My need? For true authentic sharing - and being vulnerable. Not just bragging or selling at Fraternity meetings, trying hard to persuade each other of an idea of a proper profession that in my view will never materialise. What do the academics say? It is purely a social construction.'

'Okay, that is clear,' he says, priming his next question, while wishing to make it seem as if he had prepared for this interview. 'And how would you describe your practice at the moment?'

'Hmm. Well, showing some promise, but early days. And not easy to get the work. But satisfying all the same. I started out coaching in-company - working on equalities issues with Consignia – but I have now parted ways with the firm, and practicing on my own.'

'I see.' Tony raises his head from his notebook. 'Could I ask why the move away from Consignia? I do know those internal roles are really tricky.'

'Well you can ask, but I am limited in what I can say at his point. I feel sure you understand, for reasons of company proprietary. Shall we just say I wanted to spend less time with my family?'

He giggles a little at this euphemism. 'I'm happy to I report only that your entry was through an internal route. I need to know the entry point, because people's point of departure from their previous occupation tends to shape the CPD and credentialing path they follow. If that makes sense?'

Joanna nods at this. 'Yes, it does, now you say it. Tell me more. This is quite interesting. Never really thought about it before.'

'Okay,' says Tony, encouraged by her interest. 'For example, those than come in after a redundancy pay-out - after a long time in the corporate cocoon - tend to look for a recognised professional path way to follow. Those that come into this through love and passion – a need to challenge the established organisational order, the power system – are less needing of a structured funnel. In fact, they do not trust that, reaching out instead for the support of like minds.'

'Yes, that makes sense. I am a bit of a mix of both then. You can write that down of you like, just to complicate your theory.'

'Ha! I will! So now that you are sole trader, could I ask the point of focus of your coaching work?'

'Early days as I say, but I am building a reputation for support of women at work. Glass ceilings and all of that – and have a contract now with a large bank as well as individual clients, mainly women in their own businesses.'

He notes this down, while she gazes out at the shoppers below. 'I see. So, a two-pronged attack? And are you making ends meet, if I may ask?'

Her gaze returns to meet his. 'You can. The corporate stuff is a pilot at this stage. Do hope it grows into a lucrative case study that I can market to others.'

'And your work with the independent women?'

'Well, the fees for that are low, as you might suspect. But we have set up an interesting local economy transaction system - a LET - where we barter goods and services. I exchange my coaching skills for homemade vegan jam and website design. It works well, if a bit random.'

'No, not at all,' Tony beams, enthusiastically. 'Sounds really really creative, I applaud that.'

'Oh, yes. It is really liberating. We are even thinking of setting up our own micro-bank, where we can attract and pool investment for our own projects. We are so excited about that. And of course, a proportion of our exchanges goes to charities – at the moment we are thinking of sponsoring and supporting a women's refuge. The woman who runs it is in the network.'

'Hmm, excellent. This is all so consistent with my values and practice. So, may I ask, are you financially independent at the moment?'

'That is quite a question.' Joanna looks taken aback. 'Not something we Brits often talk about, money. How shall I say it? I am in financial transition, and beyond my work situation, I am coming out of a tough separation from my marriage and finding my feet again.' She looks downwards, her hands in her lap.

Tony puts on his best active-listening face. 'That must be tough.'

'It is. But I am getting through. One day at a time. Ha ha.'

Tony notes this down, oblivious to the irony. 'So, could I ask about work–life balance?'

'Meaning?'

'Well, for many coaches, work–life balance is a big issue. Trying to balance work getting and doing, and all the travelling as well. Home parenting, caring issues. As well as keeping the financial wolf at bay.'

Joanna nods along to this listing. 'Oh yes, I am feeling all of that. I do get to see my kids and they need me, I need them, but I am still settling on where I might live, once the house is sold. Right now, my work is local. I do quite a bit of Skype support, and we women in the network are finding good ways of sharing our parenting. Many are in a similar boat to me, so we need to be there for each other.'

'I see. But you have a vision of how this might settle?' he asks, worried that his empathetic mask is slipping.

'It is emerging yes,' she replies, 'but so far I would not say that balance is there for many. I often wonder if work-life balance is only another thing to beat ourselves up with for not achieving – like wellness.'

'That is very insightful.'

'Thanks, Tony, I am capable of insight now and again. But let me go on. And sometimes corporates turn coaching into a thing, making policies for it and all the rest. Standards and compulsory trainings, which is all well and good in many ways. But then perhaps all of that well-meaning intervention could just be another way of blurring the personal and public boundaries, appropriating the whole person. At a price. Letting the company take over your whole life. Wow that was a lot. Speech over.'

'No, do carry on. You have clearly thoughts about this,' says Tony, hoping he is not patronising her. "Hard to write it all down.'

'You could have recorded it on your phone. What were you asking me?'

'Hmm. You were on a riff about corporates appropriating people's personal lives?'

'Thank you for the prompt. Yes, I have been up close and personal to the way corporations capture souls! Staff becoming dependent on their employer to provide crèches, mediation rooms, gym membership, cheap cycling. Then there is HR monitoring stress levels, and on-board coaches to mop up the mess and get you back on the hamster wheel.'

Tony cannot resist joining this litany. 'Oh yes, and the chimera of flexible working, but with smart phones and 24/7 access, staff actually have less and less discretionary time. Even when commuting, people are busy doing an extra two hours email time. That is now expected of them, but never registers on a timesheet.'

'Well said, Tony. And I must say I am finding this chat helpful. Quite illuminating. More than I was expecting.'

'Thanks. But you are doing all the heavy lifting here, ideas wise.' He ponders his next question, rifling through his notebook to seek his non-existent alt.coaching survey checklist. 'Hmm so coaching, especially in-company coaching, could be seen to be part of the problem here? Keeping the capitalist ship afloat, palliative care etc.?'

'A provocative thought. That could well be true – in fact it has been part of my experience as both giver and receiver of the same in the corporate world.'

Tony is pleased to find her in such reflective mood. 'Much food for thought there in all that you say there, Joanna, and a longer conversation needs to be had.'

'Could be. But I'm not sure where this analysis gets us. All quite anal.'

'Don't be so down! These are exactly the kind of deeper issues I would see the fearless alt.coaching effort addressing.

You know what you say of women's support to each other? I applaud it. Few men reach out in this way. There are some exceptions. For example, in the Stokes Croft environmental massive, Justin and I do support each other through some deep personal stuff, even crises. It is really helpful.'

On this mention of Justin, Joanna takes her phone off the table, quietly putting it in the patch pocket of her fawn linen jacket.

'Sorry, these phones are a distraction. Talk about the tyranny of "always on." They run our lives. But you mentioned Justin? I have not heard from him for a while. How is he doing?'

'Justin? He is doing really quite well, as far as I know. Been having a tough time at home and at work. Lots of turbulence there and I am glad that I am there for him.'

'He must appreciate that.' Her expression is impassive.

'Oh, I think he does. Nowhere to turn. Tensions in family life and on the financial front. He is now putting in all sorts of hours in the gig economy, Uber mainly. But it is hard from him. A few sources of his income have been withdrawn and Joy is no longer in a job. House sold, but nowhere specific to go. But they are working on it all. I cannot tell you more.'

'Well, that is quite a picture.'

'Yes, it is. But I guess the main thing is that they are together still, Justin and Joy, despite all. Not so sure how long it will last though. It is really fragile. Justin is really afraid she will take off, have an affair. And she has had quite enough of his weakness, of his being such a soft touch, which gets him into trouble. He is easily seduced.'

'Hmm,' murmurs Joanna. 'Sounds like Joy might have to be putting up with a lot?'

'Yes, I think so. If only Justin were there to support her, which I think she wants and needs.'

'Really? How do you know that?'

'Oh...' He reflects on his answer. 'Well he tells me so. We share everything… let it all out, no holds barred, we steer well away from the usual superficial men's' talk. I am well aware of his restlessness, his wish to break out. And of hers too.'

'I see.'

Tony decides to push this line of questioning further. 'Didn't you and he used to be quite close? I am surprised you do not know all of this?'

'Not sure if I would go that far. If we were close, then that is not the case now.'

'He said how muchhe enjoyed supporting you, how receptive you were, kindred spirits even?'

She appraises him coolly, leaving this unanswered.

'Come on.' Says Tony. 'You must know him as well as I do. He is such a romantic, I think. I mean I love him dearly as a friend, but he does get easily captivated by the things and people that float past him. And he is quite charismatic and empathic. So, he does draw people and projects towards him...'

She decides to cut across this. 'Look, are we here to talk about Justin, or to do your survey?'

Tony leans back, putting his hands deep in the pockets of his hoodie. 'No, the survey. Not even quite sure how we got onto the topic. Sorry about that diversion. Could we get back to my questions?'

'Forgiven. And do carry on, these questions of yours are interesting to dwell upon.'

Tony studies his notebook once more. 'Ah, here it is! The next prompt. Could I ask you about loneliness? Many of the coaches I talk to mention this – feeling lonely in a helping profession. No colleagues to turn to, and not much support at home.'

'Truth,' says Joanna, 'there is that sense of hidden shame about it.'

'Yes. And for many in the helping professions, especially for women, there is the issue of them outgrowing their partners, in a developmental sense. I mean to the point where conversations that need to be aired cannot be had across the dinner table - or even in bed. Whoops. But you know what I mean. Was that impasse part of the cause of your split? That you had moved on and your husband hadn't?'

Joanna allows this question to hang in the coffee-infused air. Glancing around, she sees that the room is filling up with a cross-section of the right-on great and good. She turns back to Tony. 'What a personal question. But yes, seeing as you ask, and in the spirit of transparency - that issue was there, and it did not help. I could not be open with him about the ways in which I was changing, and he did feel threatened by it all. He said he no longer knew me, wanted me to go back to the old Joanna he felt comfortable with.'

'Thanks for your honesty. I will stop taking notes at this point. But what you so painfully describe is all part of pattern that I was outlining, to be sure. A living case-study.'

'But your question was about loneliness?' queries Joanna.

'And I am not sure about lonely. "Becoming me" is not a lonely process. I am still finding my independent feet in lots of areas. I am too busy outside and inside to be lonely.'

'That is good to know,' he says, looking unconvinced. He has run out of questions, not sure how to move this on.

Sensing the silence and noticing the notebook is shut, she offers him a way forward. 'Let me ask you a question, as you seem so knowledgeable on these matters. Are you married, a parent?'

'No, I am not. Never found the right person, and besides I am not sure I want to bring kids into this world, given its current state. I need to sort the world out before I spawn. Ha ha. Meanwhile, I am a free agent to pick and choose or not. Just like you right now, I guess. We are both free to explore, to come and go as we please, if the fit is not right? Are we not? And after all...'

Joanna leans across the table, interrupting him. 'Hang on! Before you go any further, I need to know where this is going?' He looks alarmed. What do you mean? Where this is going? I was just following my questions list is all. I put all my respondents through the same process. Then you asked me a question, which cut across. Please tell me what is niggling you.'

'Hmm. What is on my mind is that - since my separation – there have been so many men of my acquaintance who have never really talked to me properly before my marriage split asunder - coming onto me. Well, offering me support, but behind the gin and sympathy, I just know that there is another agenda – one of seeking intimacy, shall I say? Even the husbands of good friends. Perhaps especially husbands of all kinds, seeking a no strings affair with what they perceive as a vulnerable woman. It stinks, frankly.'

'God, I had never imagined that sort of thing happening. How awful. Such vultures. But then, in your case, not so difficult to believe. After all, you are really attractive women, at so many levels. And whip-smart too. There are not so many women like you around. It is little wonder men swarm.'

'Really?' asks Joanna, looking incredulous.

'Yes really. So, you are being picky in choosing your next partner? Or in deciding whom you might like to date? I must say, I don't blame you.'

'Tony! I am not at all sure if any of this is within the remit of this survey? Is this to do with loneliness question?'

'Yes, the loneliness category.' Tony breathes a sigh of relief to be offered a lifeline to get him back on track. 'The need for support, companionship and intimacy?'

'I see.' Joanna spreads her fingers on the edge of the table.

'Tony, I need to ask you a question.'

'Please go ahead, I am all ears.'

'Tony, do you find me attractive?'

'Well…yes of course I do? Why? I thought you knew that? Not that it is anything to do with anything.'

'I see. Now I need to ask my follow-up question. Don't talk. Please wait for it. Are you angling for a date here?'

Tony does his best to feign the aggrieved look of the wrongly accused. 'No not at all. I am not one of those cheating husbands. But I do want to get to know you better. Most of all, I would love to support you. People say I am so helpful, so giving, without any ulterior motive.'

'And?' She looks at him, encouragingly. 'Doesn't that unconditional positive regard ever develop into something else? I could well imagine the tug...' 'Well... as for freely given support developing into a liaison – well in our case, then I would not count that out. In fact, it could be growthful for us both. Like minds and all of that, consensual, together in different ways. Without conflicts...'

'Okay. Let me summarise, as all good coaches do, at some point in the conversation. Like now.'

'Do go ahead.'

'So, I am concluding that, somewhere at the back or front of your mind, you would like to date me, to take this beyond a professional relationship?'

'Well, very much at the back of mind .... but I would have to be honest, I do find you attractive, and there would be no harm in us exploring…'

'Exploring what exactly – each other? Tony, do you think I need a man? Do you?'

'I am not at all sure about that, actually. But yes, it is a natural thing for humans to do, to pair bond. After all, you have had at least one man in your life. Sounds like you are getting plenty of offers from inappropriate men, ones that do not share your value set. So, if you do need a man, then hypothetically, given that I am free agent, then you and me - or someone like me - could fill a need. You are in your prime after all.'

She holds up both palms towards him. 'Tony, I think this has gone far enough. And please stop looking at me with those puppy dog eyes.'

'Okay I have stopped. Puppy back in kennel. On the naughty step.'

'Okay,' says Joanna, firmly, 'so, let me summarise, once again, from my perspective.' He sits back, attentively, as she continues. 'Do not assume I need a man in my life, for the reasons you describe. And also, do not assume that because of that lack of need for a man, that I am looking for an alternative amorous relationship within the sisterhood I am close too, either.'

'I would not dream of imagining that.'

'Of course not. Men never harbour lesbian fantasies about women they fancy,' her voice laced with scorn.

Tony looks downcast, fiddling with the organic sea-salt shaker, dreading her next question.

'Tony, I need to change tack a little here. Tell me - I do have to ask – did Justin ask you to contact me? I need to know? Is he fishing?'

'No, not all.' A flush of surprise crosses his face. 'Well, I did say to him that I would like to contact you – for the survey of course.'

'And he said?'

'He said that it was up to me. I am sensitive to the fact that neither of you can contact each other, that it is not safe. But there is no way that I'm a back channel to him. Please don't be so suspicious. All I want to do is to support you. Just like I want to support other alternative coaches too.'

'Possibly,' questions Joanna, 'but I am not at all sure I can trust you to confine yourself to that role.'

'Look, please do trust me. I am an ethical person. Everyone says so.'

'Tony, I am not at all sure that I want your support. For a number of reasons. I really do think you want into my knickers, even if you say you are not wanting an affair. After all, you know what they say?'

'No what do they say?'

'They say that the best way to shag a feminist is to pretend to be a feminist sympathiser yourself? Surely you have come across that duplicitous slander?'

'Ouch. No, I never have. But very funny all the same.'

'Yes ouch, you may well say ouch,' says Joanna. 'And secondly I do not need a man. Even more than that, I do not need a man to tell me I need a man. Especially when that man in question means himself. That is not to say that another man in my life is out of the question. But not you, Tony. Apart from anything, you not my type at all, actually.'

'Well that is okay then.' Tony is looking suitably chastened. 'We can confine what we do to personal support. '

'Tony, right now you are the last person I would turn to for personal support!'

'Why?' asks Tony, though not wanting to hear the answer.

'Why? Because your boundaries are so leaky is why. Just now you revealed so much about Justin, without his permission. And about Joy, too. I would have to assume that you would leak similarly about my confessions to anyone else – you may even be planning to do that right now, as we speak?'

'No, not all' Tony protests, slumping further in his chair, resisting the temptation to pull his hoodie over his face.

'Tony, listen. After all of this charade, you getting me here under false pretences, to seduce me. I am thinking of reporting you – to… to whomever will listen. The Fraternity for one.'

'Oh, come on.' He straightens in his chair, suddenly animated once more. 'This is escalating ridiculously – can't a man talk to a woman without being accused of trying to rape her? Is this your "me too" moment? The moment that you have been waiting to tell the vengeful girls about? All that posing as victims…'

'No, it is not. But I will certainly tell the sisterhood – we share everything. And they will be appalled to hear of your sneaky, crooked come-on.'

He recovers a crumbled handkerchief from his hoodie pocket, wiping his nose.

'Tony, look at me. Take that rag away from your face. I have another question for you.'

'Go ahead.'

'Are there not lots of adoring, idealistic newbies in the environmental space - as you call it - that you can more easily pick up as conquests, notches on your alternative bedpost, that are far easier pickings than me?'

'Joanna! Now you are being crazy. Of course not. I respect those young women really highly, I would never...'

'Are you quite sure?'

'Never! To be honest, one or two them have developed a... an attachment, but I well well how to manage and deflect such approaches.'

Joanna scoffs, loudly enough to interrupt the conversation at the adjacent table. 'Oh really? Don't you mean a crush? Which you encourage then exploit? Then discard the poor innocent when the next hennaed piece of fresh meat comes through the door?'

'That is not how it is – I have the utmost respect...'

She interrupts. 'Don't think I don't know what goes on with self-appointed gurus. The temptations are too great. You must become satiated with all that unconditional admiration. It is all too easy for you. So, what is this all about?'

'What is what?' His look is now one of complete bewilderment, his eyes seeking an easy escape route.

'This! Your coming on to me so clumsily. When there are girls out there who are open to your advances. Oh, I know. I get it. You cannot resist the challenge I represent. Wanting to shag your best friends ex? Go further than he ever managed? A competitive thing? And meanwhile you are totally betraying your friendship with him?'

'This is lunacy. I never knew how far you two went in your relationship. He never said.'

'I feel sure Justin told you how vulnerable I was. And told you that when I reached out to him for help, just needing to talk things over, when things were at their worst - that, at that moment, he was afraid, and knocked me back. I bet he told you about that. Didn't he?'

'Yes, he did,' confirms Tony. 'He said that he was feeling guilty for not supporting you, but he couldn't take the risk...'

'Self-preservation?'

'Something like that. But he felt bad.'

'Aha. So, you saw a way to creep alongside of me on some sad CDP pretext? Well I have to tell you things have moved along for me lately. I am not a needy woman now. Quite the opposite. I get stronger by the day.'

'Good. But I am so sorry you feel this way about me, Joanna. I think we should stop this now. No damage done? Still mates? Move on from here? Reset the whole thing? Put the whole thing behind us?'

She shakes her head defiantly, pushing back her chair as she makes to go, the scraping on the floor audible to all.

He stands too, moving towards her, his voice rising in desperation. 'Joanna, I want to make this right. A hug maybe?' He moves towards her before she can resist, taking her in his arms for a clumsy, awkward moment.

'Tony, just stop.' She raises her voice, pushing him away from her. 'I do not want a hug. I do not want you close, sniffing my scent. I do not want your lust anywhere near me. I need you to go now. I will pick up the bill for the coffee, thanks. Oh, and just one thing before you go.'

'What is that?'

She pulls her phone slowly from her pocket, pointing at the red record button. 'I have recorded the latter part of our conversation, beginning with your betrayal of Justin and Joy, as I thought this conversation might lead down this road. And a girl never knows when such a record might prove useful.'

'But that is totally wrong,' he mouths, his protest forced from his throat. 'You are betraying our confidentiality. This is my interview!'

'Hmm... just as you have betrayed all of those others.'

'This sneaky recording. How are you going to use it?'

'That is none of your business.' She looks him straight in the eye. 'I may never use it. But I need you to know that I have it here. And I really don't want to see you ever again. It is recorded on a cheap burner phone, untraceable. I really did not trust your motives in all this in the first place. Now I know my suspicions were justified. And putting up with this vileness was worthwhile - if only to have this evidence in my hands.'

His terror is plain for all in the room to see. 'But you must tell me what you plan! Joanna!'

'Stop now. You are raising your voice. People are looking. You are making a scene and a fool of yourself. So much so that I think I saw that women over there videoing your hug – you could be done for assault. I will talk to her afterwards. She looks shocked.'

Tony turns to stare at the woman, then turns away, as Joanna says, 'just go now. I will not follow. Perhaps you need to sneak off to Greggs again. Gorge on more comfort food? Or go into Wetherspoons pub to drown your sorrows alongside of the pathetic all-day drinking men?'

He makes for the stairs, his hoodie now fully over his face. As he leaves, he nods to those around her, wanting to ask the women with the phone if she had indeed caught the hug, or his shouting on camera. But he does not have the courage. He just wants to get out of there, a shroud of guilt and humiliation following him down the funky staircase.

A Leak Springs

The next day, Justin returns from a satisfying Uber shift, happy that he is in rhythm with their new life, to find Joy sobbing loudly in the kitchen. 'What is it, Joy?' he asks, rushing to take her in his arms. "Tell me all about it.'

He listens as she says, 'Justin, it is awful. My day was going so well, preparing for our house move, hearing good news from the university about me being offered some teaching work, when I opened a letter from Magic Carpet's solicitors.'

'Oh My God – and?' Justin cannot halt an involuntary spasm of fear cross his face.

'The "and" is that they have found out the source of the Magi-Leaks. And our name is implicated in it.'

Justin shakes his head. 'How could they ever have they done that? We were fireproof.'

'I did say they are excellent at surveillance. And they say that they cannot reveal the source that fingered us.'

Justin considers this. 'But surely not Dick, not Tony – he would have told me, he promised - least of all not Glynis?'

'As I said, I have no idea how they knew. And I don't think we shall ever find out who betrayed us, and I am not sure that it matters. We can ask around, but they say they have evidence. They say that their case is robust.'

Justin recoils at this turn of events. 'Case for what exactly?'

Joy steels herself. 'For us – for us reneging on the NDA. Which in some ways we have. Maybe in a lot of ways we have. We could be bang to rights here.'

'God, this is beyond belief.' Justin considers the implications of this development. 'There goes our golden parachute.'

'Yes, Justin, that parachute is now totally deflated. Grounded forever. While you were out at work, I was trying to come to terms with that. But I doubt if they will give up on hounding us out of our existing agreement.'

'Oh, that is the end.' Justin does his best to reason this out, fighting the rising emotion. 'But they have so little to go on. We were simply minor players in this. We will never reveal what our exact involvement was. They would not want another public outcry over yet another example of their threatening behaviour.'

'Even so, Justin the shame, the stress of this.' She returns to his arms for a long hug. 'Hmm that feels better. I guess the good news is that the letter says that if we accept that the existing NDA is null and void – and if we sign another NDA to bind us into perpetual silence on the fact that there was ever a NDA in the first place – then they will leave it at that. Which is a relief, I suppose. But still...'

'Hmm. I guess we had best sign up then. I am so sorry this has come out. And who knows what their game plan is in all of this is. Just trying to keep people quiet while they hunt down whomever breached their security in the first place. Though I guess they know full well that the damage is already done.'

'Well we can forget about that dream of finding the perfect home in the funky Montpelier neighbourhood now.' She sighs. 'That is our financial backstop gone. Back to the drawing board on how we make ends meet. Look Justin, I need to go for a walk, let this pain go away some. Do you mind? I need to be alone for a while.'

Justin picks up the discarded solicitor's letter, reading it once, then twice, in an attempt to make sense of it all. He learns that they can challenge the company decision, but make it clear that if he were to press for restitution of the payments, then all manner of pain might come their way. He slips into a fatalistic mood, thinking that in some ways they were fortunate ever to have scored the payments in the first place, given that it was prompted by Magic Carpet's fear of them being part of a wider conspiracy, which was never the case. Now it would seem that they may have a sliver of evidence that they were part of something wider after all. So, the Carpet want to both punish them financially for this; yet at the same time need to continue to silence them, ensuring this time that they are silenced forever. His head aches trying to figure out their motivations. Perhaps those payments were never theirs to begin with. Yet still ……. he reflexively checks his phone, to see a message on his voice mail, sent from a withdrawn number.

He listens in to this mysterious message with growing disbelief, as he hears at first Joanna's voice, then Tony's. Justin feels a degree of both shock and surprise, as Tony had never told him that he had actually arranged to see Joanna. Sure, he had said that he might, but Justin never knew that he had followed up on this vague intention. He realises soon enough that this is a recording of that conversation, though he has no idea as to where and when it might have occurred. He is curious to visualise the scene but cannot. In her house? Tony's? Somewhere outside? Listening in, he senses a growing fear that this recording could be sent to him in a spirit of anonymous malice, designed to expose and shame him. Could it be something to do with the Carpet taking action against them?

The longer he listens to this conversation, his fear of exposure subsides. Nothing that he hears makes him a guilty party. Instead it shines a floodlight of accusation upon Tony. In fact, the more he hears of this, strong feelings of anger well up at the sheer extent of Tony's betrayal of him.

So intent is he on the recording that he does not hear Joy coming in through the door, returning from her solitary walk. She is taken aback to hear voices, which she slowly recognises as those of Joanna and Tony. What were they doing in her kitchen? What was going on? But on entering she sees that Justin is alone, listening to a recording on speaker phone.

Aware that he has not clocked her entry, she listens in to the last five minutes of the exchange, yet fails to make any real sense of it, knowing only that it is a recording of a tense argument. She freezes at the sound of Joanna's voice, so vividly remembered from their last meeting. A voice she never thought she would hear in their house, a voice she would never wish to have in their house, threatening the stability that she and her husband had only recently recovered in their relationship together.

As the tape peters out, she coughs, loudly. Justin jumps at this, looking more guilty and alarmed than she had ever seen him before. Or at least not since she had confronted him on his relationship with Joanna. She asks, 'Justin, what the hell was that? Kindly let me know what is happening here? Come on!'

Justin is paralysed, completely lost for words for a moment, asks, 'did you hear any of that?'

'Well, I don't know how much of it there is, but yes, I heard the last few minutes or so, but it still makes no sense to me. I was standing at the door, but you were too lost in whatever was on that recording to notice me.'

'Sorry about that, but yes, I was lost in listening. As far as I can work out, it is a tape of argument between Joanna and Tony. And no, before you ask, I had no idea they were going to meet, though Tony did indicate that he might like to meet up with her. A notion that I strongly discouraged, but it looks like he went ahead anyway.'

'And where did they meet?' asks Joy, curious for more detail.

'No idea, but the latter part of the conversation suggests that it was in a public place, a café perhaps. I am as shocked as you are to find that someone anonymous has sent this to me, on an untraceable phone. Nothing of my making for sure. I did not invite this in. You can listen to the whole thing if you like. As I hear it, I am blameless in this – in fact quite exonerated.'

'But who sent it? Do you think?'

'Dunno,' replies Justin. 'Not Tony for sure. Maybe Joanna, though I have not heard from her since I knocked her back. Could be her. Not sure it matters. If the purpose was to let me know what Tony was up to behind my back, then they have done me a service.'

'I think they probably have, if what you say is true. Are you sure you have not contacted her?'

'No, not at all – and the tape says as much. I have been honourable.'

'So, this cannot hurt us? Any more than we have already been hurt today?'

'Not that I can see. Look, listen in with me. I will play the whole thing again, and you can help me know what any of this might mean. And what clues might be in there to indicate the sender.'

They settle with a cup of tea to eavesdrop into the whole recording. Their eyes meet at critical points, Joy allowing herself the occasional gasp, and more than the occasional harrumph. Justin listens intently for the second time, noticing nuances he had missed first time around. When he breaks to seek Joy's eye contact, he is reassured that what he was sensing the first time around was indeed what she is discerning also. As the tape finishes, she exhales long and soft, saying, 'it still spooks me to hear her voice, here in the so-called safety, the sanctuary of our home.'

'I know, I know.'

She continues, 'then hearing his voice, dripping with sanctimony, while badmouthing the both of us, simply makes me want to throw up. I know we all indulge in hypocrisy, but this is taking it to more disgusting extremes. How dare he?'

'Yes indeed, how the devil dare he?' responds Justin. 'But I thank you for listening through. I really appreciate you doing that, when you could, quite rightly, be throwing things at me.'

'Well, I am still thinking of throwing things at all three of you, especially Tony, the next time I see him. You are not off the hook yet. But tell me, allowing you a moment of grace, how are you feeling about your bestest ever radical friend right now? '

'How am I feeling? How I am feeling?' Justin dwells on this for a moment. 'I am, to put it mildly, feeling totally betrayed by him, my trust in him irreparably damaged. I cannot carry on working with him or even seeing him. That friendship is over. I feel little short of murderous towards him. Vengeful.'

'And what was that other thought, the one I saw flicker across your face, following on those murderous feelings?'

'I was thinking, along vengeful lines, that we might even think of exposing him, use this evidence among other things to tear his whole deceitful enterprise down?'

'Hm. I share that feeling, believe you me. But then I wonder if we need to be the direct agents in that. Sounds like Joanna might be plotting his downfall at this very moment, with the power of the sisterhood behind her.'

'One way or another he must be stopped.'

'How was I ever taken in?' asks Justin, his face consumed with self-reproach.

'Well face it, Tony is really seductive and charismatic, ready to plunder any signs of idealism he detects, for his own self-aggrandisement. And you, Justin, are highly vulnerable to such enticement.'

'As bad as that, eh?' asks Justin, looking hurt.

'I am afraid so. Seduced like you have been taken in many times before and since, dear chap. I know your intentions are good, but...'

'Time I wised up then. And thanks for believing in me.'

'Hmm. That was weird hearing that woman's voice. It brought all of that history back in wide relief,' sighs Joy, weariness in her voice. 'Rekindled old suspicions and fears once again.'

'I know, I know, and sorry you had to go through that. But at least you can hear her truth directly with regard to her and me.'

'Well partially yes...'

'And it shocked me too, to hear her voice again,' says Justin, 'when I thought all of that was behind us. But you need to know, as I have said before, there was nothing going on.'

She looks unconvinced. 'Well, that all depends on what you mean by nothing, does it not?'

'I am not saying nothing happened! Not that old euphemistic cliché - but whatever was going on was not consummated.'

'Well, something was going on...'

'That is true, it was... though I am not precisely sure what it was – and glad to be out of it.'

'You have protested that before. But I have to say that it does leave me fearful it will happen again. That you could be subject to the same temptations again.'

Justin is silent in the face of this, allowing her to continue.

'Look, Justin, I do not think it was her in particular. You had fallen into a set of circumstances that made you vulnerable to wanting to escape from all that was pressing on you, driving you maybe towards falling in love even – which we both know is a short-term form of delusional madness.'

'True enough.'

'So, I don't want it happening again. When a similar set of circumstances conspire.'

Justin is adamant. 'I just want you to know that I would not even think of it again.'

'Justin, I am not sure if denial is the right approach. If it all begins to happen again, then I want you to think about it, to be aware of what is stirring in the shadows. Don't completely suppress the feeling - but don't act in it. Most of all, talk to me about it before it blossoms.'

'Okay, wise words. It looks as though you have another question brewing, Joy?'

'I Do. And I have to ask - did Tony ever gift any of his drooling acolytes to you - the left-over ones - or even a fresh one?'

'No for God's sake, never. And besides which was he deeply proprietorial in respect of his female followers. They were his and his alone, even when he had dumped them. And even had they been available, I would not have defiled their innocence. And there was a sense of duty of care.'

'Good to hear. And make sure you continue to observe that duty.'

'I will do,' confirms a solemn Justin. 'And you know, besides all of that temptations stuff, I notice that today's youth, the so-called millennials, are wising up to doing their environment thing in a different way from their predecessors. Tony and his like are old news, working out of a redundant model. I must say, along with them, I am done with his form of activism. Or slacktivism.'

'That is interesting to hear. Makes sense. So, he is driven by some desperation to keep the show on the road, to keep his insatiable appetite for adoration met? I noticed how often on the tape he mentioned loneliness. Causes me to think that that might be his central problem and his major fear right now. But don't you go rescuing him, out of pity.'

'I won't don't worry. I am done with Stokes Croft for the time being. Though saddened to discover that the radical left is as politicised as anywhere else.'

'Okay, shall we drop that subject of you and your affair that wasn't an affair for the time being. It is exhausting, and we have other things to worry about. More tea?'

'Yes please.' As she pours, Justin continues, 'what a day this has been. Full of surprises. Did your walk yield any more insights into the Carpet's solicitor's letter? I have read it through a couple of times, and I think we have little option but to accept it is over with them, and sign off the new NDA.'

'Yes, I tend to agree with you. It was good while it lasted, but it always felt a little dirty. It is really odd. We were never, as they suspected, part of a wider plot… until we were, almost accidentally. I would still love to know who fingered us. It is galling.'

'I agree with all of that, and we could talk about it endlessly. But time to be getting on with our lives without those monthly windfall payments. Uber is going well for me right now, which should see is through for now. How was your day at the Stokes Croft massive?'

'Oh, I don't know. Not so great. I feel quite low with it all, after my initial evangelism. I am getting nowhere with the comedy archive and Dave does not pay me a penny. It has literally gone beyond a joke. On top of that he seems in his own mind to have given up on the archive project turning into a book as a bad job. Instead he is working up a new stand-up set based on his inability to write the history.'

'Sounds a good sideways move,' says Justin.

'He has tried out the first draft on me and it is actually very funny. Even if some of the best jokes are at his white archivist's expense. But I cannot no longer be the co-constructor of his epic for no money - he is taking up all my oxygen. And we need to be bringing in funds. So I have bitten the comedic bullet, telling him that I do not see me having the time for this any longer, and need to move on.'

'So that is it?'

'Yes, Justin, that is very much it. He took it okay, looked a bit lost, but he knew it was coming. That decision was helped along by some particularly good news today. The English department wants to hire me as an associate lecturer! Can you believe it?'

'That is great news. And you are a natural teacher. I have always said it.'

'Well, in face of the loss of the Magic Carpet stipend, this teaching news reinforces my wish to call it quits on part-time university courses for now. I mean they have been really good, but a luxury. I can always go back to study later.'

'That sounds like a plan,' says Justin, 'and I am just thinking… you could always sign up for Uber.'

'Really? You would be pushing on an open door there. I would really like that.'

'Really. Didn't think you would jump for that. What a surprise. But that is great then. We could invest in a second beat up Prius - I feel sure that Brian could negotiate the swop of an old one for the Astra.'

'Possibly. Or we could have one Prius and we split the shifts, to allow time-share of kids?'

'That would work well. But we still need to cut back on our overheads.'

 'Yes, I need to quit the Hub,' says Joy, 'those personal trainers and all of their narcissistic pectoral flexing are getting on my nerves. Now help me with this box packing, won't you? Our old life needs consigning to history.'

Joining the Dots

Two weeks later, and still surrounded by packing cases, Joy and Justin are busying themselves around their Westbury kitchen, nearly packed for the big move. Joy raises her eyes from the cause of her increasing claustrophobia to ask, 'Justin, can we just take a moment before our Uber shift changeover? Have a cup of tea together?'

'Oh yes good idea.'

'Daddy, can I hand over the sacred car keys to Mummy please?' Adam asks.

'Yes, you can, that would be fine symbolic act,' replies Justin.

'But do not forget your sacred duty to clean out the car between shifts.'

'But Daddy, we hate that job,' chimes Amelia.

'I know you do. But you must grow to love it. It is your contribution to our commonwealth. And besides Mummy and I could do with a moment to catch up on our workdays.'

'Daddy, what is a commonwealth?' asks Adam, sensing an opening.

'Well son, it a thing we all do together to ensure our wellbeing and security.'

'But Daddy,' counters a jubilant Adam, 'we learned at school that it is a special club for black and brown people that used to worship the Queen.'

'Well it is that too. Sort of. Here, take these J cloths and detergent bottle and get to work. The one with the dirtiest rag gets food first. Off you go. Now.'

Shooing them out of the kitchen, Justin regards Joy fondly over his teacup.

'How was the day shift today, Joy? You look quite fresh, I must say.'

'Oh, it was quite okay actually. Lot of rides, and quite a few tips too. I am certainly finding my way around town, or at least Google Maps is. The pious Prius is all yours for the evening, to see what Bristol might throw at you. Especially the revellers who, in their drunkenness, forget where they live.'

'Oh yes, them,' he sighs, ruefully. 'But it sounds as though you are enjoying your new work incarnation?'

'I am loving it. For now, anyway. I like doing a job where I am not directly responsible for people all day. Just random strangers that you pick up then drop off again.'

'I am glad you like it. It is fun that for once we are both doing the same job. Never done that before really.'

'True. And you have been most helpful, showing me the ropes. Though I do feel a little competitive edge from you at times?' Joy asks, in a teasing tone.

'Oh, just a little bit! I am the senior partner here you know,' he teases back. 'Any interesting rides to brighten your day? You normally come back with at least one great yarn.'

'Oh yes, one or two of the rides had an element of humour. There was one young investment banker who says he finds Uber really most useful, not only for the cash-less convenience, but also for the purpose of knowing where he was the evening before, or even the week before.'

'What, so he knows that from reading his statements?' asks Justin.

'That's it. And his statements not only tell him where he has been spending his time, but the driver ratings of him also let him know his state of drunkenness on any particular evening. The worse the rating, the heavier the night out. He says he finds that really useful, as he has little memory of where he has been, or what condition he has been in.'

'That is quite a fringe benefit. Who knew? Have you heard that Uber in London have introduced a "quiet" function? Where passengers can request that the driver does not talk to them, unless spoken to?'

'Yes,' Joy nods. 'I had a chat to Dave Allenday about that on the phone today. He said he would hate it. How is he going to promote his gigs without his captive audience to chat up? Just as he did with you, back in the day.'

'Yes, he did. If quiet function had been in operation, we might not have Dave in our lives...'

'And it would be so much duller.'

'Well, Joy, the "quiet button" might not work for Dave, but I must say I could do with some silence myself at times, when driving. Just thinking that it is a shame the driver cannot request silence in the opposite direction. But all in a day's work, hey? And how is Dave anyway?'

'Same as always. Did I tell you he has abandoned his book in preference for a stand-up routine on the impossibility of writing the book?'

'I think you did. Quite a repurposing of material, that is. Very Dave. He makes use of every scrap of life, every corner, to be re-presented as observational comedy.'

'He does that. And throughout this new act he mocks me, his glamorous white editorial assistant, mercilessly. It is borderline cruel, but really funny.'

'I am looking forward to hearing this. I would never be allowed to mock you like that…'

Joy grins at the truth in that. 'Well that is different. But worry not, there is a price to be paid for mocking me. I have told Dave that, as a riposte, I am working up a stand-up piece that exposes the darker side of working for him. Shining a light inside the unmasked funny man when desperation sets in, and he thinks no one is watching.'

'Bet that idea tickles him,' Justin smiles.

'Oh yes it does. Tickles and terrifies him in equal measure. In fact, I have tried a few lines from my improv act on him and he really likes it. He has challenged me to do the full routine at an open-mic night at the comedy club next week.'

'Can't wait for that! Please, can your husband come?'

'Of course. I need all the support I can get. It will be a gas, though I will be terrified on the night. Could be a whole new career. But Justin – moving away from the comedy, and the theatre of the absurd that our lives have become - there is something I need to talk to you about. Something that has been preying on my mind.'

'Oh yes, something about the house move?' Justin looks sympathetic. 'Don't worry, we will have these boxes shifted into our new rental place in Brislington soon enough.'

'No, it is not that, I think we will cope with that temporary disruption. We have had enough of those recently to know what to do. And it will be a relief to get the proceeds from the house into the bank. But no, it is something else.'

'Go on.'

'Well, since we sat here last month, listening to Joanna's tape outing Tony, I have been quietly seething about his betrayal.'

'I am not surprised Joy, that has been eating into me too. The fact that he could so shamelessly betray both of us to Joanna like that...'

'Yes, but beyond my anger at him for that, I have been figuring that if he could betray us to Joanna like that, then he would be quite capable of selling us down the Sewanee with other folk also. For his own nefarious gain.'

'Yes, he undoubtedly could. I would not put nothing past him, from all we have recently been learning.'

Joy nods, gravely. 'Then, after seething about that, I have been thinking about us being outed over the Magi-Leaks. That exposure is costing us plenty financially, and could still land us in trouble…'

'I know what you mean, but I doubt if it will. We have signed up yet another NDA with the Carpet confirming that the company will not take any further action for the price of our silence, and the rescinding of our monthly stipend. That should be it.'

'You are right, but my every instinct says that somewhere along the line, Tony is behind our exposure, even though he has sworn blind to you that the data leak did not come from Glynis's USB.'

'I think I trust your instinct on this one.' Justin's eyebrows rise in question. 'But how do we proceed, to find out more about his possible duplicity? Without landing ourselves in even more hot water?'

'Yes, there are risks attached,' agrees Joy. 'But I have been thinking... that the person who is most likely to know the whole truth is the journalist Dick Bellows, the one whose name is all over Magi-Leaks?'

'True enough, but he would never cough up his source. Too much is hanging on his retaining the anonymity of his sources for him to reveal who it was.'

'Worth giving him a try?' asks Joy inquiringly.

'Well, nothing ventured nothing gained. You want to make the call? My phone is nagging me, saying that is time for my shift.'

'Mummy Mummy, Adam found a sweetie stuck to the back seat. He tried to eat it, but I had to stop him!'

'Well done, Amelia – how did you do that?'

'I squirted him in the face with the squeezy spray. Look, he is all clean now.'

Adam beams. 'Look, my J-cloth is dirtier that hers. I get to eat first.'

'Okay. Children – kiss your Daddy goodbye, before he goes gentle into that dark night.'

'Why is he going gentle, Mummy? Is he afraid of being done for speeding? Again?'

'Adam, I so hope not. Now that really would be the end of our precarious little set up here. Off you go, Justin. I will ring Dick and see if he is prepared to take this conversation further.'

The following lunch time, Justin and Joy meet Dick in the Robin Hood pub, an ancient watering hole set at the top of the Gloucester Road, far away from preying eyes. Joy's call has persuaded Dick that is worth taking the risk of meeting, but he is clearly full of caution as to where this might lead.

'Hi, Joy and Justin, great to see you both. But where is the fire? You said you needed to talk with complete confidentiality?'

'Yes, we do. And thanks for taking the time. It concerns Magi-Leaks.'

'Why does that not surprise me?'

'Well, first of all, so many congratulations on getting that story out,' enthuses Justin. 'Seems a long time since we first met, by chance, in the call-centre car park.'

'Yes, it does.' Dick chuckles. 'Strange how the act of tugging on slender threads can lead to the major unravelling of a whole corporate. I do sometimes doubt my methods, but in this instance...'

'Yes,' agrees Joy. 'And it seems quite a while since I was trapped in the Carpet's maws too. I can't tell you how liberating it feels to be out of that place – especially when it is falling apart. The morale there must be at its lowest ebb.'

'Must be,' considers Dick, 'but then that is what the Carpet ushered in. What you sow, so then must you reap, and all of that. So how can I be of assistance then?'

'Well it might be just a hunch, but...' Justin begins, tentatively.

Dick shrugs. 'You might think that. But in my experience, it is rarely just a hunch. Do go on. I am listening.'

'What it is...' Justin continues, 'and this cannot go beyond this room, but we trust you...'

'Justin you need to trust me in this, if I am to be of any use at all.'

'Well, both of us have been fingered by Magic Carpet solicitors as being one of the original sources, fencing the USB with data leak.'

Dick whistles through his teeth. 'And can I ask you the direct question – were you one of the sources?'

'Yes, we were,' admitted Joy, speaking slowly. 'Along the line. Among others, of course.'

'Hmm. I never knew that. The two of you, eh? That comes as a surprise. But well done you anyway. You have done the pursuit of truth a great service.'

'Thanks,' says Joy. 'And despite the jeopardy this has put us in, we are pleased, also, to have played a part in that company's downfall.'

'It is a good feeling, isn't it, to be on the side of right?' Dick seeks their eyes for affirmation.

'Yes, it is.' Justin considers his words carefully, 'But, without going into detail on all of that – and it doesn't matter anyway, now the leak is out - we have a follow-up question. A suspicion that we are harbouring. And you could be the man to help us with the answer?'

'Uh ho. What is that?' Dick looks quizzical.

Joy looks him the eye, to ask, 'was Tony Crocker involved in your disclosure to the press?'

'I am not sure you can ask me direct questions. It doesn't work like that. But I am interested to listen to your story. And I may respond to any other questions you may have. Go ahead.'

Justin continues. 'Okay, so this is a hypothetical. Did you ask your original source to gain permissions from his or her sources, before you moved to publish? I think we all know these disclosures run in a chain.'

'Of course I did. And my fence assured me that he had asked for full consent before I went to press. I checked that several times, always need to be thorough.'

'Well, hypothetically once more, if that person were Tony Crocker, and if the USB was the source, then he never once asked us for that permission. In fact, he denied that our USB was ever involved. Hypothetically.'

Dick looks really thoughtful. 'Is there more?'

'Oh yes,' confirms Joy, warming to this disclosure. 'As a result of Magic Carpet discovering our association with the leak, they have rescinded a major monthly NDA payment to us – related to another matter entirely - and silenced us once more. This is really serious for us, as you can well imagine. They were originally suspicious of us anyway – and now they have this sword to hang over us. It is potentially very threatening.'

'Yes, it is, I can well see that,' says Dick, his eyes narrowing. 'You're in a tight spot. And your next question?'

'A hunch and a question. We suspect that Tony was the one who passed our USB to you. Or whomever, then they got it to you. And that it was Tony, under duress from Magic Carpet, that dobbed us in. What do you think?'

'As I said to you before I cannot confirm or deny any of your contentions. However, I will get to the bottom of this from my end, then get back to you. Be assured. And thanks for sharing this with me. I hate to think of informants being punished, even if somewhere down the line. Look, I need to get going. Let me make some inquiries and I might well get back to you.'

'Thanks Dick,' says Justin, 'you have been most helpful.'

Dick is more than thoughtful. He is incensed, beyond anger at what he is hearing. He thought Tony a flake, but this is beyond deceit. He makes inquiries around journalistic circles to reveal what he suspects has happened. He picks up a lead on this line of inquiry through his old colleague, Nick Dollard, a fellow investigative reporter, based in Bristol, who runs his own political blog, and has had many by-lines in Private Eye. After a preliminary skirmish on the phone, Nick agrees to meet him in the Robin Hood.

'Hi Nick, thanks for taking the time. How you doing?'

'Always a pleasure to talk to you, Dick. And doing fine thanks. Life is never dull, that is for sure. How can I help you today?'

'Well, strictly between us at this stage, of course, I am tracking down a story that may or may not have legs?'

'What is that then?' Nick looks unsurprised. 'Lots of stories come my way. And so many of them are barely able to reach the door, never mind stand up.'

'I know, I know. This story concerns Magi-Leaks.'

Nick grins. 'What else would it be about, coming from Mr Magi-Leaks himself? And? What could I know about the leaks that you don't already know?'

'Here's the thing. I have a suspicion that someone is touting a story concerning my scoop, where he claims to be the hero behind the leak.'

Nick takes a sharp intake of breath. 'I think I've got this one. Could you be talking here about Tony Crocker, that well-known environmentalist fake? He comes to me all the time with stories that he claims will bring down society as we know it. They never ever do. What a time waster, a fantasist.'

'Just to be clear. So he came to you with such a story?'

'He did. Not with more data of course, you have all of that in the bag, and all the discoveries are credited to you. What he had instead was a narrative relating to the discovery of the leak. In this story, Tony is the hero, who has safeguarded all who might be implicated before moving it on, selflessly, to a third-party, who eventually passes it on to you.'

'Quite a claim...'

'Yep, a typical Tony story really. Of course, no editor really wants to buy this story, attractive though it may seem, as it is quite unverified. And they know that if they approach you, the infamously discreet Dick Bellows, they will hit a brick wall. Why do you ask? Has Tony been bothering you about this too? Seems like he has tapped everyone in the National Union of Journalists Rolodex.'

Dick smiles at this. 'Well, I ask because, somewhere along the line, the fact of Tony touting this story around might well have attracted the attention of Magic Carpet.'

'Could well be.' Nick stirs his memory. 'Sounds like he was trying to sell this story far and wide, recklessly, without too much concern for the original source. Why, what has happened as a result of him spreading his seed with such gay abandon?'

'Well, strictly entre nous, Magic Carpet is currently fingering someone who was implicated in getting the Magi-Leaks out. Not the hacker or an employee, but someone in the chain along the way.'

'I get it. And you think the company put the squeeze on Crocker to reveal more of his sources?'

'Yes, I think that is a fair assumption.'

'That assumption makes sense to me, actually. I heard it on the grapevine that Magic Carpet was sniffing around. Didn't find out exactly why. So I guess when they got nowhere in their search for the source, that they decided to strong-arm Crocker?'

'Well this is speculation, but my guess is that Crocker, under all sorts of pressures, squeals to them as to his source, on the condition that he is kept out of other legal actions. He demands that the price for this identification of source is that this disclosure is never traced back to him.'

'What a rat, but quite consistent with Crocker behaviour.' Nick's face curls in disgust. 'What a loose cannon. Did he ever give up the hacker?'

'No. I am not even sure that he knows who the original sources might be. And from what I know of these sources under pressure from the company, they have integrity enough never to reveal where the USB came from either.'

'How much trouble are they in, can you say?'

'Plenty. But it sounds to me that they have found a way to protect themselves. On a vow of complete silence.'

'This is an appalling story. After all you have done to keep the trail anonymous. What you going to do?'

'Nick, what do you think I am going to do? I am going to have a word with Crocker. Thanks for meeting up, it has been really helpful.'

'Any time, mate. Always happy to help. Especially if it nails that chancer Crocker.'

Tony is excited to see Dick's name come up on his phone. 'Hi Dick, great to hear from you.'

'Hi Tony, how you doing?'

'Doing fine thanks, doing fine. How about you?'

'Well, up to my ears in Magi- Leaks. But all good.'

'Ah good, glad to hear it. And thanks for the monies by the way. That got through fine. Is that why you are ringing? Another instalment on my way, after your splash in the Washington Post?'

'Could be.' Dick grunts down the phone. 'I never know until they actually pay me. Takes an age. But no, I am calling about another story I may need your help on. We need to talk, in person, quite soon, please, if you can find the time?'

'Yes, of course, I am always happy to talk to journalists, especially you. Seems like a lot of news-hounds have been nosing me out of late.'

'I bet. You are a popular man. But look, we cannot speak on the phone. It is too risky. Where do you suggest we meet? Your call.'

'Ah, so maybe you don't know?' says Tony, looking rather disappointed that the world is less interested in his movements than he supposed. 'I have moved out of town now, living in Wells, down among the real Greens, not just playing around with the virtue signalling urbanites. Fixed up with a lovely new girlfriend too, Ursula. Bit older than my usual, but lovely person. I have moved in with her down this way. Thatched cottage, all the trimmings. Ha ha.'

'Sofa surfing?'

'Oh no, it is all quite serious, and she really likes my radical edge.'

'I see, okay' Says Dick sounding sceptical. 'Glad to hear you are all set up then, away from Stokes Croft. I can hear all about it when we meet. I will drive down your way then, even if green fields scare me. Please suggest a place. It is important that we do this soon.'

'How about the Crystals Café in the centre of Glastonbury? About eleven tomorrow?'

'Sounds good to me. I look forward to seeing you there, in your new habitat.'

Dick fights his way into the Crystal Café through the beaded curtain hanging in the doorway. Peering through the incense smoke that pervades the place, he sees Tony sitting at the rear of the cafe, leaning back on a hemp sofa.

'Great to see you, Dick,' enthuses Tony, brushing aside the string of purple crystals hanging from the ceiling as he stands to greet Dick, 'and welcome to my brave new world. What flavour of herbal tea takes your fancy?'

'None for me thanks. But I may buy a couple of the angels in the shop window. They seemed to be calling out my name.'

'Ha ha! You are kidding me, right?' says Tony, not wishing his new habitat to be ridiculed. 'Sure, it is all a bit sandals and togas around here, but I am loving it. Doing quite a bit of work with the radical climate change group, Extinction Rebellion. Very topical at the moment, and I have put myself at the heart of it. Is that why you want to meet? Are you onto a climate story, exposure of the oil companies? Need my help with that? Let's get going!'

'No, not that right now, but an exposé of Extinction Rebellion might be an idea at some point.'

Tony looks affronted. 'You know very well that I did not mean that sort of story. I meant having a go at the agri-farmers, the Monsanto's of this world. Or is it more about Magi-Leaks? I was central to that from the beginning, as you well know.'

'Well yes, it about Magi-Leaks that I need your help on. A few questions before we start. I have been digging around and...'

'Yes?'

'And there are questions I need answered. For starters, did you, as you said you would, ask your sources for permission for the Magi-Leaks USB to be made public? Take care as you answer. Remember your integrity and mine are on the line here, so no evasion please.'

'You know something, don't you?' blurts Tony, pushing his sofa away from the table.

Dick holds his gaze. 'Just answer my question.'

'Well, I am pretty sure I did check it out with my source. It was some time ago,' Tony says, scratching his head in Stan Laurel fashion.

Dick coughs. 'This is not an action you would forget Tony. And I am taking your prevarication as a no.'

'Okay then. Guilty as charged. Now... when I think about it...' Tony's eyes search among the dangling crystals, seeking a recovered memory. 'I forgot to contact my source. I was so excited, and it was all moving so fast. Could happen to anyone. And any way, they said to me it would be fine for me to use as I thought best...'

Dick presses on. 'And you recall that you told me that you had in fact asked for permissions? Twice?'

'Hmmm, yes I did,' says Tony, shamefaced.

'So that is that one sorted. Guilt admitted. My second question relates to you touting a Magi- leaks narrative of the data release, where you are the hero in the story. No need to deny this. It is out there on the Fleet Street grapevine.'

Tony shakes his head, remaining silent, eyes down at his feet.

'But you never found an editor that would touch it, did you?'

'Dick, you have got me here under false pretences!' says Tony, trying and failing to put on a show of defiance. 'But seeing as you ask, the media showed lots of interest in my account, but it was too hot to for them to handle.'

'Really?' Dick looks incredulous. 'Not what I hear. But then Magic Carpet got to hear about your flogging of this source. Someone, somewhere snitched on you – probably had had enough of your fantastical so-called scoops.'

'How could you ever know that? That is fake news. Totally false. You would never dare go directly to Magic Carpet!'

'I reached this conclusion through the power of deduction, dear chap. So that is confirmed then. Your face says it all. Let me continue with my saga,' says Dick. 'Magic Carpet pressured you into naming of your source – on the basis that they give you immunity...'

'This is wild speculation. You will never prove this!'

'Not sure if I need to. I now know it is true though. You give yourself away too easily. I advise you never to play poker. And I suspect that Magic Carpet is now punishing your source that you threw to the wolves.'

'How do you know that?' says Tony, casting his eyes around among the crystals to locate the exit.

'Because that is precisely what I would do, if I were the company – stands to reason.'

'It's that Nick Dollard behind this isn't it? I knew it. When he swore that he would never...'

'You know well enough, Tony, that I never reveal my sources. Unlike you.'

Tony smarts at this. 'So what are you going to do?'

'Do? Nothing at the moment. It is more what you are going to do...'

'Which is?'

'Which is that if any of this speculation is true, then you will go back to you source and confess all.'

'Hm. And if I do not?' says a defiant Tony, a pout pursing his lips.

'If not, then it something you will have to live with this for the rest of your days. Up to you. Ruining your informant's lives, for you own glory. Taking a risk that doesn't even come off. But be aware that the whole world now knows the kind of things that you are up to. Journalists will never ever trust you again. Nor politicians I would think. Nor will too many other people you would claim as friends, I suspect. Word gets around, and mud sticks, even down here in the rural backwaters.'

Dick, satisfied that his message has been received and understood, watches Tony shuffle through the beaded curtains, setting off some Buddhist wind chimes ringing on his way out. For whom the bell tolls, thinks Dick. He reaches for his phone to fix another meeting with Joy and Justin, while the memory is strong. They are keen to follow up soon, and the meet is set for the Robin Hood the following day.

Settled once more among the Robin Hood's dark oak panelling, Joy opens the conversation. 'Thanks so much for getting back to us so quickly, Dick,' says Joy. 'We are so appreciative. What can you tell us?'

Dick muses on this. 'I am afraid nothing, directly. Just to say that the matter is dealt with from my end. I suggest you get in touch with whomever it was you think exposed you.'

'And?'

'Well the "and" is quite simple. Get him or her to fess up. Confront them. Then do whatever you think necessary. Don't mention me in this though – I was never here.'

'Of course, you weren't. Thanks for dealing with this, Dick,' says Justin, resolved to follow this instruction.

'It was a pleasure, replied Dick, 'and I hope I get to see you again. Don't forget, I am always alive to a good story. And have an appetite for justice being served. Quite tigerish in that regard. I know that you two seem to excite trouble, good trouble, whether you are looking for it or not. So don't forget, come to me first.'

'Funny you should say that,' rejoins Justin. 'I may have just the thing. A story of rampant corrupt practices within a professional services body.'

'Really? I would like to hear the executive summary of that one. Go for it.'

'Not easy to summarise.' Justin responds, musing on how to compress such a long rambling saga such into short-form. 'Essentially, the professional body I have in mind, the Coaching Fraternity, is little better than a glorified Ponzi scheme, designed to rip off vulnerable and needy members, while the fat cats crown themselves with fancy titles and a life of luxury. They also cartel with other coaching bodies to keep prices high and the rules ever more arcane.'

'Interesting. Not pulling your punches on this one, are you Justin?' grins Dick. 'Tell me just a little bit more. Draw me in – but not into the weeds.'

Thus encouraged, Justin continues, 'they seem like a bunch of altruistic sweethearts, saying all the correct inclusive things, until a member crosses them, or their beloved standards. Then the jeopardy is high. Any member who stands up to the executive is likely to be defenestrated.'

'Well related, Justin. You could be writing the by-line for me. But examples? Evidence trail? This cannot stand up on pure emotion.'

'Oh yes, there evidence aplenty.' Justin composes his thoughts. 'So much of their documentation would not stand up to forensic examination. And there are quite a number of cases that could be cited. Even my own first-hand account?'

'Aha, I see,' says Dick, stroking his chin. 'Would this story be driven by personal vengeance perhaps, by any chance? A vexatious action?'

'Could be' Justin admitted. 'I leave that for you to decide, Dick, having heard the story, but I have plenty of email and meeting records to support my contention, and witnesses who may be willing to give evidence, as long as whistle-blower protection were in place.'

'Oh, I would be interested in seeing all of that. Pour over it in my own time. Bringing down the pompous and the entitled.' Dick makes to leave. 'I need to go now, but let us fix a time and we can go through this in much more detail. It is reminding me a narrative category, but I can't quite put my finger on that right now?'

'I tell you the type of account it reminds me of, if that would help,' says Justin. 'In some ways it has all the characteristics of a cult. Mind control. Not the Moonies of course, but it shares some of the underlying structures. Group-think.'

'Thanks for adding the colour. And yes, I could see that looking at this Fraternity through the lens of cult formation could yield dividends. Thanks for the tip off, Justin. I haven't done a cult since the Scientology exposé. Now I really must go.'

Joy and Justin are left in the darkness of the Robin Hood, considering their next steps. Justin reflects on their conversation with Dick. 'I am so glad that I raised the ante on my Fraternity grievances with Dick. He seemed interested. And I have nothing to lose, having left them. And I know disaffected others who might stand up and be counted.'

'Well yes, it is a good story, when you unpack it. Don't bank on your moaning mates to stand behind you, though. People have a habit of disappearing into the woodwork when asked to make witness against a power system that could leave them exposed. I know that only too well, from my attempts at Magic Carpet to confront injustices. It is a painful experience, to find you are the only complainant.'

'It would great to take that lot down, though. This pub is a good place for us to plot, the Robin Hood. Plenty of darkened woodwork for things to crawl out of. Feels a bit like we are outlaws again, aiming to defrock the Sherriff of the Coaching Fraternity, and her henchmen.'

'Justin, you are romanticising again. First things first please. You do get diverted so easily! Honestly. Now we have the tip off from Dick, and decoded his cryptic feedback, then we need to seek out Tony for his comeuppance. I have been trying to track Tony down, but looks like he has gone to ground.'

'Hmm,' says Justin, trying hard to focus on one thing at a time. 'Not sure if he has gone completely to ground. I heard down Stokes Croft's way that he was now tied up with Extinction Rebellion.'

Joy pulls out her tablet and scrolls. 'Extinction Rebellion South West. Bingo! Oh look, here he is!' She leans over, keen for Justin to squint at her discovery. 'There he is in this photograph, smirking, in the middle of that group of crusties.' She reads on. 'It says here that he is part of a group leading a protest at a deforestation site near Wells, that cathedral city in the midst of deepest, darkest Somerset, on Friday. What do you think?'

'I am thinking ambush!' Justin beams at this. The downfall of the Fraternity can be put aside for another day. 'Get our camouflage jackets out!!'

Justin and Joy approach the protest sight in a state of heightened anticipation, weaving their way past colourful tents, tarpaulins strung over trees, and make-shift barriers. These temporary structures are populated by a homogeneous collection of men with long beards, and women with braided hair. The buzz generated by their conversations is palpable. Joy whispers to Justin, 'I think we might be a might not have gotten the message about the dress code. Your Marks and Spencer's anorak does not seem to cut it somehow.' Justin looks down at his wellies, deciding that his footwear at least fits the bill, even if they were not quite muddy enough.

Joy nudges him again. 'Did you hear that conversation about the "pink boat" arriving here tomorrow? They seemed to be orgasming over that.'

Justin titters. 'Yes, I did hear that. A boat in the middle of landlocked Wells, of all places. One way to launch a new movement though, I guess. With a pink boat.'

As they move further through the crowd, feeling conspicuously out of place, they hear someone call her name.

'Joy!' a young man in a combat jacket approaches them. 'It's me, Tom! From outside the Better Bank.' He registers the blank looks on their faces. Looking disappointed, he shrugs, 'aww, no reason for you to remember me I suppose.'

Joy's eyes light up in recognition. 'Of course I remember you! And I am so happy you remember my name. In fact, I looked for you outside the bank the other day, and saw someone else had taken your pitch. I did wonder what had happened to you. But here you are, looking great. So good to see you. And sorry for not being in touch. There was no excuse not to.' She gives him an impromptu hug, which he returns with great warmth.

'Hmm,' breathes Tom, breaking off from the hug. 'Glad you don't mind me being a bit stinky. Not too many washing facilities when you are camping out here. And no need to feel guilty on my account. We itinerants are not easy to track down. In fact we often resist being tracked down – even by our own.'

Justin, not wanting to be left out, moves in for a hug, though his hug is more awkward that Joy's, more of the man-on-man kind, hips far apart. Justin breaks off from this to say, 'so good to see you too, Tom. After all that drama in the bank. How you doing?'

'Well, as you see I am keeping fine.' Tom gestures with both hands passing up and down his body, to demonstrate the truth of this. 'Got myself off the streets, with some good help. Now doing some hospital portering here in Wells. And finishing off my nursing exams. It is all good.'

Justin smiles at this. 'So glad to hear that. Must have taken quite an effort, to climb out of...'

Joy needs to interrupt Justin, to stop him putting his well-intentioned foot in it. 'You have been through a lot...'

'Yep, agrees Tom. 'Thanks for the understanding. But enough about me. How about you two?'

'Us?' Justin thinks about this. 'Doing great really. Kids are fine. Moved house. And still no bank loan!'

'Really? After you saving a banker's life in there too. That executive bloke was the worse. Treated me like dirt. Like a sub-human.'

'Yes, Dominic Cross. He was the worst, but not atypical of his kind. No idea what happened to poor old Ted Fear though. Probably in Thailand by now. Or...or...' she is ashamed that he might have passed, and that she never visited him in hospital.

'No, he is not in Thailand!' replies Tom. 'In fact, I saw him only the other day, finding him alive and well. He has moved down this way, working in the Wells Citizens Advice Bureau - and he was really good at helping me sort out a benefits problem.'

'That is such good news,' says Joy, 'and some coincidence.'

'Yes, isn't it,' Tom agrees. 'He was happy to see me, and was so grateful for all of our help during the life-saving emergency. It turns out that both he and I are living down this way, nowadays. I am sure he wouldn't mind me saying that he might even be looking for love again, after all this time alone. Ted is in strong heart.'

'Well that is really good to know,' says Justin, 'so happy you both met! And happy that we three have met again, too.'

'You could go see him, he is just down the road, and would love to see you both. Why not drop into see him today after this?' Tom feigns concern. 'But please don't give him another heart attack. And don't mention your loan!'

'No, we won't!' Joy scans the horizon.

'You looking for someone? Or just here for the protest?' Tom asks, studying their unsuitable garb doubtfully.

'Well both really,' says Joy. 'I love the vibe around this protest. Never felt the likes of it before, or at least not since student days, when we played at protesting. But, as a matter of fact we are looking for someone. You might know where to find him?'

'Okay, try me. I know quite a few of the people here. Who you after?'

'An acquaintance of ours from Stokes Croft? Tony Crocker?' she asks, non-commitally.

Tom thinks for a moment. 'Oh yeh... I have met him. He could be one of the leaders here. Quite a few claim to be, but actually it really is hard to know who are the leaders and who are the followers. I saw him up a tree over that way,' he says, pointing straight ahead, 'he was right in the middle of that clump of people earlier. He might still be there.'

'Great,' says Joy, 'and thanks. Tom, could you give me your number again? This time we must keep in touch. We just must. And so glad things are working out. And that you got out of your old life – out before the Better Bank put the spikes in the pavement.'

Leaving Tom to help one of his friends dig a deep trench, they move in the indicated direction. As the wood closes in around them Joy says to Justin, 'this is a bit spooky out here. Last time I was this deep in a wood was with Bert, on the fateful ride.'

'Oh yes, Bert the Casanova. I hear he is not out of the woods yet. Not by a long chalk.' They walk slowly, eyes scanning in every direction, when Justin grabs her by the elbow, bringing her to an abrupt halt. 'Look Joy, over there. He is bearded, but I recognise him. There! He is standing somewhat apart from the crowd, holding a sad-looking banner saying, "Solution not Pollution."'

'Oh yes I see him now! God, he does look a bit sad. Lost. Lonely.'

'Yes, he does,' agrees Justin, continuing to glance over at the lone figure. 'Good description. How shall we approach him? We hadn't really thought this through, beyond tracking him down.'

The answer to this question is rendered unnecessary by Tony glancing up, aware that he was being looked at. Recognising these two interlopers in an instant, he moves to withdraw, then stops, feeling the need to say something, as he cannot just run away. 'Well hello there. Surprised to see you. What are you two doing here? Didn't know you were protestors?'

'Why should we not care about the environment?' challenges Joy. 'Or is this just another exclusive club, closed to those not of the right persuasion or dress code?'

'No, of course not,' Tony stammers, 'but it seemed like you were looking for me, the furtive way you were shifting around over there.'

Joy states the obvious. 'Yes of course we were looking for you. And for good reason. Let us not beat about the forest. Our main protest movement right now concerns you.'

'Oh why? Come on. I thought we were mates,' he says, looking distinctly shifty.

'No, we are not mates, not anymore,' says Justin, firmly. 'You have betrayed us both horribly, Tony. But then you probably already know that.'

'I have no idea what you are talking about.' Tony attempts to look blank.

'Let us tell you what we are talking about, but of course you already know why we have hunted you down. We have at least two charges that we want to confront you with.'

'Why are you taking this tone? This is not the easy-going Justin I know and love. You must be over-reacting to something here. Being over emotional. Chill man.'

Undeterred by this appeal to his better nature, Justin continues, 'the first thing we need to talk to you about is about the tape of your conversation with Joanna.'

'Oh, so you have heard that tape?' Tony's face flushes, deeply. 'That was a really underhand thing for that stuck-up woman to do. That conversation was something and nothing...'

'Yes, we have heard the tape,' Joy clarifies, 'It was sent to us anonymously.'

'Well, it wasn't too bad, was it?'

'It was the worst.' Joy is venomous. 'You gave away all of our confidences, made up stories about us. For nothing.'

'Okay. I am sorry if that upset you. It was a bad mistake. I was trying too hard to...to...'

'To pick her up?'

Tony shrugs. 'Yeh probably – hadn't planned to, but she was coming onto me so strongly in the beginning. I was duped. She was tricking me, just to catch me on tape. What a b... b...'

'Hmm.' Joy says, her tone acidic. 'Putting that betrayal aside for a moment, there is the even more serious case of you telling Magic Carpet that we were the sources of the Magi-Leaks USB.'

'Where do you get that from?' Tony's jaw drops. 'That is ridiculous. What a thing to accuse a friend of. I would never do such a thing.'

'Tony, stop embarrassing yourself,' says Joy, sharply. 'We know it to be true that you shopped us to Magic Carpet. With dire consequences for us both. Why else would you be hiding out here, if not to try and escape from all the badness you have done?'

'I am not running away from anything!' protests Tony. 'I have nothing to hide, and I am easy enough to find. You both did! I have a good life down here. Living with a lovely woman called Ursula who thinks the world of me. She is a decent person, and delighted that I have brought her into an alternative life style. She is here now, leafleting. And I have joined the activism effort, out here in the sticks, surrounded by my new friends.'

'I am sure all of that is true,' Joy says, 'and you were not hard to find. But none of that takes away from the heinous thing you did to two good friends.'

'Okay, so who has been behind all of these vicious rumours? Who said? These accusations are despicable.' He scratches around for an answer to his own question. 'I know. Dick Bellows? Nick Dollard? I would not trust those two as far as I could throw them.'

'We cannot say,' says Justin, firmly. 'But I know you quite well. I can see from your face that, despite all these blustered denials, that you are as guilty as hell.'

Tony hangs his head, slumping his shoulders. 'So what? I know it is not true, even if you seem to think it is. So what – what you gonna do it about it?'

'First of all, we want to have this conversation with you,' says Justin, 'before we decide on the consequences for you. Which could be considerable.'

Tony sniffs at this, but has nothing to say.

'For a start,' continues Joy, 'we know that there is not much we can do legally, but we can put the word out...'

This conversation is interrupted by the appearance of a well-groomed, and certainly not dreadlocked, middle-aged woman, who steps out for a nearby clump of trees, holding a handful of leaflets.

Tony swallows hard, rigid with panic. He splutters, 'Ursula, what are you doing, creeping up on us like this? I thought you were pamphleting on the top car park?'

'Oh, I was, Tony,' Ursula says, levelly. 'My being here is quite innocent. I was in fact looking for you, to take you home for a lovely home-cooked lunch. But then I stopped in my tracked when I overheard the beginning of this unhappy exchange.' She stares directly at him. 'Who are these people, Tony? What on earth is going on here?' She eyes all three in turn, angered and needing answers.

'Ursula, I can explain,' Tony pleads, 'they are just a couple of old friends from Stokes Croft, Joy and Justin Drake, dropping by to see the protest in full swing. Nothing to see here.'

Ursula bleeds scorn. 'Well hello Joy and Justin, nice to meet you. But you don't look like you are here to protest. Neither do I frankly, but from all I overheard, you are here to confront Tony with some unfinished business?'

'And hello Ursula,' says Joy, 'Tony had mentioned you were an item. And yes, these are at least two pieces of business we need to clear up with Tony.'

'Nice to meet you Joy. Yes, I heard, and it all sounds dire.'

Tony feels a need to shut this down, before it goes any further. 'Ursula – let's just go to lunch. These two are just making stuff up.'

'Doesn't sound like it to me, Tony.' She fixes him with a stare that would have brought down one of the bullocks casually watching them from the adjacent field. 'In fact, some of what they are saying confirms some suspicions that I have been harbouring about you recently. What do you have to say for yourself?'

Tony searches for answers. 'As I said before, it is a pack of lies. They are on a witch-hunt. And you have no reason to be suspicious of me. I have given you the best of me. Exclusively.'

'Really? So you say. Could you tell me, just so I know, where this Joanna figures in your life?'

'Oh, she is nobody.' Tony shrugs this off. 'Just a jealous friend of the Drake's who set me up in a honey trap operation, then taped it and sent it to these two. Who have both made a meal of it. Joanna is ancient history. Old as Glastonbury Tor over there.'

'Is that true, Joy?' asks Ursula.

'No not at all true,' says Joy, flatly. 'No honey trap. Just Tony being Tony.'

'Tony,' continues Ursula, 'so how many more have there been? Beyond Joanna?'

'None. I just said she came before you. She meant nothing. Nothing happened.'

Ursula is clearly unsatisfied with this answer. 'Was she like me? Rich and alone? And vulnerable?'

'Hmm, well I suppose so, now that you say it. Not that that mattered.'

'Hm, Tony,' says Ursula, her resolve steely. 'I have heard more than enough. I am shocked. But not so shocked as to notice that every fibre of my being is saying that I have been taken for a fool. Tony, give me the spare keys to my house and car back right now. I mean it.'

Tony looks desperate. 'You cannot be serious? Where will I live?'

'Well, sleeping in one of these tents might prove a wake-up call for you,' suggests Ursula, not altogether helpfully. 'Try getting down with your so-called comrades, rather than being a daytime activist, with a good woman and a warm meal to go home to. Probably time for you to get back to a diet of your beloved sausage rolls. And not those of the vegan variety, but the smelly, greasy ones. They suit you quite well.'

'Stop being so horrible Ursula!' Tony raises his hands in supplication. 'This is not like you at all. How could you do this to me. After all I have done for you! In front of my friends? It is shaming. Please, shall we just go home and talk over this misunderstanding?'

'No, we will not. My keys Tony. Now,' says Ursula, thinking ahead. 'I will drop your rucksack and your collection of sweatshirts at the "lost and found" at Wells Bus station. And no, I have no intention of washing them for you before I stuff them in your rucksack. Just so you know.'

Tony shuffles around the pockets of his combat jacket to find the keys, then reluctantly hands them over. 'I have enough of the lot of you stuck-up middle-class snobs,' he blurts. 'You have no idea what I have sacrificed for the cause. I am going back to join my tribe, and there is nothing you can do to stop me.'

'No, we cannot physically restrain you' says Justin. 'But be aware that we do know at least one of your fellow tribal members who would be most interested in your betrayal of us, and of your deceiving of Ursula. These comrades of yours have principles, Tony. You cannot pull the wool over their eyes anymore. You are pretty much done here.'

'Stop, stop. I get it.' Tony looks utterly defeated. 'I am off. You will never find me, where I am going.' With that, Tony skulks away along a path leading far away from the main camp, pulling his hoodie over his straggly hair and unkempt beard while he kicks out at broken branches, muttering loudly to himself about the injustice of it all.

Ursula watches his noisy retreat. She is shaky, now that he is gone. She trembles, her face fallen. 'God, I need to get out of here. And thanks, both, for indirectly alerting me to the worst of that freeloading liar.'

'It has been good to help you with that. What's next?' asks Justin.

'Some company would be good,' sighs Ursula. 'Would you two like to come for a tea in town? I have had enough protests for one day – including his sickening, childish self-justifications. So like a petulant teenager. "It's not fair!!' You could almost hear him saying it. But enough said. I know a good place in the centre of Wells. The Strangers with Coffee café? St Cuthbert's street? Suit you?'

'Sounds perfect,' says Joy. 'As a matter of fact, we need to see a friend in town also. Shall we? See you there.'

Back in the safety of their car, Joy and Justin take a moment to catch breath. 'Well that was quite a thing. All of it!' says Joy.

'Wasn't it just!' replies Justin. 'Tony dispatched. Mission accomplished!'

'And wasn't Ursula amazing? Quite a woman. And showed a great sense of timing. Enter stage left, the scorned woman.'

'She most definitely was,' agrees Justin.

'Given the circumstances, it was nice of her to ask us for tea.' Joy's face softens. 'On other hand we inadvertently alerted her to his full duplicity. The bullshit she was already seeing through... No doubt we served up answers to many doubts that were beginning to prey on her mind.'

'Could be,' says Justin, channelling his empathic side. 'It must be all quite humiliating for her, now, having to climb down from this new life she was creating. But she seems strong.'

Joy says, nudging her husband to start up the car. 'Come on, let us go take tea with her, then bumble round the town to find Ted Fear. Who said the countryside was a place of quiet retreat – give me Broadmead shopping centre in the middle of Bristol any day.'

They find Ursula at the Strangers With Coffee café counter, ordering a cream tea. She looks happy to see them, saying, 'a real squeeze in here, but it is cosy. I used to come here a lot when I was living alone. Before... oh well I am living alone again, or so it seems. Back to the old haunts for solace,' she says, half-heartedly playing with a clotted cream scone.

Perched at a tiny pine table, in the window of the café, Joy gazes out at the passing tourists obediently following up-held umbrellas, saying, 'look Ursula, I can see you are hurting, which is hardly surprising. You don't need to talk about Tony if you don't want to.'

'I know that. Thank you. I am in shock a bit. A silly teenage infatuation. I should have known better. But I was lonely. Mind you, I was beginning to think he was a mistake – all that bullshit pouring out of him. And those horrible stinky sausage rolls.'

'If it is any consolation,' says Joy, 'we were taken in, if that is the phrase, at first, by Tony too. Many people were. You are not the first, and you won't be the last. The attraction of the noble cause – to be a partner in crime in that. It is quite a pull. Irresistible in fact.'

Justin adds, 'you were really were strong there, in the forest. He knew you meant every word you said. There is no coming back for him.'

'I am not sure I want to talk about him for a while. I am numb,' says a despondent Ursula, tidying up scone crumbs in little circles around her plate.

'Not at all surprising,' consoles Joy. She sighs, 'I am not at all sure that we want to expend too much more time and energy on him either. But that showdown in the woods was really good closure for us. It needed to happen. And you know, it was not planned, but it was really good to have you witness to our confrontation of him.'

'Same here. It was really good for me to have you both there, to witness my sacking of him too. Made it real somehow.'

'Yes, it did,' agreed Justin. 'And excellent for him to have heard a similar message from two different directions. He had nowhere to hide.'

'And now he is gone,' says Ursula, the reality of it dawning.

'Perhaps his rebellion is extinct, this time around. What is the alternative name of this cafe?

Strangers without Benefits?'

'That's more like it,' says Joy, 'except he was on benefits. If I see him again it will be "Stranglers with Coffee.'

'Do you think we will see him again?' muses Justin

'No, none of us will,' replies Joy. 'His pride - and that massive ego will be hurting too much. Such men are fragile underneath you know, beneath all that bluff and bluster.'

Justin disagrees. 'Dunno about that. His ego does need feeding. He will resurrect himself again somewhere, bound to happen. Attached to whatever expedient cause suits him at the time.'

'Was he always like this?' asks Ursula.

Joy considers this. 'I think he was sincere once. In fact, when I first met him he seemed authentic enough. But time and tide and a degree of desperation has brought out the worst in him.'

Justin looks at his watch. 'Thanks for the tea, and sorry for what has happened to you, but we need to get going. One more visit here in town, then home to feed the kids. Do you know where Citizen's Advice is?'

'Oh yes, and thanks so being here, It is just around the corner, inside the Town Hall, in the Market Square. Can't miss it. A local landmark. Are you needing advice? They are very helpful.'

'No, it is not that,' says Justin. 'Just that we have to meet someone who works there.'

'Oh, would it be Ted Fear? He is so nice. And was so helpful to me on a Council Tax issue. And he might be helpful again, in making sure I get Tony completely out of my life. Evicted for ever. No returns!'

'Yes, it is Ted! What a small world we live in Ursula,' marvels Joy.

'Wells is a very small city. Smallest in the whole land. Do give my best to Ted. He is a wonderful person. Bye bye Strangers!'

'And well-met stranger to you – with coffee!'

After the claustrophobic woods, Justin and Joy are struck by the wide streets and open squares of this historic town. Inside the noble Town Hall, they are directed to Citizen's Advice, where they recognise Ted, busy behind a desk.

'Hello Ted, guess who?' says Joy. 'It is Joy and Justin Drake. Last seen when you were considering us for a loan. Remember?'

'Oh, my goodness, how could I forget!' says a surprised Ted, his face breaking into a smile. 'You two. I don't believe it. How remarkable it is to see you. Excuse me but I am quite taken aback.' Cleaning his glasses on the end of his tie, he asks, 'what brings you to town? Or should I say city?'

'Oh, we are here for the rebellion,' says Justin, not sure how to answer this question.

Ted brightens at this. 'Oh, I say! The Monmouth rebellion! Where the rebels tried to over throw the established church? The biggest thing ever to happen in Wells. Only happened five centuries ago, but still vivid in the townsfolk's memory.'

Joy chuckles. 'No not that rebellion, but I do admire the spirit of those upstarts. But we dropped by for the Extinction Rebellion. The protest on the edge of town?'

'Oh yes, we have had lots of those protestors drifting around. Been coming in, asking for advice on squatting and the likes. Have to tell them that that is not really my brief.'

'Cheek of it,' says Justice, trying to get in the idiom.

'Quite,' replies Ted. 'But we get all sorts drifting in here. Many tourists too, asking for information on the Glastonbury Festival. Not exactly why I work here. I am more interested in working for the benefit of society. But never mind all of that, it is so good to see you both. Thanks so much for dropping by. I really don't know what to say. Apart from saying thanks for saving my life!'

'That life-saving was all Joy, really,' dismisses Justin. 'Oh, and young Tom, the homeless guy. Her able assistant.'

'Tom, yes Tom! Did you know he is living down this way? I have seen him a few times. I was able to let him know how eternally grateful I am. To you all. This is just a marvellous reunion.'

'Yes, funnily enough we met Tom today too. Unexpectedly. What a fine young man.'

'Yes, he is. Splendid chap.'

'Oh, and we also met a woman called Ursula?' says Joy.

'Didn't get her family name. She was asking after you too.'

'What beneficence you bring to brighten my day. Of course I know Ursula. She is often in here. I seem to be her preferred advisor.' Ted smiles at this recognition.

'So, how is your work here Ted? You are looking in command of things.'

 'Thanks for the vote of confidence, Justin, but I am just trying to get my head around this new Citizen's Advice website. All gobble-dee-gook to me. Oh, and they have changed the "corporate" logo. All lower case. What sort of change is that?' Ted rants on, now he is in the flow. 'Honest to goodness, it is getting like the bank in here. They will be changing the name next.' He sighs, heavily. 'But I suppose there is no escaping modernity.'

'I would think you are well out of the bank,' Joy surmises. 'And just look around you! Installed in an even finer old building than the one you graced in Bristol!'

'Oh, yes I am well out of the bank. And my life has changed so much. "Better Now," as I used to be forced to have to say. The heart attack was a blessing in disguise – sorted out my life. Got paid off. Moved to somewhere quieter. Cannot thank you two enough for ensuring that I have lived to enjoy this new phase in my life.'

'So happy to have helped you with that,' says Joy. 'Ted, just a thought. Do you ever come back to Bristol at all? We have just moved to Brislington and were thinking of having a house warming – you would me most welcome.'

'How generous of you – that would be wonderful, thanks! I will bring young Tom if I may. We can have a resuscitation reunion.'

'Ha ha! Never hosted one of those before. You must come along.'

They are interrupted by an American couple, who talk over them to ask if they could be directed to Stonehenge. 'Ted, we had best be going,' said Justin, 'you have work to do. But see you at the party.'

On the way back to the car, Joy pulls Justin to one side. "Look over there. Outside the benefits office, looking at the bus timetable. Tony! Seems like we will never shake him off.'

'Let's get out of here Joy, before he sees us. He is probably waiting for his rucksack to be returned, never to be seen again. Ever.'

Back in the car, he asks, 'and what is all this about a party, Joy? First I have heard of it.'

'Hmm me too. Just came to me. New house, new life. Much to celebrate. Including getting Tony out of our lives. And discovering friends in Wells. I like this place. Shall we move here?'

The Women's Wildfire

'Hi. Sharon, this is a fancy wine bar!' says a wide-eyed Joy.
'Yia Mas? One of my favourites. Lots of hunky Greek waiters
to make you feel young again. They can flirt with me all day
long if they wish too.'

'So I see. One of them is even making eyes at an old lady like
me.' Joy returns the waiter's attentions with a smile. 'But
thanks, Sharon, not so much for this introduction to seduction
hell, but for asking me to join your choir. I worry that I will bring
down the tone. Hope I don't disappoint you. But thanks, I am
really looking forward to something completely different.'

'No, you won't bring down the tone,' assures Sharon.
'Definitely not. It will be great to have you along. And it is good
fun, once you get into the swing. We are all merely amateur
chanteuses, not divas.'

'Maybe so,' Joy says, doubtfully, 'but I told you I cannot sing a
note, never mind hold a tune. Mind you, with all this waiting for
the next Uber ride, I get plenty of opportunity to sing along
with Radio 6.'

Sharon is distracted by the waiter. 'Great wine – thanks. But
what is the paper napkin and pen for?'

He leers at her, 'your phone number. Please.'

She waves the waiter away. 'See what I mean Joy? They are forward.'

'So I see. But back to the task in hand. So, the choir meets around the corner. The foyer of St. George's? Thank God it is not the main auditorium.'

'I know it sounds grand, but it works well – great acoustics.'

'I will take your word for that. But Sharon, it is so good to see you after all this time. And glad you thought of me. Good not to be skulking around behind the bike sheds for a sly fag as the only place for girls to huddle. This is different altogether. Seeing my Sharon in her natural element, her pomp.'

The waiter hovers unnecessarily once more, proffering the suggestive napkin speculatively to Joy, who pushes it to one side. Sharon giggles at this. 'Oh yes, Allah be praised. Behind the bins, away from the cameras, was so sordid. Embrace the new. Shake off the carpet's shackles. Sing it into extinction. Glad I was let go.'

'Let go!' echoes Joy. 'Such HR weasel words. Those mumblies.'

'Agreed. But life is good. I scored a good pay off – as did many of the other girls in the office on salary. And I am now working in a bijou flower shop in Clifton village.'

'Suits you madam,' mocks Joy. 'You are steering well clear of the Clifton Wine Bar, I hope?'

'Oh God yes! Those creepy old codgers in their waistcoats and cravats, thinking they've still got it. A couple of them even take snuff!'.

'Yuk. Give me a good honest reefer any day. So you are blossoming in the flower emporium then, Sharon?'

'Oh yes! I meet some wonderful men in the flower shop. Many of them buying peace offerings for their wives – normally driven by reparation for some sexual transgressions or similar acts of husbandly neglect. But that can lead to some interesting conversations. Not to mention promises of some quite exciting illicit trysts. Which in turn leads to more guilt laden flower sales. Winning all round!'

'Sounds really exciting? If a little bit weird. A niche flower shop indeed. Petals with benefits.'

'Well I don't take it too seriously,' says Sharon. 'And then there is the online dating for the older lady. You wouldn't believe the demand. Swipe right, swipe left, the world is your oyster. You only live once. All this useless beauty, as Elvis Costello once sang.'

'So he did. But stop, just stop, before I let my imagination run riot. Must say you are looking good on it. Keeps a girl young.'

'It does, it does. And your new life is Uber driving? I will ask for you especially when I book Uber next time. Maybe when in need of an emergency escape from a horny husband?'

'I would be more than happy to assist a maiden in distress. And please don't forget to tip. But the Uber algorithm does not work like that. First come first served. But I could be your emergency bail out number from a date gone wrong if that would help?'

'That could help a lot. There was this bloke the other day from the Wine bar...'

'Not called Bert by any chance?'

'No, but it was another cast out of the same mould. Bert. Wasn't he the one you told me about? Tried to woo you in his ancient classic car?'

'Yes, that one. It was hilarious. I would have been flattered but the patter was... well too pat. He was playing to a well-rehearsed script. On auto-seducer.'

'So what happened to him?'

'Justin and he had a bust up. One of those coaching melodramas.'

'Oh yes! Those bust ups seem to run and run in that profession. You ever hear more after your entrapment of that Brenda. The supervisor? The dare I set you? Any follow-through on that escapade?'

'Oh yes there has been,' mumbles Joy, a flicker of remorse crossing her face.

'She complained about Justin, which got him thrown out of the brownies.'

'Lucky him. He is well out of it,' pronounces Sharon, raising her glass to Joy's, 'here's to supervisors long gone!'

Joy holds back on this valediction, saying, 'I am afraid to say that she used Justin's Facebook to identify me as her mystery shopper, evidence which she put in front of the Fraternity.'

'You bad, bad girl!' chuckles Sharon.

'Hmmm,' retorts Joy, 'The covert infiltration of Brenda's lair was all your idea in the first place! I must say Justin was not best pleased.'

'So, it was all my fault then,' says Sharon, chuckling once more. 'So, moving swiftly along, what ever happened to Bert then? His villainy caught up with him?'

'Looks like it. He escaped to the Cayman Isles, chased by his vengeful fifth wife. What a pity. One less fine specimen to grace the Clifton Wine Bar talent pool.'

'Poor women of Clifton,' mocked Sharon. 'How will they cope? And talking of men, how is Justin?

'Same old same old. He does change, but then again, he doesn't. Trying hard to change recently, mind.'

'But you two are still together?'

'Oh yes. And don't make me crazily jealous with tales of life in the singles lane. Marriage is hard, but we stick at it. Not that bad actually. I do love him.'

'It is so good to catch up, Joy, but we need to get going. Waiter, the bill please.' He hovers into view. She giggles again. 'Oh look, he has put his phone number on the bill. And a smiley face. How cute. Shall we go sing? You will be fine.'

Joy follows Sharon through the fine St George's portico, then down to the brand-new atrium, to be greeted by a familiar face. 'Don't I know you?' the friendly face asks, "I'm Sarah. Sorry, I meet a lot of people in my line of work.'

'Oh yes we met a while ago. Joy? Justin Drake's wife? Your fellow erstwhile coaching buddy?'

'Oh yes, I tried to get you to steward,' says Sarah. 'Sorry. I should have remembered you. You are looking well. And of course I know Sharon. We are fellow altos.'

'So, you sing, Sarah?' asks Joy. 'And you are on the door?'

'That's right,' replies Sarah, who returns her attention to collecting money at the door. 'I join the choir once the money is in. Love it to pieces. And I get a free entry for services rendered. Please make yourselves at home. Next please! Six pounds please!.'

Sharon says to Joy, 'best to follow me to the altos, there are lots of us. It is easier to hide in our section.'

Taking a seat in the singing circle, Joy turns to check out her neighbour. 'Oh my goodness, Joanna! How good to see you here! I never expected...!'

'No, nor me you. How are you, Joy? Good to meet up with you again. I meant to ring.' Joy hesitates for a moment. 'Gosh this is a bit awkward. Look, are we okay?'

'Yes of course we are. I enjoyed meeting you last time, in the cafe. A kindred spirit, I would think. In time.'

'Oh, I am relieved. Good to know that. I would hate any awkwardness. Especially here in the choir, where our goal is harmony. Not just for us women while we are here, but for all those around us, in our various worlds.'

'No, it does not feel awkward at all,' assures Joy. 'Worry not. Water under the bridge and all of that. You like singing with the Wildfire chorus?'

'Love it – part of my new liberation, the choir is such great solidarity for all the women here.'

'I would love to hear all about it,' says Joy, clearly curious about this new world she is entering.

'Well of course,' replies Joanna, 'but not now. Crystal, our leader, is ready to get us going.'

Crystal runs her finger around a Tibetan bell that rings high and true around the room, calling the room to silence, 'Hello wonderful women!' Crystal beams a wide inclusive smile, her eyes tracking around the circle of receptive faces. 'Lovely to see you all! And new faces too, you are especially welcome. I feel sure you will get the hang of this singing together business. Really soon. Worry not. We were all new once. Especially at birth. But then those mothers among us know that. Whoops. Well, all of us know that too, not just the mothers. We were all wide-eyed at birth. So please stand up, all newcomers. Don't be shy!'

Joy rises to her feet to join her fellow newbies. As they stand, they are greeted by a rapturous round of applause, the old hands beaming welcoming smiles, and some newbies are offered hugs from those who had brought them along. Feeling a little exposed, Joy sits down, anxious for the singing to begin.

Crystal continues, once the chatter has quieted down. 'Please know that we are a women's choir. A woman's community choir. We are wildfire! We sing in harmony, in three or four parts, but don't be put off by that. Put to the back of your mind all those "I can't sing" messages from childhood. So many of us had those injunctions from early on in our lives, from school, from family, from mean friends. Hands up all who did!' Joy looks around to see a forest of supportive hands. Crystal studies this confirmation of her theory of the early suppression of a woman's right to sing. 'There you see?' she says. 'So many of us were oppressed, from early on. But in this choir, we can now break free. I have no doubt that in no time at all you newcomers will build confidence, and find your original voice.' This statement is met by supportive coos and whoops. Warming to her theme, Crystal primes them for the experience soon to come. 'It will be fun and edgy. Endorphin triggering. And you will feel good afterwards. We will all feel a sense of women coming together drawing strength from our struggles, breaking free of isolation.'

Joy absorbs all this wonderment, while taking a surreptitious look around to notice women of all shapes and sizes and ages, some still in their work clothes, others more casual. An older woman in the altos put her hand up to apologise for 'still being sweaty from tennis.'

Crystal is all instant reassurance. 'Worry not! Sweat is what we women do. Wasn't it men who said we need all these deodorants and women's products?'

Joanna looks askance at this, whispering to Joy, 'not sure I go along with that. I now work in ethical women's products, all organic. Those products are designed by women, for women, not by men. And they are products we need.'

Crystal glances across at this exchange, seeking silence before she continues, 'so, for the benefit of all our new comers, be aware that we do not use song sheets. There will be no intimidating dots on the page. We sing naturally, and we sing from our hearts. I am a trained member of the Natural Voice Network, the NVN. We aim to make singing something we can all do. After all, singing foreshadowed speech. We all cried and cooed before we could talk.'

Crystal allows the wisdom of this to sink in. 'We sing songs from all over the world. Bulgarian, Gospel, and from nearer home, from women song writers such as Carol King, Annie Lennox, Ali Burns, Helen Chadwick. Her latest song "I can feel my heart again," really touches on all we aim to do here. Touching our hearts in the most beautiful way. Opening up to each other. And by contrast we also sing the Beatles.' Joy is relieved to hear this last mention, rather hoping that they begin on known ground.

'So, let us get started with an Aboriginal women's song, drawing inspiration from the heart of the Western Desert and dedicated to Extinction Rebellion, our latest binding rallying cry to save the planet, before it is too late. This is quite a simple but powerful song. Believe it or not this song, written by the aboriginal woman Kerriane Assange, was at the heart of a PhD she gained in intersectional studies at the University of Wollongong. It is called "Singing up the Dreamtime."' Joy feels at this point that her worst fears may be realised, but she is happy to go along with the extended body and voice warm-ups that follow, before Crystal primes them for the song itself.

'Let us start with the low voices. I need you to make deep, guttural sounds. Cries of birth pain, of deep grief. That's it, but louder. Yes, now I can hear it. Great, you have got it. Everyone applaud the lows please.' The "lows" grin as the clapping rings out. Joy is relieved that she is not a low woman, as she is not sure she could sustain such growling.

'Now middles, you altos. We need a long, prolonged drone sound. It goes like this. It is easy enough, all on one note.' Crystal taps her tuning fork on her knee, then holds it to her ear. She then hums...... 'this note here. Just drone it. moan it.' She listens in to the altos' monotone. 'That is it. Let all the tedious pain of being a woman sing forth. You've got it. Well done.' Joy felt a little miffed that they were not applauded for their efforts, not like the lows, but glad nonetheless that she found the note from somewhere inside of herself.

'Next, you tenories. Pardon my Italian. You have the tune, lucky girls. It goes like this. Nothing too complex but it does go up and down a lot.' Crystal sings the song line, to show them the way, then sings along with them, many times, until they have the tune deeply grooved in memory.

'Excellent! I like the sound of that,' Crystal says, grinning. 'You show offs!

'Now, you tops. What we need from you is an ululating sound, in the style of African woman resting after a hard day's working in the fields, around the home. Can anyone of you tops do this eerie sound?'

One or two are eager to show they can, the highest note ululations shaking the light fittings. 'I know it is hard for some of you, but we need these tonal ornaments on top of the other parts to complete the wholeness of this wonderful sound. Try it, tops!'

As they sing, she enthuses, 'that is gorgeous. Now let us put it altogether. Have courage, it is no problem if you make a mistake, we are here to learn.'

Joy is glad that she has the part that is mainly on one note. Listening in to Sharon's voice, she is soon enough droning along with the best of them. And enjoying it. Soon enough she lost in the sound, not able to distinguish her voice from the rest of the women. They are becoming perfectly blended, just as Crystal predicted they would. And the totality of the aboriginal song sounds awesome, from another planet, transporting her to places and feelings beyond her experience, transported perhaps to the Dreamtime itself, where she imagines herself slowly walking in the bush, flowing with the Song Lines. Joy's confidence builds, as they move on through this evening's repertoire, from a simple song of planetary redemption through to the finale of the Beatles 'Here Comes the Sun.'

After a fine 90 minutes of "making noises with air," Crystal announces, 'tonight is our end of term party. Would you all please proceed to the bar and coffee area to mingle and rejoice. Thanks to all who have brought food to share, most of it healthy. The vegan food has been separated from the rest, as has the gluten free.'

Joy chats to Sarah over a plate of vegan quiche. 'This is delicious. Thanks for helping organise this wonderful women-full gathering!'

'Oh, so glad you enjoyed it. Certainly looked like you were rapt with the whole thing. I love to organise, have a real flair for it.'

'I loved it Sarah, really loved it,' replied Joy. 'At the beginning I was really nervous, but I was soon caught up in the wonder of it. I found that after a while my voice fitted in well, mainly thanks to tuning into Sharon. I had trouble with my breathing though.'

'Don't worry, that will come with time. The main thing is to feel that you are a part of the whole.'

'Sarah, thanks, I felt so included. Singing the Beatles at the end was great. Home territory. I never thought I would be singing aboriginal though. I will bring my didgeridoo next time. What are you working at now, Sarah, when you are not here, hosting events?'

'Well, I am glad to be out of full-time coaching. Did Justin tell you the Coaching Fraternity is falling apart, making headline news?'

'Oh yes he did. In fact he was a part of their downfall.'

'Well good for him. I thought he might push against that lot, eventually,' nods Sarah. 'I am now developing my skills in embodied performance, as well as doing interior design, which is going well. Excuse me a minute Joy, while I collect up some of these paper plates before they fall to the floor.'

Across the room, Sharon is speaking to a smaller woman with intense look on her face. They seem to know each other well. Sharon beckons Joy over. 'Joy do you remember Glynis, ex of Magic Carpet?'

'Oh yes, I think I do. You used to work at the call centre?'

'I certainly did,' grins Glynis. 'And you kept avoiding me! For good reasons I suspect, as I was never the bearer of good news. But I am now well out of that. And yes, of course I remember you, Joy.' She makes no mention of Wiki-leaks, but her eyes exude grateful recognition for the part Justin and Joy must have played in that. She says instead, 'I am now working for a women's refuge. In fact, quite a few women who have moved through the refuge are here tonight. And we try to sing in the refuge kitchen as often as we can, to lift our spirits. Oh, hello Joanna!'

'Hi Glynis, and hello again Joy,' greets Joanna. 'You were in fine voice. Great to sing with you and I hope you will come along next term?'

'Wild horses would not keep me back,' reassures Joy. 'So, you said you were back into marketing organic products?'

'Hmmm. That, among other things. Well market research anyway, mainly with women. It is miles away from my old job at Consignia. And family life has moved on too. We have sold the old house, and I now have a rental in Clifton. The kids come and go between us, and Alan is coming around to the new arrangement. This choir among other things is making a real difference to my life. You still in Westbury?'

'No, we have moved on, also to a rental in Brislington. A big place, huge unruly garden. How do you know Glynis, may I ask?'

'Oh, that is easy. Glynis is a leading light in the women's cooperative that I am proud to be a part of, that sprang out of the remains of the Chrysalis Group. We sponsor the women's refuge that she so ably runs. And she brought me along to the choir.'

'Well I hope that I make such connections here,' says Joy.

"Look, we are going to have a housewarming party soon. You

must come along Joanna. You too, Glynis you must come. Dick Bellows will be there!'

In the Garden

'Look Joy, our scruffy garden is filling up with our friends.'
Joy casts her eyes over their new space, glad that she
decided to christen it so royally with a party. 'So it is. What a
pleasure to see! They don't seem to mind the broken paving,
or the weeds breaking through under their feet.'
'No, they don't,' agrees Justin, 'though I wonder if some of the
Stokes Croft posse might be looking for weed of a different
kind later on.'
'I doubt it. After all, Tony is not here, thank God. But the idea
of the party was a good one. Well done me. Need to go top
some wine though. Yes Amelia?'
'Mummy, what do I do when they have eaten all the food off
my tray?'
'Well Amelia, you go back in the kitchen and top it up. Let me
know and I will help you. Loving your waitressing pinafore.
And as for you, Adam, in your bow tie! Quite the grown-up
man about town!'
'Thanks, Mummy. It is quite tight, but I like it. Think I will wear
it to school.'
'Well why not, Adam? Try holding the tray with two hands, it
might be safer.' Adam nudges her. 'What is it now?'
'Mummy, I was thinking, with the bow tie and everything...'
pleads Adam, trying on his best winning smile, 'that I could do
the wine serving instead of the food?'

'No, Adam, just no. Daddy and I will deal with the drinks, thank you very much. Now go look after your hungry customers, or you will be made to double clean the Uber car tomorrow.'

Justin peruses the unfolding tableau that is slowly but surely filling their garden. 'The wine is going down well...'

'Majestically,' Joy replies. 'Justin, that is the doorbell. I must go answer it.'

At the door, Joy greets Tom, Ted and Ursula. 'Well, hello you three. Welcome. The musketeers from Wells, refugees from the Monmouth Rebellion! And Ursula, Ted said you would be coming along. You are most welcome!'

'No, thank you for the invite,' says Ursula. 'Ted and I are becoming firm friends, even gone to a few concerts in Wells Town Hall together.'

Yes, we have,' agrees Ted, 'and young Tom is working at the local hospital. Good to have him on hand in case I keel over again. Eh Tom?'

'Looking around at the state of some of my patients at the hospital, then you, Ted, are the least of my worries. Loving this house, Joy,' says Tom, eyeing the long dark staircase.

Thanks, Tom,' replies Joy, 'too big for us really, but it was a real bargain. Short-term lease. And if you are ever back in Bristol then you would be very welcome to sleep over.'

'That is a lovely offer, Joy, might well take you up on it. Beats kipping outside the bank. Unless you have installed spikes in your sofa-bed?'

'Not yet, but it could be one way to stop the kids from bouncing all over it.' Joy turns to Ted. 'Ted, before you pick up a drink and join the others in the garden, I have something of yours…'

Ted looks blank. 'Whatever could that be? I cannot imagine.'

'It is a surprise. But before you win your prize, you have to remove that National Trust tie of yours, pretty though all those little sun motifs are, shining light where ever they lead you.'

Ted allows Ursula to help remove his tie, while wondering what might be coming next. 'Thank you Ursula. But Joy, whatever have you planned for me next? An execution? A Turkish shave?'

Joy pulls a wrapped present out of a kitchen drawer. 'No nothing, so dramatic. Da Da. But this. This is for you, Ted.'

Ted unwraps the gift, to find his old Singapore Bank tie, now free of stains and pristine clean. Ursula asks, 'whatever is that Ted? The sight of it seems to be making you inordinately happy?'

'Oh, Joy, this is marvellous – I will put it on the rack alongside my beloved Bedminster Bank tie, now forty years old. But wherever did you find it?'

'I found it lying on the floor of the bank after the ambulance had taken you away,' explains Joy. 'Tom and I had to take it off, before it started to act as a tourniquet.'

'Well, I never knew that?' says a still astonished Ted. 'I mean how would I have known? I was almost joining the angels.'

'Quite so. Though I am afraid we never found out what happened to your shoes.'

'Hmm,' says Tom. 'At least they never became dead man's shoes.'

'Come on, Ted, put the tie on,' encourages Ursula, fussing around him. 'There you are! That snake looks great, twisting its way down your front,'.

'Talking of snakes, Ted,' says Joy, 'I retrieved it because that soulless robot Dominic Cross wanted to throw it away. He thought it was cluttering up the place.'

'Joy, I am not surprised. He thought I was cluttering up the place too. Dead man walking. And no successor to step into the dead man's shoes. Certainly not that dopy Hank on the front desk. He lived in a world of his own.'

'Seemed like Dominic would not have been happy until he had shut all the branches and replaced you all with machines,' says Tom. 'No more human clutter inside the bank. Or outside in the doorways. Humans out, robots in. All that will be left will be Dominic and a dog.'

'What has the dog go to do with it?' asks Joy, puzzled.

'The dog is there to keep Dominic from ever touching the machines.' Tom is pleased with his joke.

'That is really funny, Tom,' says an appreciative Ted, 'but the fact is that Dominic did not survive, any more than I did. As far as I have heard on the old boy's network, he just disappeared. Better Bank found out too late that he was part of a group inventing bogus employees on the payroll, then salting the money away in the Cayman Islands.'

'Fascinating,' says Tom, 'so where is he now?'

'We think he actually fled to the Cayman Islands to join his ill-gotten gains. Evading extradition.'

'Enough of this banker chat already,' says Joy, 'come on out into the garden and mingle. Justin, could you get the door?'

Justin opens the door to find Joanna Cooke, smiling on the threshold. 'Hello Joanna,' he says, a little nonplussed. 'Good to see you! My, you are looking well.'

'Well thank you Justin,' she says blushing slightly, while handing over a bottle of wine. 'You too. Sorry I am a bit late. Traffic was at a standstill at Temple Meads Station.'

'Yes, it always is,' commiserates Justin. 'Hope you were not tailgating though, in your hurry to get here on time?'

'Oh no. I will never forget our secret motto for keeping a safe distance: "only a fool breaks the two second rule"!'

Justin looks wistful at the reminder. 'Seems quite a while since our speeding class.'

'Yes, it does. I learned from that class though. And from what passed after.'

Justin pauses in the hallway. 'Look, Joanna I am sorry if I never…

Joanna holds her palm towards him. 'No, Justin. No more on that. You did right. And you never broke the two-second rule, though we both got quite close at times. We needed to break it. And anyway, Joy and I are now firm friends – we're loving singing together. She is a natural.'

'Yes, she is. In so many ways.'

In the kitchen he places down Joanna's bottle, asking, 'what would you like to drink?'

'Oh, thanks, something soft please. No more gallons of chardonnay for me nowadays. That guava juice looks good. Can't risk my licence.'

'No, me neither, not with my Uber livelihood depending on it. Please come out the back. We are all gathering in this prison yard that we call a garden. Who might you know?'

Joanna scans the group. 'Ah… I see Joy, obviously. Sharon, Glynis from the choir. Oh, and Sarah.'

'Everyone seems to know Sarah.'

'They do, they do,' agrees Joanna. 'Funny to think that she has gotten out of coaching, just as I am still putting my toe in that particular water, along with all the other things falling off my groaning plate.'

'Well, as they say in positive psychology circles, Joanna, "get a bigger plate."'

'Really helpful, Justin, thanks for that platitude. Mind you, the further I get in, the more I can see why she got out. I do know that you have been through all of these agonies too, Justin, with the Fraternity and all.'

'Best not to dwell on that professional funeral pyre. This is a party,' says Justin, waving his arm towards his guests. 'So, how is work going?'

'Going great thanks, Justin. As well as some coaching on the side, I am working in market research for an innovative start up – organic products for women. Suits me fine, and I pick up a few coaching clients along the way. Look, loving the catch-up, but I must go join my fellow choristers for a minute. Great to see you again, and loving the house! Suits you both!'

Dick approaches Justin, wine in hand. 'Thanks for the invite Justin. This is a fine gathering.'

'Glad you are enjoying it. Always happy to entertain the fourth estate. As long as I don't become the story.'

'Great to be here,' says Dick. 'Thanks for the Coaching Fraternity tip off by the way. Made quite a splash, did it not?'

'Oh yes, that was publicity they were not expecting to come their way. Hit them right below the belt. You did a great job on them, Dick. Even used some of my quotes, anonymised. I am so glad to see the pompous president McQueen and her VP buddy Andrew Rice brought to heel. I see the Daily Mail picked up on their affair?'

Dick grins. 'Of course they did! Couldn't resist it. Right up their sordid street. And your pictures of them hustling you out of the posh hotel suite were priceless. I hear you even got the royalties for that. The affair was only a small part of the story, but lurid enough to add some sauce. Their affair started here in Bristol, so I am told.'

'Really?' Justin's eyes widen. 'At my inquisition at the Marriott?'

'The very same,' confirms Dick. 'Did you not see that post-coital glaze in their eyes the next day?

'Come to think of it – they did seem to be showing off to each other, trying to impress. Lots of sneaky sideways glances.'

'Ha ha,' chortles Dick. 'Bet it wasn't six times a night though, as the tabloids will always have it. They would have been too busy deciding on appropriate standards for nookie.

Interestingly enough, I was having a chat earlier to Sarah from St George's about the Fraternity story.'

'You know Sarah?''

'Justin, everyone knows Sarah! Anyway, she used to be a coach. She thought I had done a great job of exposing them for what they are. And the world of coaching has one less Crocker in it, I see?'

Joanna comes to join them. 'Sorry to butt in. But did I hear the name Crocker? Sorry, Joanna Cooke.' She offers her hand to Dick. 'And you must be Dick Bellows of Magi-Leaks fame? I recognise your face from the papers.'

'One and the same, for my sins,' says Dick, offering her a slight bow.

'And the very same one now bringing down the Coaching Fraternity - just after I had paid my fees and joined them?' Joanna gives Dick a mock dig in ribs.

'You cannot make an omelette without breaking egos,' ripostes Dick. 'Anyway, that world of coaching needed bringing down. So, you know Tony Crocker too?'

Ursula, hearing the mention of Crocker, drifts over to the edge of this conversation.

'Well, a little,' replies Joanna, 'through coaching circles. How did you know him?'

'Only really through work. Used to know him. He would come to me with stories. Left town now, I think.'

'Why am I not surprised? He came to me with stories too' says Joanna, winking extravagantly at Justin

'Ohhh. I sniff a lead here. Should I get my recorder out?' Dick grins.

'No chance,' ripostes Joanna. 'The story that Justin and I hold tight will never see the light of day. Though a recording did prove useful. Ha ha.' She says, giving Justin a stage wink.

Justin says, 'so if you can't have our story, Dick what are you currently working on?'

'Hm. Another major business scandal. A group of high-level bankers ripping off their own. Then working with shady characters in the Cayman Islands to launder their money. Even a few white-collar criminals from Bristol involved.'

'Fascinating. Oh Dick, meet Glynis,' Justin says, as Glynis breaks off from the sisterhood to come and join them. 'Hi Glynis, do you know Dick?'

'Hello Dick,' she says, shaking his hand. 'We have never met before. I only caught sight of you from time to time around the Magic Carpet, in the days before the Carpet began to leak.'

Dick's interest pricks up. 'Oh, did you work there, Glynis?'

'Well I used to. Got laid off with many others, but back on my feet now. Glad to be out of the place. By the way, your exposure of the Carpet's management practices was excellent. The whole office cheered when we saw the headline – then the evening news. Great work.'

'Thanks,' said Dick, 'but you know I was just the channel for the news. The story would not have been possible without the brave hackers, and those that risked a great deal to get that data out the gates.' Dick holds up his glass. 'Cheers to each and every one of them!' Glynis and Justin glance at each other, only too happy to join Dick in this silent tribute to the unknown hackers and their secret accomplices.

'What you working on now, Glynis?' Dick asks, clinking her glass.

'Oh, working full time at a women's refuge. Now there is a place packed full of stories. And the ill treatment of women, not just by men, but by Social Services too. A disgrace. Want to drop by sometime, Dick?'

'Sounds great. Here is my card.'

Joy approaches the group. 'Sharon, can I take you away a second?'

Sharon giggles. 'Hope you don't mean, "borrow me," Joy? I am allergic to that term, since Magic Carpet. I am not a library book.'

'No, not wanting to borrow you at all. I could never afford the fines for your late return. I want to introduce you to two men that could be of great use to you. Stop looking at me in that tone of voice, Sharon. You know perfectly well I do not mean "use" in the Greek waiter sense. Follow me,' she commands, moving towards Brian the mechanic and his perpetual shadow.

'Sharon, I want you to meet Brian and John; they are the miracle workers who service our cars. You need to get to get to know them, with all of the trouble you have with your old banger. Come to think of it - Joanna, come over here too – this introduction might be worthwhile for you too. As well as meeting two lovely people. I seem to remember that you are vehicularly challenged.'

'Joanna, Sharon, meet Brian and John. They can help you with anything car related. Pick up your car at the door, no job to small. Drop it off like brand-new afterwards. Even have a cashless payment machine.'

'Good to meet you both,' says Joanna, 'and yes, cars are the bane of my life. Mind you, driving has proven to be a lot less stressful since I saw the light at the speed awareness class.'

'Oh,' says Brian, while John follows his every word, as befits a trusty shadow. 'You have been on one of those bad girl classes? I heard Justin did the same.'

'He did. In fact, weirdly enough, we both did the same class! Learned the error of our ways together.'

'That is weird,' said Brian, with John nodding in grave assent.

'My ex-husband thought my being caught brought shame on the whole family,' sighs Joanna. 'He was big into cars, mind you,'

'Really?' Brian shows immediate interest, as does John. 'A dealer? Or a small garage owner like us?'

'No, Alan is into parts. Big time into parts. Parts big and small.'

'Alan...' Brian ponders. John whispers in his ear. 'Oh yes, thanks John. Surely not Alan Cooke?'

'Yes!' replies Joanna. 'Small world. Do you know him?'

'Of course – we use him all the time. Don't we, John? He is excellent at sourcing obscure parts for older cars.'

'Like yaw rate tracking sensors?'

'My God,' say the collective mechanics, 'you do know a lot about cars.'

Joanna shakes her head. 'Not really – just some terms stick in my mind.'

Hearing talk of cars, Dave Allenday leaves his chat with Tom to come to join them. 'Hi there, Dave Allenday, resident token black comedian. What every party needs to keep up the diversity quota.' Dave shakes Brian and John warmly by the hand, squeezing firmly, deciding that the option of a fist bump might not be understood. 'Did I hear that you were in the bend em and mend em business?'

I am,' says Brian. 'Both of us are. Never a dull moment.'

'What do you think of the Prius then?' demands Dave. 'I'm an Uber slave, like Joy and Justin here.'

'Prius?' Brian does not give this much thought. 'Hate them!'

Dave looks hurt. 'Why is that then?'

'Easy! They never break down is why. Give me Joy's old Astra any old day. But please do recommend us to other Uber drivers. Except not the Prius drivers, obviously.'

Dave turns his attention to Sharon. "And you must be?'

'Sharon – best friend of Joy!'

Dave considers this admission. 'Well good luck with that. She will only let you down.'

'Let me down? How come?' asks Sharon.

'Well, she abandoned me in mid book.'

'Really? I heard it was defeating you more than it was defeating her. You chickened out first!'

'That is true enough.' Dave pulls a rueful face. 'Seriously she was - and is - a wonderful help. What a sounding board.'

'She is,' agrees Sharon. 'And she in fearless in responding to dares, too! She was telling me funny story about you? About your new stand-up act being based on her supposed failure to help you? Being a white woman and all?'

Dave beams. 'Oh yes. That act is going down a storm!'

319

Sharon smiles. 'But, to get her own back, she is now doing own act based on her experience of working for you?'

'Yes, she is. Too clever for her own good. She debuted that act last week at the club. Had the place in paroxysms.'

Joanna's imagination is sparked by this tale. 'I would pay good money to see that act.'

Dave jumps to the rescue. 'No need to part with hard earned. We'll get her to do it right now. Joy. Oii! You are needed!'

Dave's shout brings the whole party together, all eagerly clustering around him.' Joy! – the whole world needs to her your debut turn! Now.'

Joy blushes. 'Now? It is not worked up enough.'

'Oh, no!' says Dave, 'it came out all in one piece. Perfectly! Do it!'

'But in front go the children?' protests Joy, 'they are still busy distributing snacks! And it really is adult material.'

'Oh no, Mummy, we want to hear it too,' demands Adam. 'All of it!'

Joy composes herself then begins, 'Here before you stands an average white woman. The worst job I ever had was being editor to this mountainous black comedian, who was writing the history of black stand-up comedy in England. Except that his writing skills never stood up. Nor indeed did other aspects of him stand-up that much either, despite his bragging. He delegated everything to me, except the ganja smoking, though he did trust me with the Rizla papers and the ritual rolling process. He did say that one of my duties was to answer the phone, the only problem being that he was permanently on it. If he had been dictating the book down that phone that would have been all well and good. Except he was never onto his agent, only his dealer. For the first week I did not take too much offence at being referred to as Vera Lynn, though it did begin to wear thin after a while. And I really regret ever confessing to him that my family used to watch the Black and White Minstrels back in the day. In fact, sometimes Dad blacked up to enhance his viewing pleasure, while Mum was busy tapping out letters to Mary Whitehouse complaining about Alf Garnet. Oh, and Dave's tales about his role in heading the resistance in the Black and White Café in St Pauls during the 1980 riots. I am not sure how you lead a rebellion from a pram, but I let it pass. Then the way he used to treat me ... Let me tell you about the time when my bra strap broke and....'

Joy continued in this vein for a while, growing into her voice, as the guest gathered round in a happy cluster, applauding her lustily at her grand finale song and dance. Blushing, she tries to retreat from the limelight as her guests swarm around her in a feast of congratulatory acclaim, before beginning to make their reluctant way homeward. All too soon, the guests were finally gone, leaving Joy, Justin and the children alone once more in the broken-down garden.

'Did we do okay with the nibbles, mum?' asks Amelia. 'Adam ate most of the ones on his tray.'

'Did not. And I was the politest,' boasts the bow-tied one.

'You have some really nice friends Mummy,' says, Amelia.

'Yes, I do. They are daddy's friends too. They are our tribe. Our homies.'

'How did you all meet?' asks Adam.

'Oh, through work, through singing, all sort of places and things brought us together. We are blessed.'

'Well, the tribe all seem to like each other,' ponders Amelia, 'not like some of the tribes we learn about at school.'

'Were any of them Ponzis, Daddy?' asks Adam, never tiring of this theme and its potential for dad ribbing. 'Why did we not have pizza for them to eat? If they were Ponzis?'

'Well yes, a few of them were, but not too many. A lot of the Ponzi tribe have drifted out of my life.'

'Dick seemed popular,' says Adam, struggling to release his bow tie. 'Everyone wanted to talk to him! He was magnetic! And I was an iron filing!'

'He is famous,' said Justin. 'No wonder he drew you and all the other human filings towards him. He writes amazingly popular stories about smoking the bad guys out of town.'

'Oh. And is he a Ponzi?' asks Amelia.

'No definitely not. He is the anti-Ponzi. They experience reverse magnetism around him.'

'And Mummy, you were so funny,' sings Amelia, swirling her pinafore around her head as she mimes her mother's dance.' We loved your act.'

'You didn't understand it, Amelia!' blurts out her scornful brother, now relieved of his neckwear.

'Well neither did you!' squeals Amelia. 'But it was funny anyway. All those faces Mummy pulled. And that little dance she did at the end.'

'And the way your women friends burst into that lovely song.'

'Here comes the Sun?' Joy smiles, fondly. 'Yes, they sang beautifully, Adam. A perfect ending to the evening. And to our moving in to this fine house. And Dave's voice booming out for a solo verse when we all thought it over.'

'Trust Dave!' says Justin, 'always wanting to hog the limelight.'

'Well, Daddy was singing too,' insists Amelia, 'he was the best man singer.'

'Dick was good too,' says Justin. 'It could be that we need to start up a men's choir. Or at least sing a few shanties. We men need solidarity too.'

'You were brill, Mummy,' says Adam.

'Yes, she was, kids, so she was. As ever. Brilliant.'

30588359R00192

Printed in Great
Britain
by Amazon